## "I like the women

Emma's brows rose. "We're not dating."

"According to some people, we are."

"Creed, what are you afraid of?"

"The man on that yacht was shot and left to go down with the ship. If there was anything on that boat worth killing for, it likely went down with it," Creed said.

Emma frowned. "That doesn't mean we'll be targeted next."

Creed stared at her, at her gray eyes dark and troubled. He tilted her chin upward. If the man he was after thought Emma had anything that belonged to him, he'd pursue her relentlessly. "Promise me you'll be careful. And you'll call if you need me."

He was already on the precipice, standing far too close to her. The thought of something happening to her sent him over the edge.

In one motion he pulled her into his arms, crushing her lips with his. He kissed a path down to the base of her thoat, where her pulse beat erratically.

"Creed, this is wrong."

No, that was far from the truth. For the first time, nothing felt so right.

Dear Reader,

I had fun building the little vacation seaside town of Cape Churn and populating it with characters you'll see again. But the most fun I had in *Deadly Engagement* was researching the scuba diving and boating aspects of the book.

I took scuba lessons about twenty years ago and have yet to scuba dive in the ocean. I took my open-water dive in a murky lake, and I've snorkeled in Cancun, Hawaii, Guam and Florida, but never scuba dived in the ocean and never in Oregon, where the Pacific Ocean is cold and requires a wet suit to maintain body warmth. However, it's on my bucket list. I had pictures of equipment, dive boats and rocky coastlines bookmarked while I pounded away at the keyboard.

While writing this book, Cape Churn became such a part of my life I wanted to join Emma Jenkins and Creed Thomas Ruckman aboard the *Reel Dive* on the hunt for the cargo aboard the *Pelageya* and then go in search of the *Anna Maria.* What an exciting journey!

Nothing like a little suspense to make the setting even more interesting, right?

Happy reading!

Elle James

# DEADLY ENGAGEMENT

—

## Elle James

**HARLEQUIN® ROMANTIC SUSPENSE**

Recycling programs
for this product may
not exist in your area.

ISBN-13: 978-0-373-27855-8

DEADLY ENGAGEMENT

**Printed in U.S.A.**

HARLEQUIN®
www.Harlequin.com

## Books by Elle James

**Harlequin Romantic Suspense**

*Deadly Reckoning* #1698
*Deadly Engagement* #1785

**Harlequin Intrigue**

*Dakota Meltdown* #938
*Lakota Baby* #961
*Cowboy Sanctuary* #987
*Blown Away* #1014
*Alaskan Fantasy* #1033
*Texas-Sized Secrets* #1052
*Under Suspicion, With Child* #1080
*Nick of Time* #1100
*Baby Bling* #1127
*An Unexpected Clue* #1156
*Operation XOXO* #1172
*Killer Body* #1191
*Bundle of Trouble* #1226
*Hostage to Thunder Horse* #1244
*Cowboy Brigade* #1281
*Engaged with the Boss* #1306
*Thunder Horse Heritage* #1357
*Thunder Horse Redemption* #1382
*\*Triggered* #1433
*\*Taking Aim* #1439
*\*Bodyguard Under Fire* #1446
*\*Cowboy Resurrected* #1451

*Covert Cowboys, Inc.

---

## ELLE JAMES

A Golden Heart Award winner for Best Paranormal Romance in 2004, Elle James started writing when her sister issued a Y2K challenge to write a romance novel. She has managed a full-time job and raised three wonderful children, and she and her husband even tried their hands at ranching exotic birds (ostriches, emus and rheas) in the Texas Hill Country. Ask her, and she'll tell you what it's like to go toe-to-toe with an angry 350-pound bird! After leaving her successful career in information technology management, Elle is now pursuing her writing full-time. Elle loves to hear from fans. You can contact her at ellejames@earthlink.net, or visit her website, at www.ellejames.com.

This book is dedicated to my family, whose loving support has encouraged me to continue to pursue my writing career. My husband, who believes in my abilities and asks, "Why aren't you writing?"; my sister, with whom I brainstorm and share my successes; my father, because he taught me the value of hard work; my mother, who is my first line of defense beta reader; my oldest daughter, who reads my work and always looks forward to the next story; my son, who is proud of his mom and her writing; and my youngest daughter for keeping me on my toes. I love you all!

# Chapter 1

Creed Thomas Ruckman's smart phone buzzed and he pulled the rental SUV he'd picked up at the Portland airport to the side of the road just outside Cape Churn, a quaint Oregon seaside town. The caller ID displayed Blocked Sender. Probably The Man, his boss, who'd sent him on the red-eye flight from Alaska late the previous night, bumping mission status to urgent and a matter of national security.

Royce Fontaine orchestrated the band of Stealth Operations Specialists from their headquarters in Washington, for the most part. On occasion, he ran missions himself. The man was fearless and demanded no less from his operatives than what he expected of himself.

Creed hit the button on the headset hooked over his ear. "Thomas." He used Thomas and other aliases as his last name when he went undercover—Ruckman had become just a name in his file back at headquarters.

"You in Cape Churn yet?" Royce's deep voice filled his head as if he were there in the vehicle with him.

"Just pulling into town. Any word on Phillip Macias's whereabouts, or the location of the yacht I tagged in Russia?"

"That's what I'm calling about and why you're where you are. The GPS tracking device stalled off the coast of Cape Churn. Satellite images aren't picking up the boat at the location. Either they scuttled the boat or the boat sank. That's where you come in."

"I figured as much. None of my associates in Russia could tell me what's on board, or why it's so important to Macias."

"I put a bug in the ear of one of my contacts in the National Security Agency's electronic surveillance and monitoring division. He just sent word that something big is about to go down on the west coast, and Macias is at the center of it. There's a lot of subversive chatter by some of the people on their watch list."

"Any idea what?"

"Only hints at some type of explosions with the potential of killing entire cities of Americans."

Creed's heart sank to the bottom of his belly, then bounced back with a kick of adrenaline. "I figured it was something big. Macias is known for drama. When he's involved, it's go big or go home. Though they couldn't prove it, my informants told me he was responsible for last year's attacks on Chicago and D.C. in an event similar to the Greek Conspiracy of Fire Nuclei of 2010."

"Right," Fontaine agreed. "And he was only using

pressure-cooker bombs in those instances. From what my NSA source said, he's going for a bigger bang, possibly dirty bombs." Royce paused, then continued. "The situation is critical. Since all of this is conjecture at this point, keep it on the down low. We don't know who Macias's contacts are, and we can't trust anyone. If it leaks to the press, we could lose the connection. You have to find out what Macias is up to, his contact for uranium, if that's his angle, and stop Armageddon from happening. Millions of lives are depending on you."

"No pressure, right? And what you're saying is that for all these years people have been prophesying California would one day fall into the ocean, that event may come earlier than we think."

"As soon as I can pull some of the others in on this mission, I'll send them your way. In the meantime, you're the lead man."

"Sounds like I'm the *only* man."

"For the moment, you are. I'm working intel from this end. I'll feed you everything I know as soon as I know." True to his word, Royce would do everything in his power to help him. The head of SOS kept his promises. "You've got all the information and the cover you need to find that yacht. Go get 'em."

"I'm on it." Creed hit the button on his earpiece to end the call, drew in a deep breath and drove into town, to the Cape Churn police station. He climbed out of the rental and entered the office, wearing shorts, flip-flops, sunglasses and a T-shirt with the image of a sailboat emblazoned across his chest. Pasting his friendliest insurance-adjuster grin on his face, he extended his hand to the man he presumed was the chief of police, the one person in town who would know a local from a transient, and where to go to get what he needed. "Hello, I'm Creed Thomas. Are you the police chief?"

"That would be me." He gripped Creed's hand in a firm handshake. "Tom Taggart. I don't believe I know you. New resident in town, or here on vacation?"

This was where his cover came into play. Until he knew the trustworthiness of the locals, he couldn't reveal the potential danger lurking in the quiet seaside town. "Actually, I'm here on business."

"What kind of business brings you to Cape Churn? Setting up a golf tournament? Team building weekend? Searching for a vacation home?" The chief smiled. "Just ask—we're likely to have what you're looking for."

Creed removed his glasses, liking the older man's open, friendly face. "I'm looking for a boat."

"A boat?" Taggart's brows rose. "Renting, buying? Anything special you got in mind?"

"A missing boat, to be exact." He handed the chief his fake business card with Thomas Brothers Insurance written in bold lettering across the top. "I underwrote an insurance policy on a yacht we believe went down off the coast of Cape Churn in the past couple days."

"Is that so?" Taggart scratched his chin. "I don't recall receiving any reports of a ship in distress or BOLOs on missing persons."

"That doesn't surprise me. The owner probably didn't know he was in distress until the ship went down, and his family won't be missing him for several days. I understand there was a significant amount of fog the night before last?"

"True." The chief nodded. "Folks around here call it the Devil's Shroud. Nothing but misfortune happens when it slides into the coast. Could be your boat got caught up in it."

"That's my bet. Fortunately, we have tracking devices on the yachts we insure, and I believe I can locate it. All I need is a guide to get me out to it. That's what I was hoping you could help me with."

"Depends on where you're going. The shallows around here are pretty treacherous, even on a calm day. If you have the GPS coordinate, and it's not in the middle of the rocks, I recommend Dave Logsdon's dive boat and Emma Jenkins as your guide. She's not a full-time diver, but she has the most diving experience all around the cape."

"Where can I find them?"

"Logsdon docks his boat at the Cape Churn Marina. It's early in the summer season, and schools aren't out yet. You might catch him, if he's not chartered."

A man wearing a navy blue police uniform entered the building behind Creed and removed his uniform cap.

The chief turned to the officer. "Gabe here can show you the way."

"Where to?" Gabe stuck out his hand. "Gabe Mc-Gregor."

Creed introduced himself.

"Mr. Thomas needs to hire a boat and a guide to look for a potentially sunken yacht his company insured."

"Think it got caught in the fog the other night?" Gabe ran a hand through his dark blond hair. "We haven't had any distress calls or bodies wash ashore."

"The GPS tracking device we installed on the craft

indicates it's offshore, not moving. Too far to be anchored, which leads me to believe it's at the bottom."

"You'll want Dave Logsdon and—"

"Emma Jenkins," the chief finished. "I've already briefed him on the best guide in the area. Would you show him how to get to the marina? I've got a meeting with the mayor in fifteen. We'd send a diver with you, but we're short staffed, and diving isn't necessarily a requirement for the job. I can put a call into the coast guard and have them start a search for survivors."

"Thanks." Creed would rather not get the coast guard involved just yet. "In the meantime, I'd like to check the location and make sure the boat wasn't stolen or the GPS device tossed overboard."

"I'll put out the word to be on the lookout for any casualties that might have washed ashore." The chief stepped around Creed and Gabe. "Gabe can take you to the marina and get you set up."

Gabe waved toward the door. "I can take you there, or you can follow me."

"I'll follow," Creed said.

"Dave's the most reliable captain in the area. He can get you just about anywhere, or close enough you can swim in. And Emma is the most experienced diver. Can't go wrong with her."

"Good to know." He didn't really care as long as he had a boat to get him to where he needed to go. He didn't necessarily need a local dive master to guide him in. Having received his training courtesy of the U.S. Navy SEALs, Creed could dive circles around most recreational divers. But to keep his cover, he'd go along with the locals and maybe learn something about who Phillip Macias was planning to meet with his Russian cargo.

The sooner the better. He had a feeling the yacht going down wasn't part of the plan, and whoever was expecting it would be in a hurry to get his hands on whatever was on board. If that happened, it could initiate a chain of events that could potentially destroy the entire western coast of the United States.

*They're cancelling the Children's Wing Project.*

The words echoed in Emma Jenkins's head as she shoved her duffel bag with her wet suit and regulator into the backseat of her Jeep. She slipped behind the wheel and headed for the marina, her chest hurting so badly she could barely breathe.

If she hadn't scheduled the week off, she might have been tempted to call in sick to the hospital where she worked as a nurse. The same hospital her former fiancé had swindled out of the funds raised to build the new children's wing eight months ago.

Laura Kurtz had called that morning with the news. "I wanted you to hear it from me first, and to assure you it's not your fault and no one thinks that way."

*Yeah, right.* If she hadn't introduced Randy Walters to the board of directors, he wouldn't have been offered the consultant position for raising funds for the new children's wing.

"If you're at fault," Laura had said, "then so am I for not seeing through his lies."

Emma had been so gullible, thinking Randy was trustworthy, loved her and really had planned to marry her in June. Her wedding dress still hung on her closet door, a painful reminder of the fool she'd been to trust a man.

"Take this week off as an opportunity to get yourself together, have some fun counting starfish or whatever it is you do on your dives, and come back refreshed. We need you here at Cape Churn Memorial. You're the best nurse we have."

At that point Emma had faked an incoming call, her voice choking on a sob she refused to release. Randy didn't deserve a single tear. He'd hurt her, but worse, he'd hurt the children of Cape Churn and the surrounding seaside towns by absconding with the money meant for the addition.

Emma's only hope at redemption lay in the sea. Call it a hunch, but today was the day her luck would change. She could feel it in her bones and flowing in her blood, the same blood that flowed through the long line of Cape Churn Jenkinses, who'd helped establish this little town on the coast of Oregon in the mid-eighteen hundreds. The sole surviving Jenkins, she had an obligation to redeem the family name.

As she turned her Jeep into the marina parking lot, her heartbeat slipped into an unsteady rhythm, her breath coming in shorter bursts as excitement mounted.

Today would be the day she found the wreck of the *Anna Maria,* a ship legend told of having sunk in the Devil's Shroud in the late 1700s. She climbed out of her vehicle, grabbed her duffel and hurried toward destiny.

The boat that would get her there, the *Reel Dive,* rocked gently against its mooring. Dave Logsdon trotted along the dock carrying a cooler, probably filled with beer, his flip-flops making soft slapping sounds. He wore a worn U2 T-shirt and cargo shorts stained

from fish guts and bait and frayed at the edges. An
L.A. Dodgers baseball cap perched on his curly blond
hair, tipped back so that he could see. "Some fog we
had the past couple nights, wasn't it?"

"Unfortunately." Emma climbed aboard, unzipped
her bag and slipped her diving mask and headlamp
over her head. She adjusted the straps and removed it,
laying it aside while she dug out the rest of her diving gear. "Had plenty of accident victims in the emergency room."

Dave shook his head. "It was pretty bad out here.
Must have been a disturbance farther out to sea. We
had plenty of waves to go along with being socked in
with the Devil's Shroud."

"Not a good night to be out on the water." According to the legends and the written records, a similar
night, over two hundred years ago, had led to the dis-
appearance of the Spanish galleon, the *Anna Maria*.

Nothing penetrated the choking blanket of fog the
locals had nicknamed the Devil's Shroud. Ships caught
in its deadly clutches ran aground in the deadly shallows of the reefs surrounding the jut of land called
Cape Churn.

The *Anna Maria* had been spotted out to sea, nearing the Cape on its northern journey to the mouth of
the Columbia River, navigating the jagged coastline
between the rocky islands peppering the ocean floor.
She'd been due to dock the next morning in the harbor town of Cape Churn, laden with gold coins and
priceless china from the Far East. When the shroud
descended, the ship and all aboard had perished.

Records kept by colonists placed the ship near the

rocky shallows, but all efforts to locate the ship had come up empty.

*Until now.* Emma laid out her equipment, one piece at a time, going over her dive plan in her head. The dive that would fix everything in her life. Failure wasn't an option. Her life, her reputation at the hospital and in the community, depended on her finding a treasure sufficient to cover the cost of the new wing.

A moment of doubt slipped beneath her forced bravado. Why did she think she had a chance to find the *Anna Maria* when no one else had? Any sane person would conclude she had the same chances of winning the lottery as finding the two-hundred-year-old wreck.

"Ready?" Dave asked, leaping aboard.

"Almost." Emma shoved aside her misgivings and tested the flow of compressed air from the tank to the regulator, sucking in a deep breath and letting it out. She looked around at the equipment stacked on the deck. Buoyancy control device, or BCD, wrist dive computer with a built-in GPS, cylinder, regulator, booties, fins, wet suit, gloves, mask and diving knife. The most important item was the map she'd drawn of Cape Churn after researching her great-grandfather's logbooks and journals that had been kept by the long since deceased lighthouse keeper from the late eighteen hundreds.

Emma straightened. "Do you have the location entered in your GPS?"

"Done."

After a great deal of research and studying old letters and documents, she'd calculated a back azimuth from the locations reporting a sighting of the *Anna Maria* and determined the coordinates accordingly.

Three years ago, she'd established a grid extending six hundred yards outward from that location, taking into account tide and ocean currents. Over the years, she'd dived the grid, meticulously ruling out one section after another until now. The final grid, her last hope to find the *Anna Maria* and keep alive the dream of a hospital addition benefiting the children.

A tentative thrill of anticipation shimmied across her skin.

Dave climbed the ladder to the helm and paused at the top, his back still to her as he faced the dock. "What's with the police car?"

Emma glanced up, her gaze scanning the parking lot.

An SUV with Cape Churn Police written on the side pulled to a stop, and Officer Gabe McGregor got out.

Emma smiled and waved. Gabe and his fiancée, Kayla Davies, were friends of hers, though too often she felt like a pathetic odd man out to their loving family.

Another car pulled into the lot, parking next to Gabe's SUV. A tall, dark-haired man unfolded himself from behind the wheel. Wearing sunglasses, a T-shirt, swim trunks and flip-flops, he strode toward them, carrying a large duffel bag, his broad chest and thick arms a testament of a firm regimen of weight lifting. Maybe even a little Native American ancestry, with those high cheekbones and square jaw. The stranger met the officer at the back of the vehicle. Gabe spoke and pointed toward the boat and Emma.

Emma's pulse quickened, and she frowned at the realization.

"They seem to be pointing at us," Dave commented. "Should I wait and see what they want, or take off?"

Emma wanted him to take off. She had a lot of sea-floor to cover on her days off. But Gabe was her friend. If he needed to talk to her or Dave, she could spare him a few minutes. "I can wait."

Gabe strode across to the dock, headed straight for them, the stranger keeping pace behind him. "Emma, Dave, glad I caught you."

Feeling at a disadvantage, standing below the two tall men, Emma climbed out of the boat and stood on the dock, still staring up at the stranger with the officer. "Hi, Gabe. Good to see you. How are Kayla and the baby?"

Gabe smiled. "Both doing fine. Tonya had her first full night of sleep without waking last night. Kayla got up twice to make sure she was breathing." He turned toward the man behind him. "This is Creed Thomas. He arrived in town this morning, looking for assistance in a case he's working."

Emma's frown returned. "Case?"

Gabe nodded toward Creed. "I'll let him tell you."

The swarthy-skinned man stepped forward.

Dark, piercing eyes shone down on her, sending a ripple of trepidation across Emma's nerve endings.

"As Officer McGregor said, I'm working a case for my insurance company, and I need the expertise of a diver familiar with this area to help me."

Gabe grinned. "That would be Emma. She knows these waters better than anyone around."

Emma nodded. "Why? What are you looking for?"

"A boat that disappeared off Cape Churn maybe last night or the night before."

"Devil's Shroud," Dave said from his perch on the boat. "People from around here know better than to get caught out in that fog."

Creed nodded. "Officer McGregor informed me you'll be diving off the cape today, and I could use a boat." He glanced toward Dave before returning his attention to Emma. "And, as I said, an expert diver to help me find the boat that went down. It was expensive, and my underwriters want to make sure it did go down and wasn't stolen."

Her chest tightened. "I had other plans for the day. If I can fit your search in around my plans, it's a possibility." Emma's eyes narrowed. "Do you intend for me to find the boat, or are you going down, too?"

He nodded. "I'd planned on diving."

"Are you an experienced diver?" She hoped so; otherwise, he'd slow her efforts.

Creed's lips curled upward. "You could say I am."

"Good." Emma's mouth firmed. "I don't really have time to give lessons or rescue a new diver from getting the bends. I've got work to do."

His dark eyes twinkled in the sun as if he was laughing at her. "I'll try not to inconvenience you."

Her frown deepened. "You won't be carrying a speargun, will you?"

His forehead wrinkled. "No. Should I?"

"I'd rather you didn't." Emma smiled, softening her words. "I don't want you shooting me by accident."

Creed chuckled. "I take it you've been out with inexperienced divers before?"

She nodded. "I give lessons."

"So," Dave said from the deck, "do we have an additional diver today?"

Emma sighed. "I suppose." She glanced at Gabe. "You owe me."

Gabe tipped a finger off his hat. "He seems to be on the up-and-up, or I wouldn't have suggested he join you." He patted Creed on the back. "You're in good hands with Emma. Not only is she an expert diver, she's also the best nurse in the county. She helped deliver our baby girl."

"I don't think I'll need a labor-and-delivery nurse on this dive."

Emma laughed. "God, I hope not."

"Be careful out there." Gabe left Creed and Emma standing on the dock.

"Guess you're stuck with me." Emma stepped from the dock onto the deck of the dive boat.

Creed followed with his bag. "When are we leaving?"

Dave climbed down to the deck and flipped open the engine compartment, wiggled a hose, tightened a clamp and straightened. "How about now?"

"Do you have your own gear?" Emma eyed the man's bag.

"I do." He set the duffel on the deck and yanked his T-shirt up over his head, tossing it onto a nearby bench.

For a moment, Emma couldn't focus on anything other than the broad expanse of dark skin. Wow, the man had way too much going for him in the looks department. Not that she was interested. Once bitten... and all that.

Creed bent to unzip his bag.

Emma tore her gaze from his attributes, glancing at the bag's contents, hoping she wouldn't have to waste valuable time fitting him out in skins and breathing apparatus.

After moving another step away from the man, Emma pulled her sundress up over her head, remembering too late that she should have untied the string in the back first. With her arms caught and the dress over her face, she struggled to find the string.

"Here, let me." Large warm hands gripped the strap around her back, loosening the tie. The back of his knuckles brushed across her bare midriff as he pulled the dress up and over her head.

Standing in nothing but her bikini and feeling more than a little exposed, Emma glanced up at Creed to offer her thanks. Her words died on her lips as she gazed up at the dangerously handsome man standing so close she could almost smell the sunshine on his tanned skin.

Dark hair hung in loose waves over his ears and neck. Deep brown eyes smiled down at her.

Emma blinked once, then swallowed hard and backed up a step. Unfortunately, she backed right into a bench seat and would have fallen if Creed hadn't reached out and snagged her around the waist, pulling her hard against his naked chest.

"Er...thanks." She extricated herself from his grip, careful not to fall on the bench again.

"My pleasure." His deep voice washed over her like warm butter melting into every pore.

Off balance, Emma nodded toward his bag. "Do you have all the gear you'll need? Namely, a wet suit suitable for these cold waters?"

He grinned. "For the record, I've been diving a time or two. I believe I have all I need." He pulled from his bag the same type of equipment Emma had amassed for the underwater expedition to explore the barrier reef on the outer edges of Cape Churn.

Emma mentally ticked off all that he would need, and then nodded to Dave. "Let's go."

"On it." Dave fired up the engines while Emma unhooked the rope from the dock at the bow. Creed freed the stern rope, and Dave backed the forty-seven-foot boat away from the dock and out into the choppy waters of the bay. As he pulled away from the marina, a warm steady breeze lifted Emma's hair from her face. She entered the passenger cabin and tucked her sundress into a cubby.

While Dave steered the boat toward the coordinates Emma had instructed him to, she sat on a bench and pulled her wet suit up over her legs, then stood and tugged them up to her hips.

Creed pulled a handheld GPS tracking device from his bag.

"You put a tracking device on all the yachts you insure?" she asked.

"Only the ones we think are at risk of disappearing."

"From poor handling or theft?" Emma asked.

"Either."

"And which one was this?" Emma glanced up.

He shrugged one gorgeous shoulder, making Emma catch her bottom lip between her teeth. "Both."

"Let's compare your coordinates to mine. Hopefully, they're nearby and we can swim between the two." And she wouldn't waste too much time. She had only one week to find the *Anna Maria*. One week to change the hospital board of directors' minds on scrapping the children's wing. If she could find a treasure worth salvaging, they might reconsider.

Creed followed Emma up the steps to the helm, entering behind her, making the small space feel even smaller, filled with his large, overpowering presence. Having trouble concentrating on coordinates, Emma forced herself to compare the two sets of numbers.

For once her luck held. Creed's coordinates were within the same vicinity. Considering it was the most likely place on the reef for ships to go down, Emma wasn't terribly surprised. "Good, we're going the same way."

"Are you looking for another boat that got lost in the fog?" he asked.

"You bet," she answered.

Dave grinned over his shoulder. "Emma's ship got lost in the Devil's Shroud over two hundred years ago."

Creed's brow rose. "Going for the historical value or treasure hunting?"

Her lips twitched, and she gave him his own answer. "Both."

"Interesting." He studied her for a long moment, his gaze lingering on her mouth. Then, clutching his GPS tracking device, Creed exited the cabin, made his way to the lower level and out onto the bow where he stared out over the bay. He leaned against the railing, his jaw tight, gaze glued to the rocky outcropping ahead.

From her perch above, Emma studied the man. He had the build of an athlete. Maybe he did know a little about diving, enough that she didn't have to babysit him while she explored a particularly treacherous area.

She climbed down the ladder and continued gearing up for the dive. Leaving the suit's torso hanging around her waist, she slipped her feet into the diving boots and zipped them. The cold Pacific Ocean didn't allow divers to go without the wet suit. Too long in the chill waters led to hypothermia and death. A dry suit was even better, but today was sunny and warm enough that Emma would risk the cold with the thickest wet suit she owned.

Booties on, wet suit halfway there, Emma joined her dive buddy at the rail. "Maybe we should get a few things straight before we go under."

He turned, his gaze passing over her, eyes narrowing slightly, assessing her. "Like?"

"I haven't seen you around Cape Churn. Since I'm familiar with the area and its dangers, I'm in charge."

Creed nodded. "Fair enough."

"In fact, if you aren't a master diver, tell me now. Where we are going isn't for amateurs."

His brows rose. "As I said before, I can hold my own."

"That doesn't tell me much."

"I've logged over a hundred hours diving."

She studied him, looking for a crack in his shield, the lie behind the handsome face, and found nothing. "Okay, then. Dave is going to drop us as close as he can, and we'll swim in closer beneath the surface to avoid the waves. Once we're in the water, Dave will move farther out to keep his boat from banging up against any submerged rocks. There's a significant riptide and undercurrent that might cause us some issue."

"If it's so dangerous, why are *you* going out there?"

"I'm a wreck diver, and I've been doing it for years. The Devil's Shroud and the cape have claimed its share of ships over the years. If you want to get to them, you have to get into the shallows around the submerged rocks off the cape's point." She stared hard at him. "Still interested?"

He nodded. "Sure. Sounds like fun."

"Fun." Emma snorted. "You have no idea." She nodded toward his duffel. "You might want to suit up. We'll be there in less than ten minutes."

He popped a sharp salute and spun in a tight military about-face toward his gear.

As she dragged the rest of her seven-mil wet suit on, Emma watched Creed closely for any sign of hesitation, ready to pounce if he showed any lack of knowledge of his own equipment.

Regrettably, or maybe fortunately, he slipped into the wet suit as if it was a second skin. A quick check and testing of his regulator, dive computer, tank and mask indicated a proficient knowledge of his equipment.

*Darn it.* Emma had hoped to rule him out of this trip, claiming inadequate experience with the necessary diving apparatus.

By the time he had booties, fins and BCD strapped on, Emma had to concede the man knew his gear and wore it like he meant it. Much as she wanted, she couldn't fault him there.

Would he be an idiot in the water? Taking off instead of staying within eyesight of his dive partner? She'd be damned if she'd chase him all over the ocean floor.

This trip was important to her. She really felt as though it could be *the one.* And so much rode on her finding the *Anna Maria.* She didn't need a cocky diver with an attitude swimming off into trouble. "So what's your story?"

A grin slipped across Creed's face. "Are you always this direct?"

"I'm a nurse in my day job." She crossed her arms over her chest. "It pays to be direct."

He nodded. "A nurse, huh?"

"Yeah, so don't get stung by a jellyfish or stab yourself with a knife." She pulled her hair back off her face and secured it with an elastic band at the back of her neck. "I'm off duty, and it will only slow me down."

"I'll make a note of that." He chuckled. "Do you reserve your *good* bedside manner for the day job?"

"Absolutely." Emma smiled, loosening up a little. The man had a sense of humor and could give as good as he got. She didn't want to like him, but when he smiled like he did at that moment, she couldn't help herself. "If you're such an experienced diver, why are you out wreck-diving without a partner?"

He shrugged and stared out across the bay. "I could ask you the same."

"I do it all the time. I live here." She tipped her head toward him. "Where are you from?"

"Around."

Evasive as well as handsome, with his thick dark hair and penetrating dark eyes. They still had a few minutes to kill and Emma was good for a few more pulled teeth, so she asked, "Why the interest in the lost boat?"

"Besides the owner being missing and possibly dead? I want to protect the company interest and make sure the boat *is* in fact at the bottom of the ocean. It could be the owner found the tracking device and chucked it, taking off with the boat." He crossed his arms. "Why so interested?"

"The more I know about you, the better prepared I am for anything that happens below. So if there's anything I need to know, spill now."

His brows rose. "I just need to find the boat."

Emma opened her mouth to argue, but was interrupted by Dave.

"Get ready," the captain said. "I'm as close as I can get to your coordinates without becoming a statistic."

Emma glanced around at the rocks protruding out of the ocean. Sea lions basked in the sun on the smooth ledges. Some slipped off into the water, disturbed by the nearness of the boat.

Dragging her neoprene hood over her head, she tucked her hair beneath, then strapped her fins to her feet and shoved her hands into her gloves. Since she was the one in charge, she snapped the line for the surface marker buoy to her BCD and slipped her arms into the straps, hiking the BCD and cylinder up onto her back. Last but not least she pulled her mask onto her head and positioned it over her eyes, popped the regulator into her mouth and turned to see if her diving partner was anywhere near ready.

He stood fully equipped, mask and regulator in place, waiting for her.

Humph. So he was fast at getting geared up. That didn't mean he would be a good dive buddy. Emma waddled toward the edge of the boat and grabbed the railing as the boat pitched in the choppy water.

One last thumbs-up to Dave and to Creed, and she back-rolled off the end of the boat to plunge beneath the surface. The water took her breath away, even through the thick neoprene, making her second-guess her decision to use the wet suit versus a dry suit. But once she got moving, her body would warm the water trapped between her and the suit.

As soon as she submerged, she released the surface marker buoy, allowing it to float to the surface where it would mark the divers' progress beneath as they drifted along the ocean floor. That way Dave would know where to go to pick them up. Emma would make sure they swam away from the rocky protrusions when they were ready for the boat to retrieve them.

As Emma resurfaced, a splash beside her heralded Creed's entrance into the ocean.

He held on to his mask and regulator as his head broke through the water, and then he gave her a thumbs-up.

Together, they signaled Dave with a thumbs-up and waved.

The captain waved back and set the boat in motion to pull farther out to sea, where he'd wait until Emma indicated for him to come retrieve them from the water.

She checked her dive computer, confident that she had plenty of air for a couple hours, as long as she didn't have to go too deep. The deeper she dove, the more time she had to save for decompression coming up.

Emma loosened her mask, filled it with seawater, swished it, emptied and fit it snugly over her face. With one last glance at the departing boat and a double check on the surface marker buoy bobbing on the surface, Emma sucked in a gulp of metallic-tasting air and dove beneath the choppy waves. She headed straight for the rocks that had been partially submerged in the waves. Based on her calculations, the *Anna Maria* had last been seen there before the Devil's Shroud rolled in that evening over two hundred years ago.

A school of lingcod swam by, their dull gray bodies slipping past like silent shadows.

With nothing but the sound of her breathing and the bubbles rising from each exhalation, Emma basked in the silent underwater world, the ebb and flow of the current less pronounced the deeper she went.

As they neared the bottom and the base of the outcropping, a startling array of sea urchins and anemones colored the moss- and lichen-covered rocks and ocean floor with their spiny bodies. A curious sea lion swirled past Creed, twisting and looping gracefully through the water.

Emma shone her diving headlamp onto the rocks, swimming into what appeared to be a small city of stone sprouting from the seabed.

Creed lagged behind, his own headlamp panning the area all around him.

She waited until he looked toward her, and then Emma urged him to catch up. The wreck of the *Anna Maria* had to be hidden somewhere among the black rocks, and she was anxious to find it before her air ran out.

As soon as Creed was within twenty feet, Emma swam between two house-size boulders, her feet flipping gently, propelling her ever deeper into the maze.

As she passed by another boulder twice the size of the first, she stopped, her breath catching in her throat when she glimpsed the outline of something with a sharper edge and straighter lines, not the rounded contours of objects natural to the ocean world. As her headlamp beam played over the object, her excitement waned. It was a boat. Not nearly big enough to be the *Anna Maria,* nor as old.

A boat would be underestimating the craft that appeared to be more a luxury yacht, shiny white and fairly new at that. By the looks of it, the craft had been freshly sunk, lacking the barnacles and lichen that quickly laid claim to objects resting on the ocean floor.

Disappointed, Emma made a mental note of the name on the stern. *Pelageya.* Emma checked her dive computer. She had sixty minutes left on this cylinder before she'd have to surface. If she wanted to find the *Anna Maria,* she'd have to move on soon.

She wondered if this was the boat Creed referred to, and if so, how long Creed would want to investigate the wrecked yacht before they could continue on. Emma glanced behind her.

The light from Creed's headlamp reflected off the huge boulders as he swung it right and left. He had yet to focus in on what lay ahead of Emma.

Emma approached the yacht, making note of the large hole in the port bow. As her gaze panned upward, she caught movement behind the glass portal of the enclosed helm.

Curious, Emma swam closer and pushed open the door to the cabin. With a quick glance behind her to locate her dive buddy, who was closing in fast, she eased through the narrow opening, careful not to let her tank and BCD get hung up in the confines of the interior.

As she neared the few short steps up into the helm, her regulator hose snagged on something behind her.

She reached back to unhook the hose so that she could move on. Unable to pull free, she reached out to the walls in front of her, ready to push back the way she'd come.

As she laid her palms flat on the smooth surface of the helm's doorway, it gave way and a bloated face drifted out of the helm, coming straight at her, eyes white-filmed and vacant.

Emma let out a squeal into her regulator, the sudden appearance of the bloated face igniting her flight instinct. She back-paddled to get away, her clinical side overwhelmed into panic mode.

Something gripped her ankles and pulled hard, jerking her free of whatever had hold of her and out of the cabin.

Realizing she was breathing too fast, Emma tried to calm herself, but her head spun and a gray fog threatened her vision.

Creed's hands clasped her shoulders in an iron grip, forcing her to focus on him through her mask.

He tapped her regulator, as a reminder to breathe normally or she'd use up all her air before she could resurface. His gloved thumb and forefinger formed an O for the signal that she was okay.

Emma's gaze clung to Creed's as she fought to slow her breathing and regain control of her senses. When at last she could think straight, she motioned for her and Creed to go up. Her heart still pounded hard against her eardrums, drowning out the sound of air moving through the regulator.

Creed refused to move, pointing toward the yacht.

Emma shook her head and jabbed a finger upward, wanting to surface immediately, to get away from the floating, ghostlike body she'd seen in the cabin.

Creed squeezed her shoulders, tapped her chest with his forefinger and signaled okay.

*No, I'm not okay,* she wanted to say. As a nurse, she'd seen blood and gore. But she'd never had a body float out at her while diving. The abrupt appearance had thrown her off-kilter, and her pulse had yet to slow to normal.

Creed pointed to his chest and then to the yacht.

Emma shook her head, refusing to go back inside the confining space. A shiver rippled across her at the thought.

Creed's fingers squeezed her shoulders once more and he swam back into the yacht, leaving her hovering over the deck.

*He better not get stuck. If so, he's on his own.*

Several minutes passed, each longer than the last.

A shadow moved over the boat, shifting, swirling, circling, like a…

Emma glanced up. A great white shark hovered over the boat between rocky bottom and the open sky above. The sea lion that had been swimming along with them had disappeared. Her heart racing, Emma froze, praying Creed would remain inside the yacht until the shark grew bored and swam away. If Creed emerged with the body, the shark could attack, seeking the ready food source.

The sleek sea creature seemed to know Emma was there and wanted to toy with her as she debated whether to stay put or join Creed in the yacht with the dead man.

Emma kept an eye on the shark, checked her watch and her air supply several times before Creed finally emerged from the cabin.

A quick glance upward reassured her that the shark had indeed grown tired of waiting and moved on.

Creed backed out fins first, his hand clutching the arm of the dead man. Just what a shark might be interested in.

Emma shivered and looked again, praying the shark truly had moved on and hadn't swam out of view around a big boulder, intent on backtracking and surprising them.

A shadow swirled over them. Her heart pounding, Emma glanced up, only to see a school of lingcod blocking the sunlight between rock formations.

Their best bet was to get out with the body as quickly as possible. She touched Creed's shoulder and made the hand signal for *danger*, steepled her hands for *shark* and circled her finger, then motioned up with her thumb.

He nodded, his head swiveling in an attempt to find the shark.

With so many big rocks surrounding them, it would be difficult to see the shark until they swam up on it or vice versa.

Emma kicked out, moving swiftly through the water, anxious to get away from the shark before it decided they were fair game for lunch.

# Chapter 2

When Creed had back-paddled out of the yacht's cabin and turned to face his dive partner, he'd been happy to see Emma had shaken out of her panic. Although she still glanced around nervously.

*Good girl.*

When she'd indicated a shark in the area, he knew how dangerous it could be floating a dead man alongside them. With a brief glance at the body hovering like a specter in the underwater current, Emma kicked off, heading back the way they'd come, probably wanting to get out of the water before the shark returned.

Creed grasped the dead man's arm and followed, carefully dragging the man through the narrow crevices until they cleared the maze and swam out into the open. All the while he looked over his shoulder for the shark.

A school of small shiny fish swarmed around him, pecking at the body. Creed waved a hand to shoo them away, then flipped his fins harder to catch up with Emma.

They had to get the dead man out of the ocean before the shark decided the dead man and the live one would make easy prey.

Barely skimming above the ocean floor, a starry skate floated over a patch of strawberry anemones, its wide winglike fins fluttering gracefully. Creed wished he was there for reasons other than investigating a potential terrorist plot. He'd take time to examine the flora and fauna of the Oregon sea life. The job and a looming shark had him kicking hard for the dive boat. Sightseeing was for tourists. He had a job to do.

Emma stayed ahead of him, the line linking her to the buoy above trailing upward and at an angle behind her.

She hadn't been happy about his choice to bring the body up, but he had to determine without a doubt whether or not this was the boat Macias had made contact with and had arranged to meet. The GPS coordinates had been right on. Perhaps the identity of the dead man would help to shed more light on who Macias was involved with.

The captain had been a fool to hover close to shore in murky, foggy weather like it had been last night. The seas had been rough, a deadly combination with the fog. The hole in the yacht's hull had probably been caused by running aground on one of the jagged rocks hiding just below the surface. If the occupants had been able to abandon ship, their rubber raft would have been slammed into the rocky coastline.

Creed made a mental note to check local police reports of bodies washing ashore over the next couple days. If they didn't turn up soon, there wouldn't be much left to identify. The creatures of the sea scavenged anything dead, picking the bones clean within minutes in an all-out feeding frenzy.

Had the cabin door been open, the dead man's body quite possibly would not still be intact. Hopefully, they'd at least get a decent fingerprint off the victim.

When they'd traveled the same distance away from the reef as they'd come, Emma motioned for them to ascend. She moved with deliberate slowness, sure to make her rise to the top at the same or slower speed as the bubbles exiting her regulator.

She moved with grace, her slim legs flexing and bending, her fins gliding through the water with firm strokes.

Apparently she'd overcome her panic at finding a dead man and had restored her tight control over the dive.

Creed admired that control. He'd trained with the best as a navy SEAL. Being calm in stressful circumstances meant the difference between life and death when you were in an environment hostile to humans.

His navy days long past, he hadn't been diving as often, but he retained everything from the thorough instruction. The importance of paying attention to details had been imprinted in his memory for life.

As he rose to the surface, the dark waters lightened until he broke through to the sunshine warming the air above. The body bobbed on the surface, bumping against him. This was the part that made Creed wary. Underwater, he could see what was coming. With his head above the surface, anything could swim up to him and he wouldn't know until it hit him. Sharks normally didn't skim the surface waving their dorsal fins for all to see. That was what Hollywood fiction was made of.

To a shark, humans appeared like sea lions, a tasty food source.

For several long minutes, Emma waved at the boat bobbing in the waves a hundred yards away. Captain Dave sat at the helm, his hat pulled down over his face, napping, for all intents and purposes.

Creed ducked his head below several times to make sure the shark hadn't followed. So far so good.

Emma pulled a whistle from a strap around her neck and blew hard in short sharp bursts.

Dave's head popped up, and he stumbled to his feet. In seconds, the boat's engine revved and the craft made a large circle, heading directly toward them. He drifted to a stop a few yards away.

Emma was first to reach the dive boat, shaking out of her BCD.

While Emma readied to get out of the water, Creed kept a vigilant watch for the shark.

"Whatcha got there?" Dave squinted, then his eyes widened as he recognized what floated beside Creed. "Holy smokes."

"Dave, could you focus here? There's a shark lurking around here. I don't plan on dying today." Emma shoved her BCD toward him.

Dave leaned over the side and grabbed the gear and then her fins.

Creed ducked his mask into the water in time to see a large mass swirling below him in tighter and tighter circles, edging upward. "We got company." He let go of the body long enough to give Emma's fanny a shove, boosting her up the ladder faster than her hands and feet could keep up. "Go, go, go!"

Emma scooted up the ladder and fell over onto the deck, stripping off her mask and hood. "Get out of the water, Creed. That shark might decide live bait is better than dead."

"Not going without him." Still treading water with as little movement as possible, Creed waited until Dave lowered a cable attached to a small crane mounted near the rear of the boat, the kind used to lift divers and rescue crafts in and out of the water, when necessary.

Creed hooked the straps around the dead man's body and gave a thumbs-up, trying not to wonder where the shark was and if he had time to get himself out of the water.

The crank engaged, the metal-on-metal sound clanking in the still air as the body rose from the water.

Emma stood at the side of the boat, bending over the edge, staring into the water. "He's circling. Creed, get out of there!"

His pulse thundering in his veins, Creed yanked off his fins, threw them over the side of the boat, then grabbed for the ladder, hauling himself, BCD, tank and all, out of the water.

Emma grabbed his arm and pulled as a large gray shape angled upward, breaking the surface with a gaping maw of razor-sharp teeth. He snapped at Creed's heels, missing by inches, then fell back into the water, bumping his nose against the buoy marker still floating nearby.

Once topside, Creed dropped his gear to the deck

and pulled his hood off, shaking water from his hair, sucking in a deep, shaky breath.

Emma faced him, mouth pinched tight, gray eyes flashing. "Damn, that was close." She planted her fists on her hips, her lips pressing into a thin line. "What part of 'I'm in charge' didn't you get?"

He backed a step, holding his hands up. "I wasn't certain we'd be able to find our way back to the wreck. This guy's family would probably want to know he didn't make it and want something left to bury."

She stared at him a long time with a narrowed gaze and finally huffed. "Fair enough. But that was way too close for my comfort level. Nothing like trailing bait for a shark behind you. Don't *ever* do that again." She shivered as she yanked her wet suit off her shoulders and tugged the sleeves off her damp arms, muttering, "Which shouldn't be a problem, since you obviously found your boat and won't be going down with me again." Emma jerked the remainder of her suit down over her legs, only for them to get stuck around her dive boots. She grumbled a few choice expletives and pulled at the zippers on her boots.

Creed helped Dave tug the body to the side and slip a tarp over him to keep the gulls from sniffing him out. He shot a glance toward the cabin where Emma was pulling off her boots. "Is she always wound so tight?"

"Nah, she's usually happy and gets along with everyone." Dave chuckled. "Kinda nice to see her blow a fuse. But don't worry about her. The lady's fire blazes hot, but she burns out pretty quickly."

"Nice to know I rub her the wrong way." He didn't know why, but it gave him a kick that he got under the pretty diver's wet suit. Not that he wanted to get into her wet suit, but it had been a while since he'd been even moderately interested in a woman. They all seemed to be the same, going for the ring and commitment, something he couldn't do. Not in his line of work.

Falling for someone would make him vulnerable and make the woman a target. Not to mention, it wouldn't be fair to the woman left behind each time he was deployed to a new assignment.

His gaze slipped to Emma as she pulled the wet suit off her ankles and bent to pick it up from the floor. She had a great body, all lean muscle and nice curves where they counted.

Dave straightened beside him. "She dives every one of her days off, in case you're interested."

"Not really," Creed lied. "Are you available for another dive tomorrow?"

"I can be, but if you're not interested in diving with her…" Dave nodded toward Emma. "I can't help you. She's got me booked all week."

Not exactly what he had planned. "I'll check around for another boat."

"Not many dive boats around willing to get close to the point. Most recreational divers just dive close to the shoreline." Dave unhooked Emma's regulator off the cylinder and stowed the cylinder in a rack. "Come to think of it, the only other dive boat is being serviced right now, getting ready for the full-on summer season. You could see if one of the fishing boats would be willing to take you, but it's the beginning of tourist season and most of them are busy taking fishermen out who want to get a jump on the families. They'd want an entire group, and since there's only you…" Dave shrugged. "You might be stuck with me and Emma."

Creed nodded. "Sounds that way. Not that it's a problem. Will she be going out near the same place?"

"I'd assume so. You guys weren't down long enough to suit her." Dave climbed the ladder to the helm. "Hang on, we're headed in."

"Dave, could you radio ahead?" Emma came out of the cabin, pulling the sundress down over her bikini, the fabric clinging to her wet skin and swimsuit. "Notify the police we'll be bringing in a body."

Creed's gaze skimmed her lithe, graceful figure, the gentle curve of her waist and the swell of her breasts where the dress fit tightest.

His groin tightened, and he had to turn away to avoid embarrassing the dive master as he stripped out of his wet suit.

"Don't get your bikini in a wad, Emma," Dave called out. "I've got ya covered. I'll have them meet us with transportation for our additional passenger."

"You do that. I'd rather have left him down there and let someone else bring him up." Emma rolled her eyes at Creed. "But someone had other plans."

His wet suit off and shoved into the waterproof duffel, Creed faced Emma. "Sorry, didn't know it would upset you. Are you sure you could have found your way back to the wreck?"

"Absolutely. I know these waters. Besides, I have the GPS coordinate of the place we went down."

Creed shrugged. "My mistake."

Emma sighed and padded to the railing in flip-flops. "No. I just wasn't expecting a body to float out in my face. I guess I lost it." She shivered. "Thanks for forcing me to focus. If you hadn't intervened, at the rate I was breathing, I'd have run out of air in no time."

Creed patted her shoulder. "You're a good diver. You'd have kicked it soon enough."

She nodded, casting a sideways glance at him. "Yeah, but sooner was better. Thanks." Then she smiled, and her entire face lit. The sun chose that time to skitter from beneath a puff of clouds and shine down on her smooth, soft skin, igniting the highlights in her drying sandy-blond hair. The soft yellow, floral sundress made her look all feminine and girlie.

It made him want to reach out and pull her into his arms, to crush her to his naked chest and feel her gentle curves against him. *Whoa.*

"Uh, excuse me, I need to stow my gear." Creed dropped his hand and backed away, grabbing his duffel. He shoved it under a bench to keep it from getting wetter. Then he disconnected his regulator from the air tank, setting the cylinder in the rack beside Emma's. With nothing left to do but wait, he walked around to the front of the boat to watch as Dave deftly guided the craft into the dock, effectively avoiding further contact with his dive buddy.

As soon as he could, he needed to touch base with his boss, Royce Fontaine, at the Stealth Operations Specialists headquarters in D.C. Royce had promised he'd send backup as soon as Creed found anything of significance on the case that had started out as a rumor. All the SOS agents were tied up. Steel was wrapping up an operation in St. Thomas. She could arrive in Cape Churn within the next twenty-four hours. But that might not be soon enough.

Macias could beat her there with his contingent of hired thugs and stir up a whole lot of trouble for the tiny vacation community.

The dive boat bumped against the dock, shaking Creed out of his musings.

In the parking lot, lights flashed on top of a Cape Churn police vehicle. Gabe McGregor climbed out and strode across the dock to meet them.

Turning into the parking area surrounding the dock, an ambulance, lights off, bumped across potholes and came to a stop beside the police car. The driver and his partner climbed out. Together, they pulled a gurney from the rear of the wagon and rolled it across the pavement toward the marina.

When Dave brought the dive boat to rest against the dock, Creed jumped out and secured a rope to the bow, then climbed back aboard. Emma tied off at the stern.

Emma hefted her equipment bag from the floor of the cabin, slipped her feet into sandals and stepped over the side onto the dock.

Grabbing his duffel bag, Creed stepped out behind her.

"You guys are back sooner than I expected." Gabe met Emma halfway across the dock. "Dave tells me you found something out there." He tipped his hat as Creed neared him. "Was it what you were looking for?"

Creed dropped his duffel on the dock. "Found my yacht off the cape, probably sunk last night in the fog. It had a big gash in the starboard bow."

Officer McGregor nodded. "It happens. Any other unfortunate souls still down there?"

Creed shook his head. "No. I checked all the cabins to make sure."

"I'll contact the state crime lab and see how they want to handle this investigation. Appreciate you bringing him up. Saves us a little time."

Creed risked a glance at Emma's face. "I didn't know how long he'd last in the sea."

"Unless they wash up quickly, we usually don't get much back, if anything." McGregor's brows furrowed as he glanced at Emma. "You look a little pale. You okay?"

She nodded. "I'm fine. I've located bodies before. It was just that I wasn't expecting it to float out at me."

"Did you find the *Anna Maria?*" McGregor asked. "Kayla said you were pretty excited about this dive."

Emma shook her head. "Not this time. Too busy bringing up a dead body to get too far into the rocks." She shrugged. "I have a few more days off. If the weather holds, I'll find her."

Creed glanced at Emma. "I didn't realize you were looking for anything in particular. I thought you were just diving."

"I have tomorrow." Emma slipped the strap of her bag over her shoulder and glanced up into Creed's eyes. "The important thing was to do what you did and bring the body ashore."

Creed found it interesting that she didn't volunteer any further information on what she was looking for.

McGregor watched as the EMTs bagged the body and hefted it over the side of the boat and onto a gurney. "As it is, we had a report of a body found washed ashore a couple miles down from here. The current must have carried the others away from the boat."

Creed's head jerked up. "Have you had a chance to identify the body yet?"

"No. The coroner has him now. He'll have his work cut out for him. He was pretty pecked over." The officer turned to the woman. "Emma, any identification on the boat? That would help a great deal."

She nodded. "The boat's name was *Pelageya*. I don't know if it means anything. Might be someone's name."

"It's Russian for 'of the sea,'" Creed offered.

Emma's brows rose. "You're a master diver *and* you speak Russian?"

Creed shrugged. "A little." Fluently when necessary, as it had been just days earlier.

"Mr. Thomas, are you staying in Cape Churn?" Officer McGregor asked.

"Call me Creed." He nodded. "I'll be staying for a couple days, filing paperwork for the insurance company."

"Good." McGregor smiled briefly. "Where can I find you if we have any questions about the yacht?"

"I don't know yet." Creed hefted his bag, settling the strap over his shoulder. "Do you have any suggestions?"

Emma's lips twitched. "Officer McGregor's sister runs a B and B. You could stay there. She makes a mean clam chowder."

Officer McGregor grinned. "That she does. Mom's recipe. I'm not sure how full she is, with it being the start of summer season, but I could make a call and find out."

Creed nodded. "I'd appreciate that." On second thought, he almost changed his mind. If Phillip Macias arrived and discovered Creed had found the yacht first, he might come after him. The B and B could be the recipient of Phillip's brand of collateral damage.

Before Creed could stop Officer McGregor and tell him never mind, the man had walked back to his cruiser. Emma met with the EMT crew, exchanging pleasantries like they were old friends.

Creed shouldn't be surprised at how much each member of the community knew about the others. Small towns were like that. One of the main reasons he hadn't stayed long in one of them. As usual, he was here on a mission, and once it was done, he'd be gone.

Frankly, he hadn't expected to find what he was looking for as quickly as he had. When he'd been at the police station and asked who had a boat that could take divers out to the cape, he'd fully expected to run into difficulties. But like all small town police forces, they knew everyone and every place a person could go to get the services he needed.

Now that he'd located the *Pelageya,* he needed to move fast, before Macias learned of their find.

When the anonymous tip that Macias was dealing in large amounts of cash had reached SOS headquarters a week ago, Creed had been dispatched to Moscow, his assignment to follow Macias.

The high-powered businessman had met with Vladimir Zakharov, a Russian heavy in international trade of legal as well as black-market commodities, some stolen from the Russian government.

After the meeting, Macias stayed an additional week in Moscow enjoying Zakharov's hospitality.

Creed had taken the opportunity to ask questions of some of Zakharov's staff, discovering the purpose of the meeting between the two businessmen had more to do with terrorism than trade. Macias was awaiting the finalization of a shipment that would leave from the resort town of Vladivostok, off the east coast of Russia, carrying special cargo. Macias would take possession of the cargo off the western coast of the United States in four days.

Creed had met with one of the undercover CIA operatives he knew in Moscow. Royce had tagged him with the responsibility of reporting Macias's movements to SOS headquarters. Then Creed had pulled in several markers to find swift transportation to Vladivostok, and crossed the vast expanse of Russia. The trip took two days.

There, his grasp of the Russian language had stood him well. The locals at the marinas had been more than willing to share what they knew, pointing to the empty berth where a yacht with English lettering was preparing for a trip to the American west coast.

Fortunately, the man had spoken to the yacht captain, who'd bragged about his upcoming trip to the American continent, to a place called Oregon.

Creed paid a midnight visit to the dock and stuck a waterproof GPS tracking device on the hull of the *Pelageya*.

Creed notified Royce of the shipment and caught the next flight out, landing in Anchorage, exhausted and jet-lagged. He found a hotel and slept for ten hours, conserving his energy while the gurus back in Washington pulled twenty-four-hour shifts scanning satellite feeds until they spotted a possible yacht approaching the western United States. Based on the boat's vector, the shipment would have arrived on the Oregon coast the next night.

The evening had brought with it a fog so heavy, the locals called it the Devil's Shroud. According to Royce, the last satellite image before the fog engulfed the yacht placed the boat at the tip of Cape Churn.

The ship had disappeared. Creed had come to find it before Macias, to discover what cargo the Russian and the American had arranged to be delivered.

Creed dragged in a deep breath of the salty air and let it out slowly. Thank God they'd found the boat on his first dive. It might buy him a little time to get back down there and locate the cargo.

With a dead man in tow, Creed doubted the discovery would fly below Phillip's seemingly endless radar. An autopsy would be performed, the wreck becoming public record.

When Macias went looking for his yacht, he'd find it fairly easily.

If not for Emma, Creed could have spent days searching.

The woman foremost on his mind followed the emergency personnel to the ambulance and met with Officer McGregor.

Creed turned to Dave.

The dive boat captain had his head down in the engine compartment. Creed waited until Dave stood and dropped the door in place.

"Dave, since it looks as though I'll be going out with you tomorrow, do I need to unload my gear?"

Dave wiped a streak of grease onto his cargo shorts. "Leave it. I'll be sure to lock it up."

"Thanks." Creed jumped on board and stowed his duffel in the cabin. When he turned to leave, he thought better of it and faced Dave again. "One other thing."

The dive boat pilot straightened. "What's that?"

Creed inhaled and let out the breath slowly. How did he tell the guy to keep his mouth shut without divulging everything about his operation? "I wouldn't give the coordinate for our dive to anyone."

The other man's brows dipped. "Why?"

How much information could he reveal and not put the guy in danger? Not much. "Look, Dave, you don't know me, and you have no reason to trust me, but I have a bad feeling about that wreck. If anyone comes asking, I'd keep it to myself."

"I'll keep that in mind." Dave's eyes narrowed. "Besides, the coordinate belongs to Emma. She's the one who directed me there. You think the yacht sank for other reasons besides running up on the rocks?"

"No, I think the yacht hit the rocks. I'm just concerned over why they were out there in the first place in such bad weather."

"We have some yacht owners who don't have the brains God gave a gnat. I've seen stupider things happen."

"Still…"

Dave waved. "Gotcha." He twisted his fingers next to his lips like he was locking them.

Creed waved at the dive boat captain and strode toward the parking lot.

Emma met him at the end of the dock.

The police officer had climbed into his vehicle and was leaving the parking lot.

"If you're done here, you can follow me to the B and B. Molly's expecting you." She motioned toward a bright red Jeep Cherokee sitting in the parking lot, its ragtop down, the roll bar and leather seats warming in the sun.

"I can find my way, with a few directions."

"Yeah, I figured you could, but Molly insisted on feeding me lunch for bringing her a new customer."

Emma's lips quirked. "As a single woman with odd shifts and no time to cook, I'm not turning down a free meal."

"By all means, lead the way." Creed waved a hand in front of Emma.

She started toward her Jeep. "What were you talking to Dave about?"

"Just making arrangements for tomorrow's dive."

She stopped so abruptly, Creed bumped into her.

His hands came up around her waist to steady her.

"Tomorrow's dive?" she asked, her brows rising high.

Creed couldn't help grinning at her surprise and chagrin at the news. "That's right. Looks like we'll be dive buddies tomorrow, after all."

"Really?" Emma shot a glance toward Dave and the boat, then down at the hands on her waist. If Creed wasn't mistaken, her body trembled just a little beneath his fingertips.

He wanted to pull her back against him, but thought better of it, releasing her as he replied, "Really."

She smoothed a hand over her dress where his fingers had been, the color high in her cheeks. "Just so you know, I had plans of my own."

Creed smiled. "So noted."

Her brows dipped. "Good. Then follow me. Molly will be waiting."

As Creed slipped behind the wheel of his rented SUV, he was still smiling. He shifted into Reverse and was about to back out of the parking space when he looked out at the bay.

A large yacht rounded Cape Churn's rocky point, its

gleaming white hull cutting through the water, headed directly for the little marina.

His foot left the accelerator, and Creed braked to a stop.

The yacht came to a halt in the middle of the bay.

A honk dragged his attention back to the red Jeep with the impatient driver pulling out of the parking lot.

Creed backed out and fell in behind Emma.

In his rearview mirror, he could see a smaller boat leaving the yacht and heading into the marina.

His bet was Phillip Macias had just arrived in Cape Churn.

*Damn.* Things were about to get a lot more interesting…and dangerous.

# Chapter 3

All the way to the McGregor B and B, Emma coached herself.

"Yes, he's great looking and knows how to dive. That doesn't mean he's unmarried or available." Though she hadn't noticed a ring on his finger. "Ring or no ring, I don't need a man in my life." One lying, thieving bastard was enough to keep her from going down that path again.

Her hair blew out behind her, drying in the wind generated by exceeding the speed limit along the curvy coastal highway. The entire drive out to the B and B, she couldn't stop thinking about how his hands felt resting on her waist, warm, large and strong. Nor could she get over the urge she'd had to fall back against him and feel the solid wall of his chest against her back.

She couldn't drive fast enough to get away from her

thoughts or the man who'd generated them, now following her to Molly's.

Thank goodness the B and B was several miles out. It gave her time to gather her wits, so that when she pulled up in front of the quaint old mansion, she wouldn't be drooling over a man she'd just met.

Emma climbed out of her Jeep and tried to smooth her hair into some semblance of order.

Molly McGregor burst through the door, her face wreathed in a smile. "Emma, honey, so glad to see you. It's been ages." She hurried down the stairs and engulfed Emma in a hug.

"Hey, Molly. Don't be silly. I was here a week ago. Clam chowder night, if I remember correctly."

"Two, sweetie. It's been two weeks since I had the chowder." Molly held her at arm's length and stared into her face. "You look tired. Are you taking care of yourself?"

Great, not only was her hair a mess, she looked like a hag. "I'm fine. Just got through with a dive, and you know how the water takes it out of me. I brought you a guest."

As if on cue, Creed's black SUV pulled in beside Emma's Jeep and he got out.

Molly's brows rose as Creed straightened. "Oh, my. And I thought I was doing *you* a favor," she whispered. In a louder voice, she held out her hand. "Hi, I'm Molly McGregor, owner, operator, chief cook and bottle washer of the McGregor B and B."

"Creed Thomas. Nice to meet you." He grasped her hand and smiled down at Emma's friend.

A stab of something unfamiliar jolted Emma, followed by the sudden urge to break through their connected hands. Instead she cleared her throat. "What's for lunch?"

Molly blushed and released Creed's hand, her own hand rising to push her strawberry-blond hair behind her ear. "Lunch," she sputtered. "What was it? Oh, yes, seafood chowder." She waved toward the house. "Do you want to settle in your room first, Mr. Thomas?"

"Call me Creed." He smiled again at Molly.

A stab of irritation spiked Emma's blood pressure, and she bit down hard on her lip to keep from saying anything. What was wrong with her? She never got angry. And why should she care a fig if Creed Thomas smiled at her friend Molly? The woman deserved a little flirtation; she'd been living the life of a nun since she'd taken over the B and B. And Creed Thomas was a handsome man.

As Molly led Creed into the house, Emma studied the insurance adjuster. Dressed in his shorts and a pullover, he displayed muscular legs, a tight abdomen and shoulders broad enough to fill any doorway. He didn't look like any of the insurance adjusters she'd ever met. In fact, he looked more like a cop or bouncer at a bar.

Sure, he was great to look at, but he didn't follow directions and he'd disrupted her search for the *Anna Maria*. And from the sound of it, he'd be diving with her again tomorrow. Emma knew Dave could use the money. The more divers he had on board, the more he made to help him pay off his loan on the boat.

She couldn't forbid him from taking on more divers. At least Creed would be diving in the rocky shallows at Cape Churn, and he'd proven he was capable.

Emma hoped they spent less time on the submerged yacht and more time searching for the *Anna Maria*.

Molly led Creed up the stairs to a door off the upper landing, ducking inside with him to explain the facilities.

Emma wandered around the great room shared by all the occupants of the B and B. The house had been left to Molly and Gabe McGregor on the deaths of their parents. Unable to afford the upkeep on the huge old house, Molly had converted it into a comfortable and thriving bed-and-breakfast. She seemed happy about her work and what she'd done with the place and was content with her choices in life.

Gabe had met the young artist Kayla Davies, the love of his life, who'd moved into the old lighthouse cottage.

Emma had made friends with Kayla, and they'd met for coffee once a week down by the marina until Kayla had her baby.

As Molly descended the stairs, she smiled at Emma. "Such a nice man. Where did you find him?"

"I didn't find him, Gabe did. He came out on the dive boat with us today."

"Oh, a diver?" Molly nodded. "Come, help me set the table. You can fill me in on Mr. Thomas." She marched into the dining room and pulled plates, bowls, napkins and silverware from an antique buffet.

"Creed," Emma corrected, opting to place the plates. "He wanted you to call him Creed. Anyone besides us three having lunch today?"

"No. The other guests are out enjoying the sunshine. It's just the three of us."

Emma groaned. "I'll be a third wheel."

"As if that could happen. We're just having lunch. Emma, you can be so melodramatic at times."

"I'm much more comfortable cleaning up scraped knees and diving than I am talking at a dinner table. Besides, he's not my type."

"What type would that be? You haven't had a type since Randy left town. And *that* type you can do without."

A stab of anger, guilt and longing settled over Emma. She'd thought she had a type once. Had even been engaged. Randy had been attentive, loving and accepting of her sometimes crazy work schedule at the hospital. He'd also been lying, cheating and stealing from the funds raised for the new hospital wing.

"Besides, if anyone is a third wheel," Molly continued, "it would be me." Gabe's sister laughed, her joy of life infectious, making it hard for Emma to hold on to her anger or her guilt. Still, she didn't want to tell Molly about the new guy in town. Her own thoughts about him were far too confusing, and she hadn't had time to process them thoroughly.

"So, where's he from?" Molly wasn't going to let her off lightly.

"I don't know." Emma folded a napkin and laid it on the plate.

"Why's he in town?" Molly persisted.

"He's an insurance adjuster, or something like that. He came looking for a yacht his company insured." At least Emma had one answer. *Please, Molly, no more questions.*

"Is he married?"

Emma stepped back. "Why don't you ask him?" She hadn't thought to inquire, nor was she interested. Having been engaged once, she had no intention of repeating that heartache. "He's not wearing a ring, if that matters."

"Good grief, woman. You've been in the man's company for how long, and you haven't gotten the basics?" Molly shook her head.

"I'm not interested." Emma headed for the kitchen. "Don't we have some chowder that needs to be served?"

Molly followed. "If you're not interested in the man, then do you mind if I am?"

With her back to Molly, Emma poured the pot of chowder into an empty soup tureen. The thought of Molly dating the handsome diver didn't sit right with Emma, and darned if she knew why. "Be my guest. He's all yours."

"Am I interrupting?" The object of their conversation pushed through the swinging door into the kitchen.

Emma spun, her face heating.

Molly clapped a hand over her mouth and giggled like a schoolgirl.

Pushing her embarrassment to the side, Emma answered, "No." *Thanks, Molly. Let's not be too obvious about who we were talking about.*

Emma lifted the heavy tureen and shoved it toward Creed. "Do you mind taking this into the dining room?"

"Not at all." He carried the container into the other room as if it was as light as a feather, the door swinging closed behind him.

Molly burst out laughing, her eyes filling with tears. "What timing."

Emma grabbed Molly's wrist. "Let's get this straight—I'm not interested in Creed Thomas, and I don't want to talk about him. Got it?"

Her lips still trembling, Molly nodded. "Got it." She grabbed a basket of bread sticks and pushed through the door, a smile on her face. "So, Mr. Thomas, are you married?"

Emma groaned, glanced around for a door to escape through, then thought better of it. No telling what Molly would be saying to the newcomer. Emma might need to be there to make sure she didn't get in trouble. She armed herself with a pitcher of lemonade and followed Molly.

Creed glanced across at Emma as she entered, the lemonade in front of her like a shield to ward off handsome men and her attraction to them. Damned if it wasn't working.

"I almost got married once, but it didn't work out."

"Why, if you don't mind my asking?" Molly happily quizzed.

Emma almost turned around, lemonade and all, and retreated into the kitchen. Molly didn't know a stranger and wasn't afraid to ask the tough questions.

Creed's voice made Emma stop before she'd half-turned. "Seems she liked my partner better."

Something tightened in Emma's chest, and she turned back to the dining room.

The diver had answered Molly, but his gaze captured Emma's.

Emma knew betrayal and loss and, by the look on Creed's face, he knew them intimately, as well. A brief flash of connection blazed between them.

"I'm sorry. I shouldn't have asked." Molly reached out and touched Creed's arm. "That must have been hard for you."

Creed shrugged Molly's hand from his arm and held

out a chair for her. "Not too hard. The incident made me realize that a commitment wasn't in the cards for someone in my line of work. I'm away too often."

Caught up in the conversation, despite her best effort to remain immune, Emma asked, "Insurance adjusting keeps you away from home a lot?"

Creed rounded the side of the table and held Emma's chair for her before he answered. "I investigate special cases. It takes me all over the country and sometimes the world."

Emma sat, her attention captured by his nearness and the scent of sun, salt and ocean permeating the air around him. "You're kind of like a government agent then, like the FBI or CIA, only for a commercial company?"

He scooted the chair back across from Emma and folded his long form into it. His moves were smooth and deliberate as he settled, his gaze rising to meet Emma's. "My job's not as glamorous."

Caught off guard by his pointed stare, Emma blurted, "You don't strike me as an insurance agent."

"No?" His smile spread across his face and warmed some long dormant areas inside Emma. "What do I strike you as?"

"A bouncer, a cop, or maybe a spy or special agent." But not an insurance adjuster.

His lips twitched, and his eyes twinkled. "Now, if I was actually a spy or special agent, would I tell you I was?"

Emma's breath caught. The impact of his sexy smile hit her like a hammer to the chest. "Of course not."

"And if I did…" His eyes narrowed dangerously.

Molly laughed and finished. "You'd have to kill her?"

Her heartbeat racing as if she'd been running, Emma hated admitting the man affected her far more than he should have.

Then Creed laughed, breaking the tension in the room. "Nothing quite so dramatic. Suffice it to say, I'm one of the good guys, working to keep insurance rates down by finding, reporting and sometimes recovering lost, stolen or damaged property."

Emma's eyes narrowed, her focus sharpening on the man. His words rolled off his tongue effortlessly. Maybe a bit too easily. As if practiced.

"You must have been to some exotic places. Sounds interesting." Molly lifted the ladle, dipped it into the chowder and scooped some of the creamy liquid into a bowl, handing it across to Creed first.

"The job sounds too good to be true," Emma commented, accepting the next bowl. "How does one luck into such a position?"

Twirling his spoon in his fingers, Creed's smile slipped. "By getting fired from my previous job for ratting out a bad egg."

"That doesn't sound good. Why would you get fired for doing the right thing?"

"The bad egg was my boss."

"Oh." Molly's wide gaze dipped to her chowder.

"I take it he wasn't happy about being outed." Emma sipped chowder from her spoon, the rich flavor barely registering. Her attention had been riveted to the man she'd been trying to ignore since he walked on board the dive boat earlier that day.

"No. His supervisor chose to believe him over me."

The rest of the meal passed in silence.

Emma finished her chowder and immediately stood. "I hate to eat and run, but I need to get back to town."

Creed stood, dropping his napkin on the table.

Molly pouted. "You can't stay and chat?"

"No, I need to get some things done before tomorrow." She really needed to get away from the man who was already occupying too much of her time and space. She reached for her bowl.

Molly raised her hand. "Oh, honey, don't worry about cleaning up. It'll give me something to do."

"Thanks for lunch. As usual, it was great." Emma hugged Molly and shot a look at Creed. "I guess I'll see you tomorrow. If the weather holds out, I'm leaving the dock at eight. Don't be late."

"Yes, ma'am." He popped a sharp salute.

Emma frowned. The man had all the bearing of one who'd seen military service. What had he left out of his hard-luck story?

*No.* She reminded herself that she wasn't interested.

"Bye, Molly." She nodded toward Creed. "Mr. Thomas." Then she left the dining room, striding across the living area to the door. She made it all the way down the front porch before she heard a voice behind her.

"Ms. Jenkins."

Her feet came to a halt, and she braced herself before she looked up into the dark brown eyes of Creed Thomas. "Yes, Mr. Thomas."

"Please, call me Creed." He smiled, letting the screen door close behind him.

"Creed." She tipped her head, staring up the steps

at him, trying to ignore the way her heart fluttered. "What is it you want?"

"Since I'll be your diving partner again tomorrow, could you tell me what it is you're looking for? What is this *Anna Maria* Officer McGregor mentioned?"

She hesitated. It wasn't as if the *Anna Maria* was a huge secret. Anyone who'd grown up in Cape Churn knew the story of how it had disappeared off the coast of Oregon in the late seventeen hundreds. Some thought it was a legend with no substance. "It's a Spanish galleon that sank over two hundred years ago. I'm getting close to finding it and only have three days left to do it."

"Why only three days?"

Since her fiancé had died in a car accident while absconding with the funds destined to build the children's wing onto the small Cape Churn Memorial hospital, Emma had fought to find a way to recoup the loss. As a nurse, she didn't make the kind of money needed to pay back that large a sum. Not anytime soon. She'd hoped to convince the board of directors not to cancel the wing the community needed so badly until she could come up with a way to repay the amount. Her last hope was the project she'd been working on almost since she'd been old enough to fit into a pair of fins.

So far, she hadn't found any physical evidence that the *Anna Maria* had gone down off Cape Churn. But Emma hadn't given up hope, nor would she as long as she could dive and explore the ocean floor. But the next three days were her last hope of finding it in time to change the hospital board of directors' minds, thus redeeming herself for introducing Randy to them.

Emma stared out at the ocean, visible between the branches of red alder trees.

"I'm sorry." Creed descended to the same level as Emma and took her arms in his grasp. "I didn't know that would be a hard question."

Her gaze dropped to where his hands rested on her arms. God, she liked how strong they were and how warm and safe they made her feel.

She stiffened, hating that she could so easily have leaned against him and forgotten the burden she bore from her past mistakes. Emma stepped out of his arms. "Let's make a deal. I'll tell you about the *Anna Maria* when you tell me the truth about why you are really here?"

His hands dropped to his sides. "I don't know what you're talking about. You know I came looking for a boat that went down. We found it."

"And you're sticking to your story about being an insurance adjuster?"

For a long moment Creed stared down at her. She could almost see the lie poised on his tongue, as his lips pressed into a tight line. "That's my story."

It didn't explain the vibe she was getting. The man seemed too disciplined, too sure of himself to be just an adjuster. "And the job you were fired from?"

He glanced away, a dark shadow clouding his gaze. "I was a navy SEAL."

Her head shook side to side. "No wonder you knew so much about diving." She laughed, a short, sharp burst that lacked any humor. "I feel like you're playing me for a fool."

"Never." He gripped her arms again.

She shook her head. "Oh please, don't spread the lies thicker."

"No really. I think you're a great diver, smart and too pretty for your own good."

Butterflies fluttered in her belly at his words. He thought she was pretty. "If we're going to be dive buddies, don't lie to me."

He grinned. "Does that mean you're going to let me dive with you again?"

"You're a SEAL. You don't need me to dive."

"I need Dave's boat."

"Why?" She stared up into his eyes. "You found your boat."

"I need to see if it or anything in it is salvageable."

She crossed her arms over her chest. "Why should I help you?"

"Because you know where to look and you know this area. And, admit it, you kind of like me." He reached out and brushed a thumb across her cheek.

"I wouldn't go that far." Her insides warmed. Was she that transparent?

His grin disappeared. "I have a favor to ask."

He stood close enough that she could smell the salt of the sea on him. She swayed toward him. "Yeah?"

"Could you not tell anyone about finding the yacht?"

She straightened. "Why?"

"I suspect it was carrying stolen or illegal property, and someone might want to recover it."

"But you want to get to it first."

"That's the idea."

"How do I know *you're* not the crook?"

"I guess you'll just have to trust me."

"What if I don't?"

"That would be a shame." He gripped her arms again, his head dipping close to hers, his mouth within kissing distance. "Then I'd have to steal this kiss."

"Oh, no, you're not." Her heart raced, her breath seizing in her lungs.

"If I'm not stealing it, then you'd be giving it to me freely."

"Never," she swore, her gaze firmly fixed on his descending lips.

"Oh, sweetheart, never say never." He bent to capture her mouth with his, pressing down hard.

She gasped, her teeth parting enough that his tongue slipped through, stroking the length of hers, wiping away all thoughts of lies, subterfuge and treachery. Emma couldn't think past how incredibly wonderful his lips felt against hers, his chest pressing against her breasts and the hard ridge of his fly nudging her belly.

When he came up for air, he whispered, "You'll keep our secret?"

She scrambled for a brain cell and what to say next. "Why is it so important?"

"It could get really dangerous if you don't."

"For you, or me?"

"Both. Can you pretend I'm on vacation and you're my dive master, taking me out to dive the reefs?"

"That would be lying." She couldn't drag her focus off the way his lips moved to form words.

"I don't want the danger to come to you. Please," he said, the word a puff of air tickling her mouth, a soft reminder of how his kiss stirred her.

"Okay," she whispered, though she suspected the danger was not in the yacht or what it held, but with the man holding her in his arms.

Emma climbed into her Jeep and drove away, her head lost in a fog of lust and longing. When she neared town, her gaze fanned out over the harbor, and she spotted a shiny white yacht resting in the center. She wondered if anything Creed had told her held a grain of truth. It was still early in the summer season for the yachts to start filling the cape, and how coincidental was it that this one showed up the day after the other yacht sank?

For that matter, how likely was a former SEAL like Creed to take a job as an insurance adjuster? Not likely. If not an adjuster, what was he and why had he lied to her?

# Chapter 4

Creed didn't stay at the B and B long. Once Emma left, he gathered binoculars, his cell phone and his computer and headed back into Cape Churn, determined to find out who owned the yacht anchored in the bay. If it was Phillip, the race had begun and he didn't have much time to find what cargo was on board the *Pelageya*.

Nearing town, he hit the speed dial for headquarters. On the first ring, Royce picked up. "Thomas, what did you find?"

"The yacht and a body."

"The cargo?"

"Not readily obvious. I'm diving again tomorrow to look a little closer."

"The body?"

"Appears to be the captain, from what I could tell."

"Died because of the wreck, or did he wreck because he was dead?"

"Someone killed him. I found a bullet wound hidden in his hair." It had been hard to spot, and there had only been an entrance wound. The shell probably bounced around the inside of the man's skull, scrambling his brain.

"What about the rest of the crew?" Royce asked.

"The local police reported another body washed ashore this morning."

"Condition?"

"I'm headed to the morgue to find out."

"Still vacationing?"

"Working vacation. Us insurance adjusters can't just fly from place to place without doing some work to claim our trips on our taxes."

"Right." Royce chuckled. "Still can't picture you as an insurance adjuster. You have too much hair for the job."

Creed ran a hand through his dark thatch of hair. "Should I shave it?"

"No. Then you'd look like the SEAL you were born to be."

Creed's foot left the accelerator, the old anger burning in his gut like acid.

"I know you only did what you thought was right. Sometimes what's right to some isn't right to others."

"He couldn't get away with blaming someone else for the death he caused," Creed said through clenched teeth.

"I know," Royce agreed.

"And what kills me is that I got kicked out and he's still in the navy."

"My selfish side is thanking the stars that it gave me the opportunity to snatch you up and make you a part of SOS."

"And I'm still a part of defending the country I love against attack." Though he missed the members of his SEAL team, his band of brothers, Creed had come to care for the members of the small team of agents belonging to SOS, an organization so secret, they were called in when the CIA and the FBI were too public to handle the situation.

He'd found a new home with Royce and the others, and he was still working to protect his country, both from outside threats and internal decline due to terrorism or corrupt leadership.

Yeah, his life was that of a secret agent. Someone who never stayed in one place long enough to get involved emotionally with the inhabitants. He established only enough of a relationship to solidify his cover or gather information he needed to finish the job. Then he was off to another assignment, possibly on the opposite side of the world from the last.

"Steele is scheduled to fly back from St. Thomas tonight. As soon as she arrives, I'll brief her on the mission and send her your way."

Nicole Steele, aka Tazer, was a lethal weapon in SOS. Model-beautiful and skilled at self-defense, she brought men twice her size down before they knew what hit them.

"Good. I'm not sure how sticky it'll get here, or how quickly. I called to let you know another yacht arrived in the cape today. I'll see if I can get a boat name or registration letters so that we can find out who owns it."

"Damn. You think Phillip's already there?" Royce's voice was tight.

"The yacht is big and flashy. It has Phillip Macias written all over it."

"I can get Nicole Steele and Casanova Valdez out there by tomorrow, and as soon as I free up, I can come myself. I might even be able to snag Sean McNeal."

"If Macias is really involved in dirty bombs, the more people we have out here the better. I can't be everywhere at once. First things first, though, I'm going down tomorrow to find whatever's on that boat before Phillip does."

"You sure tomorrow will be soon enough?"

He stared out at the clouds rolling into the cape. "I think the Devil's Shroud has me covered for tonight."

"The Devil's Shroud?"

"It's what the locals call a fog so thick you can't see the rocks before you hit them."

Royce laughed. "Sounds like Phillip's transport yacht got a dose of it. Any trouble establishing a convincing cover?"

"Insurance adjuster seems to be working fine. Tomorrow I'm vacation diving."

"Good. I'll have Tazer contact you as soon as she's boots on the ground in Seattle."

"Roger," Creed acknowledged.

"Out here."

The phone clicked in Creed's ear, and he laid it in the console's cup holder of the rented SUV. At the morgue, the M.E. had yet to identify the latest body, but both dead men had tattoos on their upper forearms with words written in Russian.

When he left the morgue, Creed drove to one of the high points in town overlooking the bay and parked.

He pulled out his binoculars and focused on the yacht, trying to catch a glimpse of a man rumored to have started wars, but too slippery to be caught red-handed. No government had the goods on him that would put him away for life or sentence him to a firing squad. He was just that good at covering his tracks.

Few people stirred on the deck of the yacht. The sun faded behind a bank of fog slipping over the shoreline, creeping into the little town. Before long, the fog surrounded him, blocking his view of the water.

Creed sighed, set the binoculars aside and drove into town, armed with Emma's home address. He'd told Molly he wanted to thank Emma for her patience on the dive boat by taking her out to dinner. He really needed an excuse to go where the locals ate in order to get the latest gossip. If he had Emma with him he'd raise less suspicion and blend in with the natives more readily. Molly, the romantic he'd pegged her for, had happily handed over Emma's information, including Emma's personal cell-phone number.

Molly had only met him that day, but had determined he was a man she could trust. Her gullibility might get her killed some day. And that would be a shame. She was a good-hearted woman and pretty, with her strawberry-blond hair and green eyes.

But it wasn't her face he was imagining as he drove through town searching for Sand Dollar Lane, where Emma's quaint seaside bungalow overlooked the cape. Just as Molly had described, the sides were painted a soft, sea foam-green with pale yellow and white trim. There were colorful blooms spilling out of the window flower boxes, and a white picket fence surrounded the lush green yard.

Everything about the cottage screamed "home," hitting Creed like a slug in the gut. He'd never really had a home. His father had run out on him and his mother when he'd been five. Without a man to support her, his mother worked two jobs at minimum wage to keep a roof over his head and food in his belly. He'd been a latchkey kid in one of the poorest neighborhoods of Los Angeles, fighting in gangs as soon as he was big enough to carry a stick.

If not for a lenient judge, he'd probably have been dead or in jail by now. Instead, he'd been given a choice to join the service or go to jail.

He'd opted for the navy. His mother had been so proud of him when he'd enlisted that he'd pushed to be the best sailor, and to be the best he had to be a SEAL.

Now here he was in Oregon, ten years later. His mother had passed away from breast cancer, and he'd been kicked out of the navy. Life hadn't ended there. As a member of the SOS, he was still fighting the good fight.

But he'd never known the kind of cozy home Emma's house represented. He pulled up in front, parked the SUV, climbed out and pushed through the gate.

The sun was hidden behind the fog, making the low-hanging clouds a pale shade of pink and gray.

A light shone through the windows, and the filmy curtains over the glass did little to block the view of the interior.

For a moment, he stood on the walkway leading to the front door, staring up into the windows—on the outside, looking in. The story of his life.

A movement in a hallway inside caught his attention.

Emma's silhouette was outlined against the light pouring out of a room. She reached up to run her fingers through her hair, the backlight emphasizing her slender waist and the curve of her breasts and hips.

Creed's gut tightened, and he had the confusing urge to run forward and backward at the same time.

Emma was the type of woman who didn't need a man in her life, but if she had one, she'd want him to be full-time and committed to a relationship forever.

She deserved a forever kind of man.

That wasn't him. He hesitated, hating having to get her involved, but his mission to save the west coast pushed him forward and he knocked on the door.

A dog barked at the back of the house and all the way through to the front where toenails clicked against hardwood floors, skidding to a stop behind the door.

Emma's voice sounded through the solid wood. "Sit, Moby." The knob twisted. She opened the door and her eyes rounded, her mouth opening on a soft gasp. "Oh, it's you."

He frowned at the short shorts and skimpy tank top she wore, exposing a vast amount of skin tanned golden by the sun. If possible, the tank top and shorts were even sexier than the bikini she'd worn under her wet suit.

Creed's groin tightened automatically. "You really should verify who it is before you open the door to just anyone."

"Excuse me." Her hand found her left hip, and she looked down her nose at him. "I've been living on my own for eight years. I don't need a stranger telling me how to open my door."

A golden retriever slipped past her and barreled into Creed's midsection.

Emma's mouth twitched, and her frown eased. "Now, if you want to tell me that my dog is loud and unruly, I might be inclined to agree with you."

As if he knew he was being talked about, Moby proved his vocal acuity. *Woof!*

With Moby's paws planted firmly on his chest and a long, wet tongue angling toward his face, Creed had his hands full. He ruffled the dog's ears and set him back on all fours. "Down," he said firmly.

Moby glanced back at Emma, tongue lolling, then jumped on Creed again, managing a long wet kiss on the side of his face this time.

Emma laughed out loud. "I'm sorry. Moby rarely has company, and I haven't spent enough time teaching him manners."

"That's okay. I like dogs." He set Moby on his paws again and moved around him. "One adopted me when I was growing up."

"Oh, yeah? What kind?"

"If I had to guess, he was pure junkyard dog. Mean to everyone but me." He hadn't thought about that old dog for years. He'd named him Leroy, after an old Jim Croce song his mother used to sing out loud when she was in the shower. It brought back one of the few good memories he had of his childhood.

Emma grabbed Moby by the collar and hauled him inside the house. "Did you forget something? Or are you here to tell me you aren't diving tomorrow?"

He glanced up and down the street, then into the house. "Mind if I come in?"

"I don't let strangers in my house," she said with a straight face, her brows rising in challenge.

"Touché."

"You can come in as long as you don't mind Moby. He thinks anyone who sits on the couch is furniture."

"I'll keep that in mind."

Once she had the door closed between Moby and the road, she turned to face Creed. "Again, why did you come?"

"I wanted to go out for a bite to eat and didn't want to go alone. Since you're the only person I know besides Molly, who, by the way, is busy serving dinner to her guests, I thought I'd see if you were interested."

"I was just about to heat up a scrumptious frozen mac 'n' cheese dinner. Care to join me?"

He shook his head. Although the idea of staying in her house sounded intimate and far more appealing than eating out, he needed to listen in on the gossip. "Much as I love mac 'n' cheese, I'd rather eat something a little heartier. I'd hoped you could recommend a local restaurant."

"That would be the Seaside Café." Emma tugged the fringe on her cutoffs and stared down at her tank top, drawing attention to the fact that she wasn't wearing a bra.

Creed gulped. Soft brown nipples showed through the thin fabric, puckering as if a switch had been flipped.

Emma crossed her arms over her chest. "I'd have to change into something nicer."

"I'll wait here with Moby." He scratched the dog's ears.

Moby sat beside him and leaned against his leg.

Emma frowned down at her dog. "Traitor." Then her gaze rose to Creed. "I have been craving one of their spicy seafood wraps." She inhaled and let out the breath. "Okay. I'll be right back." With a quick about-face, she spun on the balls of her bare feet and headed for the hallway.

"Don't take too long," Creed called out. "My stomach's growling louder than Moby's."

"Poor baby," she called over her shoulder. "You wouldn't have a stomach if that shark had decided you were going to be his meal today."

"I meant to thank you for pointing him out. Dinner's on me."

She ducked into a doorway and half closed the door.

He couldn't see her, but he could see a dresser with a large mirror reflecting her bedroom. Emma moved into range of the mirror, her back to the dresser, as she pulled the tank top over her head and flung it onto the bed.

Creed groaned.

"Did you say something?" Emma's head ducked around the door.

"No, not a thing," he hurried to reassure her.

Again, she left the door half-open, and the mirror gave away her every move as she turned to the dresser, her breasts bobbing in front of her, full, rounded and tipped with the rosiest, perfect nipples.

Creed couldn't look away, his gaze captivated by perky perfection. So captivated he wasn't aware he was being watched until the door slammed and cut off his view.

"Really, Creed, you could have told me I was flashing you."

He laughed. "Not a chance I'd have missed that for the world."

"You know you can go out to eat without me." She emerged from the bedroom, wearing another dainty sundress, carrying a sweater over one arm. "That wasn't very gentlemanly of you."

"I'm sorry, did you mistake me for a gentleman?" He held out his elbow. "I never claimed to be one. A kid from the poor side of L.A. doesn't acquire those kinds of skills in street gangs."

"Street gangs?" She looked up at him. "I'm intrigued. Should I be wary?"

"My lips get looser on a full belly." He opened the door to her cottage and held it for her as she stepped through.

Moby made a dash for open air, but Creed stepped in front of him before he could claim freedom. "Stay."

His ears drooping, Moby stopped short of making another attempt at escape.

"You're better at that than I am." Emma shook her head. "I don't have the heart to talk to him sternly. I'm gone a good portion of the day or night, and he's all alone. But he's always here for me when I am home."

"As a woman who lives alone, it's a good thing you have a dog."

"Yeah," she snorted. "If I ever have an intruder, Moby will lick him to death."

Creed pulled the door shut and Emma locked it with her key.

"We can take my car," Creed suggested.

"Or we can walk. It's only a couple blocks and it's a nice night," Emma said.

"Nice?" Creed looked around at fog coating the

landscape as thick as smoke. He didn't like that he couldn't see, especially if someone was looking for them, like Phillip Macias.

Emma grinned and pulled him along. "We can see a whole five feet in front of us. Come on, I'll get you there. Unless you have issues with a woman telling you what to do?"

"No problem whatsoever."

"Good." She led him to a diner at the center of town, with a wide porch filled with tables that most likely would be used on a sunny day. Had the fog lifted, he was certain they'd have a great view of the cape.

"Inside or outside?" Emma asked.

"Inside. It's a bit cool and damp to be outside."

She led the way into the diner. Older couples, young families with small children, and a table of older men wearing gum boots and fishing hats crowded around the tables and booths. All the tables were full; the place was well lit and bustling.

Just what Creed had hoped. "We can sit at the counter." He indicated two seats being vacated as they waited.

Emma slid onto the bar stool, her long athletic legs dangling toward the ground, her sandals hanging off her toes, tipped with pretty pink nail polish.

Creed dragged his mind back to the business at hand—finding out whose large yacht was anchored in the cape.

A short, gray-haired woman set menus in front of them.

Emma smiled at her. "Hi, Nora, what's the special tonight?"

"Grilled tilapia," she answered. "Who's your date?"

Emma blushed. "Oh, he's not my date. We're just having dinner together."

Nora rolled her eyes. "Are you single?" She addressed the question to Creed.

Creed grinned. "I am."

"Then it's a date, unless times have changed so much this old woman isn't keeping up." She stuck her hand out. "Nora Taggart."

"Any relation to Chief Taggart?" Creed asked.

"She's my better half." Chief Taggart stepped up behind them and slid onto an empty stool on the other side of Creed. "Have to come to the café to get my wife to cook for me." He winked at Nora. "Got quite the crowd tonight," he commented to his wife. "Keep this up and I can retire and let you support me."

"Like you would." Nora snorted softly, her eyes twinkling. "You love your job."

"Some days better than others." The chief's gaze slipped to Creed.

Emma and Creed both placed orders for the special, grilled tilapia.

Nora wrote their order and one for her husband and clipped them to what looked like a clothesline over the window into the kitchen. She turned back to wipe the counter in front of Creed, Emma and Taggart with a clean rag. "More packed than usual for a foggy night," Nora noted.

"Everyone's ready for summer. I noticed a few new faces in town, including Creed here." Chief Taggart clapped a hand to Creed's back. "Folks are trying to get a jump on the warm weather."

"Too bad the weather's not cooperating much," Emma said. "At least it was clear during the day."

"I hear you found your boat." Taggart lowered his voice. "Although I'm not happy to report, the M.E. says the man you brought up was shot in the head."

"What?" Emma leaned closer to Creed, the scent of her shampoo teasing his senses. "I thought he drowned when the yacht went down."

Creed hadn't told her what he'd discovered. With all the blood washed away, the man's hair covered the entrance wound enough that it took a closer look to determine cause of death was by gunshot wound. He didn't comment, guessing it would stir up Emma's ire that he hadn't bothered to tell her what he'd already determined.

"He thinks it was a small caliber pistol and the shot was taken at close range," Taggart continued.

Creed nodded. "Probably someone he knew."

"I suspect it was one of his own crew."

"Nice crew," Emma said. "Should we warn Dave not to hire deckhands?"

Chief Taggart faced Creed. "'Fraid I'm gonna have to ask you to hang around in case we have questions."

"Needed a bit of a vacation anyway." Creed leaned back. "Emma's taking me diving tomorrow."

"I called the Oregon Criminal Investigations Division. They're sending someone out to investigate as soon as they can. Hopefully tomorrow. You two should steer clear since it's now considered a crime scene."

Creed nodded, although he had no intention of staying away from the yacht, any more than whoever had arranged for the yacht to be at Cape Churn. If there was booty on board, he had to get to it before Macias, or the entire west coast was in jeopardy. For all he knew, whoever killed the captain could have gotten off the boat with the cargo. "Have they identified the man from the yacht or the one who washed ashore?"

"No, but both had tattoos on their upper forearms written in Russian. The criminal investigators might have better luck identifying them. I just hope they complete their investigation before next weekend."

"Why's that?" Creed asked.

Nora set glasses of ice water in front of Creed and Emma. "It's the official kickoff of the summer season. All the schools will be out, and we'll be inundated with new faces. It would be harder to find a killer in a sea full of strangers."

"Speaking of strangers, did you see the yacht that anchored in the bay?" Emma asked.

"They got here just in time," Nora said.

The chief nodded. "The fog followed them in. They won't be leaving anytime soon."

"Good." Nora smiled. "Maybe they'll get bored and come ashore and spend some of their money. Lord knows we could use the business."

Creed prayed for the opposite. If they were working for Phillip, they were some of the most ruthless murderers in the world.

"Gabe said they sent a dinghy to shore this afternoon to purchase supplies."

"Order up!" a voice called out from the window to the kitchen.

Nora spun, gathered steaming plates of grilled tilapia, arranged in a bed of steamed long grain rice and asparagus, and set them in front of Emma, Creed and Taggart.

"Did they say where they were from?" Nora continued.

This was the reason Creed had come to the café. News spread like wildfire in small towns.

"No," the chief said. "But Joe down at the grocery store said they spoke to each other in a foreign language. Maybe Spanish. When they checked out, they did so in English."

"Maybe they're from California." Nora topped off their glasses of water. "Anything else I can get you two? Not much of a date sitting with my husband, is it." She gave them a twisted smile and shot a pointed look at the chief.

Creed liked that Emma blushed again.

"We're not on a date. I'm here for the great food." She glanced at Creed and added sternly, "I'll pay my own way."

He smiled, and her color grew warmer. "You're in charge. I'm just on vacation."

She snorted. "So was I."

Nora turned back from the kitchen. "That reminds me. I heard today that the hospital board of directors cancelled the children's wing addition. Is that true?"

The warm color faded in Emma's face, and she stared down at her fork. "So they say. I'm not giving up yet."

Nora reached out and patted Emma's arm. "I'm sorry, dear. I didn't mean to open old wounds. But you must know that no one blames you for what Randy did."

"Sure," she said, not very convincingly.

A female guest waved Nora down, and the older woman set off across the floor to talk to the woman.

Creed ate a bite of tilapia before asking quietly, "Who's Randy?"

Emma paused with her fork en route to her mouth. "Nobody." She popped the fish into her mouth and chewed, probably to keep him from asking another question.

Creed didn't give up easily. "Had to be somebody if he did something that people are blaming *you* for. What are they blaming you for?"

"You heard Nora—they're not blaming me. And I don't want to discuss it." She set her fork on the counter, dug money out of her dress pocket and laid it on the counter. "If you don't mind, I'm tired and need to get back to walk Moby before I hit the sack." She dropped down off her stool.

When Creed moved to follow suit, Emma raised her hand. "No, don't get up. I know my way home, fog or no fog. Stay and finish your meal. Nora's café has the best food in town."

Nora returned to the counter as Emma was leaving. "Leaving already?" Her gaze took in the full plate of food. "Was the tilapia bad?"

"No, no," Emma reassured the older woman. "I'm not very hungry."

"Then let me box it for you to take with you." Nora didn't wait for an answer, but charged through the swinging door into the kitchen, returning a couple seconds later with a foam to-go box. She scooped the fish and trimmings into the container and handed them to Emma. "In case you get hungry later, pop it into the microwave for thirty seconds. That ought to do it."

Emma thanked Nora and all but ran for the door.

Creed counted to twenty and followed, determined

to get answers to all of his questions. Number one, what had this Randy done to make Emma react so strongly?

With the mention of the cancellation of the children's wing heavy on her mind, Emma hurried toward home and the promise of a hot bath with fragrant salts and oils to soothe her frayed nerves. She doubted the day could get any worse. From the news about the wing to the dead man floating into her face and a shark eyeballing her for lunch, it had been eventful, crazy and scary.

What scared her most was the way Creed had been watching her. Every glance he sent her way made her blood burn and her thighs ache for more than just a look. She wanted to pound her head against a wall and beat the image of his sexy smile out of her head so that she could concentrate on what was important. Finding the funds to build the wing.

Carrying the box of tilapia, Emma hurried toward home, glad to leave behind the diner filled with all the townsfolk she knew and cared about. People who had contributed their hard-earned cash toward a project they stood behind wholeheartedly. An addition to their small hospital that would be dedicated to the children of the community.

God, she felt lower than snake spit. It *was* her fault Randy had stolen the money. Had she not been gullible and in love with the idea of being loved, she might have seen the signs and stopped it before it happened.

"Emma," Creed's voice called out behind her.

"Leave me alone." She didn't turn around. Instead, she walked faster and faster until she was running through the fog.

She stumbled on a curb in front of the picket fence surrounding her house and would have fallen if strong hands hadn't reached out and caught her, pulling her against a wall of muscles.

She leaned her head back against his chest, too disheartened to fight him and finding his strength incredibly hard to resist. For too long she'd been on her own, the only person she could count on. Even if it was only for a moment, leaning on someone else felt damned good. "You really do have a problem with following orders, don't you?"

He turned her in his arms and crooked a finger beneath her chin, tipping her face upward. "What did this Randy do that made you feel you had to run away from your friends?" He brushed a damp strand of hair from her cheek.

"He stole the money for the children's wing," she said, her tone flat, matter-of-fact.

"And why would that be your fault?"

"You're going to love this."

"Try me."

"I introduced him to the board of directors. They hired him based on my recommendation." She glanced away from his gaze, her heart squeezing hard in her chest as she admitted, "He was my fiancé."

"Again...why does it make it your fault?"

Emma was glad she still carried the to-go box of fish; it put just enough distance between her and Creed, plus occupied her hands. She swallowed hard before answering, "He wouldn't have had access to the money if not for me. Don't you see?"

"I see you beating yourself up over a bastard who didn't deserve to call you his fiancée." He brushed his lips across her forehead. "Want me to take it up with him?"

She laughed, the sound choking on a sob. "You can't."

"Why?"

"He's dead."

# Chapter 5

"Then why can't you get the money back?"

"He died in a car wreck. No one knows what he did with the money. The state crime investigators could only trace it to a bank in the Cayman Islands, and from there it just disappeared." She sighed. "It doesn't matter. They cancelled the project today. I had hoped to find…" Her words faded off.

"The *Anna Maria?*"

Emma walked toward the house, digging in her pocket for her key. "I know it's a long shot, but I'd hoped to find the *Anna Maria* and maybe a treasure aboard that could be used to replace the money Randy stole."

"You're right, that is a long shot."

She paused with the key in her hand, her jaw tightening and lips forming a straight line. "Maybe it's stupid, but I have a couple more days of vacation."

"And I interrupted one day you could have spent looking for the ship." He smiled. "Now I understand why you weren't very happy with me."

"Laugh all you want." She jammed her key into the lock and twisted it. "It's my only hope," Emma whispered.

"Of redeeming yourself for something you didn't do?" He pushed the door open.

"Of getting a new wing built on the hospital." Emma entered her house, immediately attacked by Moby. "We need it. Don't we, boy?" She bent to hug the dog and scratch his ears. "The community has outgrown what we have. Young couples are moving into the area with children or having babies, and they need to know they have a hospital nearby in case of emergencies. A hospital that can handle the needs of their small children."

"You don't have to sell me on the idea. It sounds great." As soon as Creed spoke, Moby launched himself at the man.

Emma grabbed for Moby's collar, missed and cringed as Moby slammed into Creed. A hit that would have knocked most men to the ground only made Creed stagger backward a step before he braced himself and shoved the animal to his feet.

"Sit."

Moby squatted on his haunches, his tail swishing across the floor, and then he grew still, his ears twitching upward.

Before Emma or Creed could stop him, the dog dashed through the door and out into the fog.

"Moby!" Emma cried.

Creed spun, ran after the dog and grabbed him before he could leap the short white picket fence and disappear into the Devil's Shroud.

"Thank goodness you caught him." Emma grabbed Moby's collar, but the animal wasn't content to return to the house. He lunged at the fence, dragging his master with him, growling at the dark fog.

"Let me." Creed regained control of the dog and led him back into the house.

Moby fought him every step of the way, as if there was something hidden in the fog on the outside of the fence he had to get to.

A chill slipped like a spider crawling across his skin. Creed pulled Moby into the house. As soon as Emma cleared the door, he closed it and inspected the locks.

She had a dead bolt on the front door. "Where's your back door?"

"Through the kitchen. Why?"

"Do you have a dead bolt on it?"

"Yes."

"Show me."

She crossed her arms over her chest. "When you tell me why."

"I like the women I date to stay safe."

Her brows wrinkled. "We're not dating."

"According to Nora, we are." He glanced around, found the kitchen and headed for the back door. After testing that the dead bolt was indeed locked, he glanced at the window in the door and frowned. "You should get this door replaced with a solid one. Anyone can break that window and open your dead bolt."

"Yeah, genius. And anyone could break one of the windows and get in even more easily. What are you afraid of?"

"You heard the chief. The dead man on the yacht didn't drown. He was shot and left to go down with the ship."

"So? *We* didn't shoot him, nor did we see who did."

"We were on the yacht. I suspect whoever killed the captain didn't plan on the yacht going down when it did and probably had to abandon ship. If there was anything on that boat worth killing for, it likely went down with it."

Emma's frown deepened. "You're sounding all conspiracy theory now. It was just a yacht that sank in the Devil's Shroud."

"With a murdered man on it."

She shook her head. "It doesn't mean we'll be targeted next. We have nothing to hide."

"Just promise me you'll lock the dead bolts."

"I do. Every night."

"And don't walk outside in the dark without Moby."

"He wouldn't let me." A smile slipped across her face. "Are you scared for me, squid? Because if you are, I can take care of myself."

"Do you have a firearm?"

Her frown disappeared. "As a matter of fact, I do. An HK380."

"Do you know how to use it?"

"I took lessons at the place where I bought it, and I go to the firing range with Gabe once a quarter."

"Good."

"And I also have a can of mace." She gave him a level stare. "I believe I can take care of myself."

"Mace is only good if you get close enough to spray them in the face, and that's assuming you keep it readily available and they don't shoot you first."

"Okay, you're scaring me." She shivered, her face growing pale. "We're in Cape Churn, not Portland or Seattle. Things don't happen here."

"What about the serial killer they found here a few months ago?"

"You heard about that?" Emma started to say something, then bit down on her bottom lip. "Okay, I'll lock the doors and keep my mace and my pistol handy. Satisfied?"

No, he wasn't. Macias was known to send his hired thugs in to do his dirty work with carte blanche on how they went about it. Some of his targets were shot point-blank, others were electrocuted in their own bathtubs and still others were stabbed multiple times or tortured before they were allowed to die.

If Macias thought for a moment Emma had anything that belonged to him, he'd pursue her relentlessly.

Creed stared across at her. She'd already shed her sandals and stood in her feminine sundress and bare feet, her sandy-blond, sun-kissed hair hanging down to her shoulders, her gray eyes dark and troubled.

"Say something."

He stepped closer and tipped her chin upward. "Listen to Moby. If he's disturbed, call me. I'll be here as soon as possible."

"I don't see how you'll do that. It's a long, winding road out to the B and B," she said, her voice breathy, her gaze shifting from his eyes to his mouth.

Creed was already on the edge, standing far too close to her. The scent of body wash and shampoo filled his senses.

When her tongue slipped out to moisten her lips, he groaned and pulled her into his arms. He crushed her lips with his, cupping the back of her head, his fingers threading through silky strands. One hand slipped around her waist and down over her hip, drawing her closer against the ridge beneath the thick denim of his jeans.

She opened to him, tasting of lemon and spices, her mouth warm and wet.

His tongue stroked hers, teasing her into a sensuous dance, twisting and tangling until they both came up for air.

Creed kissed a path from her mouth to the side of her neck, tasting her skin beneath her earlobe and downward to the base of her throat where her pulse beat erratically.

"This is wrong." She pressed her palms against his chest, but didn't push him away. Instead, she curled her fingers into his shirt. One of her long slender legs slipped up the back of his, the juncture of her legs rubbing against his thigh.

He slipped her sweater off her shoulders, and it fell to the floor.

Moby sniffed it and moved away, flopping on the floor, panting.

Creed pushed the strap of her sundress to the side and nibbled the soft skin of her shoulder, angling downward, shoving aside the fabric to expose the lace of her bra and the smooth swell of her breast.

He cupped the clothed swell in his palm and squeezed.

Her back arched, pressing her breast more firmly into his hand and against his lips. A moan rose up her throat and left her parted lips on a sigh.

Creed pushed the bra down over her breast and a perky, rosy nipple sprang forth, inviting him to taste.

He nipped it, rolled the beaded tip around on his tongue and sucked it into his mouth.

Her hand pressed to the back of his head, urging him to take more.

Caught up in a wave of lust, he barely heard Moby woof until he woofed again.

The dog sprang to his feet and ran to the door, barking. He scratched at the door and growled, then barked again.

Creed straightened and spun toward the door. "Does he do that a lot?"

"Only when there's someone at the door." Emma tugged her bra back in place and slid her dress straps up over her shoulder. "Someone must be out there."

"Stay here with Moby. Don't open the door unless it's me." Creed ran for the back door and slipped out quietly, closing the door behind him. Without even the glow of a streetlight, the darkness was made even darker by the heavy fog blanketing the coast. He inched his way around the house, staying close to the bushes, afraid if he stepped away from the building too soon, he'd get lost in the fog and fall over the fence before he saw it. Walking home, they'd made their way along the sidewalk without too much trouble with the concrete as their reference point.

By the time he'd rounded the back and side to the front, he'd adjusted his senses to listen for any noise. The fog dampened the ground, moistening sticks and leaves so that footfalls would be muffled.

Creed stopped at the corner and strained to hear anything, the snap of a twig, creaking knees or the rustle of fabric as someone moved through the night.

Nothing.

He slipped along the hedges to the front walkway and followed it to the gate. It stood open.

Creed had been the last one through, closing it behind him, knowing Moby was a loose cannon likely to make a run for it. He stepped through the gate and walked along the sidewalk until he came across his rented SUV, locked up tight and appearing the same as it had when he'd left it before they'd gone to dinner. He ran his hand along the base of the doors and around the fenders, feeling for any added devices. If someone was following Emma, they might be following him, as well. Creed wasn't foolish enough to believe he was the only one smart enough to use a GPS tracking device.

Short of crawling beneath the vehicle, he did the best search he could by feeling his way around the edges, finding nothing.

He left his vehicle and returned to the fence, walking the perimeter outside and inside the white pickets, feeling his way along and finding nothing. When he was certain he'd searched every inch of her little yard, he returned to the front door and knocked softly.

Moby raised a ruckus, barking and clawing at the door. When Emma got him quiet enough she called out, "Who is it?"

"Creed."

She opened the door and peered into the night, her can of mace pointed at his eyes.

Creed ducked, not wanting to risk being accidentally blinded by a nervous trigger finger.

Emma grabbed his arm and dragged him through the door. "Well?"

"I didn't find anyone out there."

She let out a long, slow breath and then glared at

him. "All that for nothing? You scared me half to death."

He pulled her against him and smoothed her hair back from her forehead. "Sorry. But I'd rather you were scared and safe than oblivious to the possible threat."

"What threat?" When he started to say something, she raised her hand. "Next time, let me stay blissfully oblivious. I have Moby. He'll let me know if someone's lurking around my house, and hopefully all the noise he makes will keep an intruder from attempting a break in." She grabbed the door handle and opened the door. "If the fog clears, we'll have a busy morning. I need my rest. Go."

Having received his marching orders, Creed bowed out gracefully. Reluctantly, but gracefully. Unconvinced of her safety after the way Moby had behaved.

He touched the side of Emma's cheek and bent to brush her lips with a kiss, risking a possible slap in the face. When she returned the pressure, he was glad he'd taken the risk.

"I'll see you in the morning." He left, closing the door firmly between them.

He stayed on her porch until he heard the dead bolt click into place. Walking slowly, he found his way to the SUV and climbed in. The fog hung like a heavy blanket over the road. When he cranked the engine and turned on the headlights, the glow reflected back in his eyes, penetrating no farther ahead than a few feet.

Shifting into Drive, he cast one last glance toward her house. The only indication it was there was the soft glow of her front porch light, muted by the tiny droplets of moisture.

He hoped she was right and there was nothing to

worry about. Moby might not be ferocious or a warrior, but he'd generate enough noise to make an intruder think twice.

Creed eased his foot onto the accelerator and leaned forward, as if that would help him to see any farther ahead than the front of his vehicle. Keeping the SUV between the lines on the road, he moved forward. Half a block away, he nearly hit a car parked on the side of the road. He made a mental note of the license plate and moved slowly past. The interior was dark and, at first glance, it appeared empty.

As he passed, a brief flash of light caught his attention, as if from the display screen of a smart phone. Creed slowed and peered through his window into the vehicle beside him. He couldn't swear to it, but he thought he saw a shadowy figure hunched over the console. It could have been a jacket left behind or a blanket, but his gut told him it was a person. Someone hiding from view.

All Creed's warning bells went off. He drove by, creeping farther down the street. He turned at the first road to the left, driving past the shadows of a couple houses before he parked and turned off his headlights in front of an empty lot.

Whoever was parked on the side of the road had hidden from view. Why would he not want to be seen, unless he was there for nefarious reasons? A secret teenage assignation? A desperate man spying on his ex-wife? A terrorist looking for the goods he needed to build a dirty bomb that could potentially kill millions?

Creed wasn't leaving Emma alone on her quiet little street. If he returned to the B and B, he'd be too far away to respond quickly. He sat in the SUV, debating whether or not to walk back the way he'd come and confront the person in the car.

Instead, he entered the phone number Molly had given him and waited for Emma to answer.

"Hello?" Her voice was clear and soft with a slight gravelly quality, melting over him like milk chocolate. His body reacted accordingly, warmth spreading throughout, his groin tightening.

"I forgot to give you my phone number."

"I don't need it," she said. "Nothing's going to happen."

"Well, now you have it on your cell phone as a recent call. If you do happen to need anything, don't hesitate."

"I won't be calling," she assured him.

"Good night, Emma."

"Good night, Creed." The way she spoke his name with the rumble of gravel deep in her throat chased the cool dampness away, if only for a moment. Then she clicked off the phone, and the interior of his vehicle grew dark.

The next call he made was to SOS headquarters, reporting the license plate of the vehicle parked on Emma's street. Maybe someone back in D.C. could track down the stalker, if he was a stalker.

Creed leaned his seat back and settled in for the night, a block away from Emma. He'd be tired in the morning, but had he gone on to the B and B he wouldn't have rested at all knowing he'd possibly put Emma in danger.

Tomorrow, he'd try to get close enough to the shiny white yacht in the bay to read its markings and send the information to Royce. If the yacht could be traced, he'd have the capabilities to do it at SOS headquarters with their powerful computers and the equally powerful Geek running them.

Creed's sense of urgency made him fidget through the night, even more so than the discomfort of his long body being cramped in the confines of the vehicle.

Time was running out.

He reasoned that if the cargo had been moved from the yacht before it sank, Phillip would have it by now and would leave the area immediately. Yet the big yacht in the bay had been there as the fog settled in. The fact someone was watching Emma's house led Creed to believe Phillip didn't have what he'd come to collect, and he'd do anything to get it.

# Chapter 6

Emma tossed and turned through the night. If she wasn't waking to every little woof Moby emitted, she was dreaming about lying naked with Creed, making love until their bodies glowed with sweat and fulfillment.

Twice she woke, having kicked off the blankets and sheets. The skimpy nightgown she wore was a twisted knot around her middle, and her body ached with an unsatisfied desire. Ever since he'd kissed her… Her lips still burned from the feel of his brushing across them. Even after she'd brushed her teeth, she could taste his tongue against hers. Her throbbing core reminded her that she was young, female and had needs. Needs Creed had stirred in her when she thought a man was the last thing she wanted in her life.

At two in the morning, Moby got up from his pallet

on the floor and trotted through the house like a guard making his rounds, toenails clicking against hardwood.

Aware of his movements, Emma remained awake until she heard slurpy lapping from the vicinity of the kitchen where she kept Moby's water bowl. When he finally returned and lay down beside her bed, Emma was able to relax, her hand draped over the side of the bed, rubbing the dog's silky head.

Moby licked her with a cool wet tongue, reassuring her that he'd be there to warn her should someone get close to the house.

She finally fell into a deep sleep and didn't wake again until six in the morning. The gray light of pre-dawn crept over the back of the house, finding its way through the cracks in her blinds.

Emma stretched, feeling better about the day as gray morning turned to muted sunshine, filling the room with light, brightening her mood. Today she'd find the *Anna Maria.* Today things would change for the better. She had to believe it.

Worry had weighed far too heavily on her the day before. Action was what she needed.

Throwing back the covers, she leaped from the bed, barely missing Moby as he lumbered to his feet and headed for the front door.

Emma pulled on a pair of shorts, a T-shirt and her running shoes. She clipped Moby's leash on his collar, tucked her house key in her pocket and headed out for a morning run.

With Moby taking the lead, Emma headed south on Sand Dollar Lane, turning left at the first corner. A dark SUV was parked against the curb in front of a vacant lot. The vehicle looked suspiciously like the one Creed had driven up to her house the night before.

Emma stopped beside the vehicle, blatantly peered in and almost laughed out loud. Creed lay in a half leaning, half lying position in the driver's seat, his cell phone on the console beside him, an arm curled up behind his head, eyes closed.

Her heart warmed. The man had stayed there all night because of her. Guilt warred with irritation. She'd told him she didn't need anyone to look out for her. She could take care of herself. If she'd known he was out there...what? Would she have invited him in? Had him sleep on the couch? Offered him a pillow from her bed? After that kiss, would he have ended up *in* her bed?

Her body heated.

*Damn it.* She didn't need another smooth-talking man in her life. They were nothing but trouble, and she was still paying for the last one.

Emma raised her hand and rapped on the window loudly.

Moby barked, raising a big enough ruckus to wake the dead.

Creed whipped a pistol from under his shirt and pointed it at the window.

Emma backed away, her hands in the air, heart hammering, the wind sucked out of her sails.

As soon as Creed realized it was her, he tossed the gun to the seat beside him, shoved open his door and got out. "You scared the crap out of me."

"*I* scared *you?*" She pointed toward the pistol on his passenger seat. "What the hell are you doing with a gun?"

"I'm licensed to carry concealed."

"I don't care what you're licensed to do. You could have shot me."

"I'm not trigger happy. I make sure of my targets before I shoot."

Still shaken by having a gun pointed at her first thing in the morning, Emma wasn't ready to let it go. "So you've shot a person before?"

He shoved a hand through his hair and then jammed his hands into his pockets. "Look, I didn't want to be so far away if you needed me."

She crossed her arms over her chest. "Moby and I did just fine without you."

As if to emphasize Emma's point, Moby jumped up, planting his paws on Creed's chest.

Creed laughed. "I can see that." He scratched Moby's ears and shoved him off his chest, glancing out at the lingering haze of fog hovering over the cape, obscuring the view. "Are we still headed out at eight this morning?"

"The weatherman said this fog will burn off around nine. If you're there at eight, we can prep the boat and tanks and be on our way out as the fog lifts." She gave him a narrow-eyed glance. "Are you rested enough to go out?"

He stretched and tilted his neck to each side as if testing functionality. "I'm good."

Oh, she had no doubt he was good. It was the *at what* she was worried about. "Are you going to run out to the B and B before you head to the marina?"

"I don't see a need. I'd rather find breakfast."

"That's what a B and B serves, and you're paying for it." She shook her head. "I have eggs in my fridge. If you can cook, you can have breakfast at my house."

As soon as the words left her mouth, she wondered why she'd offered. Spending more time with him wasn't helping her resolve to stay clear of men.

He grinned. "I've been known to make a mean omelet."

"You're on." She nodded toward Moby. "I'll be back this way in fifteen."

"I could go with you," he offered.

"I prefer to go it alone." She smiled at Moby. "Well, almost. It gives me a chance to clear my head."

"Fair enough. In the meantime, I'll see about finding a place to wash up."

Emma sighed. "You have a perfectly good room at the B and B. You should have stayed there, and you wouldn't be in this predicament."

He rolled his shoulders. "I'll have to give the bed at Molly's a try tonight."

"Fine. I'll be back in ten minutes, and you can use the bathroom in my house."

He grinned. "I'll be counting the minutes."

"Come on, Moby." Already hyperactive, the dog leaped forward, practically jerking Emma's arm out of its socket. At least her overly exuberant dog got her away from Creed before she offered her bed along with breakfast and a shower.

What had she been thinking? The more time she spent with the man, the more she found to like about him. Then again, the gun was disturbing. What was an insurance adjuster doing carrying a gun and setting up camp down the street from her? Hadn't she learned what a handsome face could get away with? All the lies and subterfuge. And here she was, falling again.

Running faster, she couldn't outrun the truth. She

was attracted to the man, and that was bad news all around. She should tell him to get out of her life and stay out. On the other hand, what was it Sun Tzu said in the book *The Art of War?* Something like "Keep your friends close and your enemies closer."

Was Creed friend or enemy? Whatever he was, Emma was convinced he wasn't telling her the whole truth. After Randy had duped her and the hospital, she refused to be gullible, naively expecting the best from everyone, especially handsome men. It might pay to find out just what Creed was up to.

She glanced down at her watch. Five minutes had passed. Circling in the middle of the street, she turned and ran back the way she'd come, her heartbeat quickening when she rounded the corner to find that the SUV and Creed were gone.

Disappointment filled her. Maybe Creed had changed his mind and gone back to the B and B. That would be the logical thing to do, considering he was paying for a room and he'd left a duffel bag there.

At the next corner, she jogged onto Sand Dollar Lane and spotted the SUV in front of her house. Butterflies kicked up a flutter in her empty belly. Creed leaned against the gate to her white picket fence, a backpack at his feet, his arms crossed over his chest, his eyes hidden behind mirrored sunglasses. Too darned handsome, by far.

Sweat beading on her brow and trickling down between her breasts, Emma felt sticky and at a disadvantage. Nothing like a sweaty woman to turn a guy off. She passed close to him, pushed open the gate and released Moby's leash.

The dog ran up the steps of the porch and turned circles at the top.

"There's only one bathroom in the house." Emma unlocked the door, and Moby raced inside. "You can have it first, while I feed the dog."

"I don't mind waiting until you've had first crack."

"You might not mind, but Moby does." She smiled down at Moby and patted his head.

Creed carried his backpack down the hallway and ducked into the bathroom.

Emma fed Moby, refreshed his water bowl. By the time she pulled out the skillet, eggs, cheese, onions and peppers, Creed appeared in the doorway to the kitchen.

His face was cleanly shaved, his black hair damp and combed back from his forehead. He wore a T-shirt with the words I'd Rather Be Diving emblazoned below a picture of a scuba diver. But it was the way his muscular arms and chest stretched the shirt that made her stare. He filled the doorway and made the kitchen feel much smaller than a few moments before. Emma swallowed hard to tamp down the urge to drool.

"Your turn," he said.

His words broke her trance, and she spun to face the gas stove. "Everything you need is here." She didn't want to face him with her cheeks burning. Her hand bumped the skillet and sent it flying across the stove.

Creed reached out and snagged it before it fell to the floor. "Relax. I'm only cooking omelets. It's not like I'm going to attack you."

"I didn't say you were going to attack me."

"You're as skittish as a wild kitten."

"I'm not used to having a man in my kitchen."

"Seems you've had one in your kitchen before me."

In her peripheral vision, she watched Creed thumb the photo she kept stuck to her refrigerator with a magnet.

"Why is there a big red line through him?" he asked.

"As a reminder not to lose my perspective when it comes to men."

"I take it this was your fiancé that you lost your perspective with," he said, his voice so close she could practically feel his breath on her neck.

"You got it." She faced him, realizing too late that he stood too close. Her hands rose to his chest. Whether to push him away or hold him close was a moot point. Once she touched him, she couldn't stop.

"Are you afraid of me, Emma?" He captured her fingers in one of his hands, the ridge beneath the fly of his cargo shorts pressing into her belly.

"You do have a big g-gun." Her heart slamming against her ribs, Emma dared to stare up into his eyes.

"Are you afraid I'll kiss you again?" He bent to brush his lips across her forehead. "I won't, if you don't want me to."

Her tongue swept across her suddenly dry lips. "I don't."

His hands squeezed hers for a moment longer and he appeared to hesitate, his gaze burning into hers. Finally, he released her hands and stepped back and winked. "See? No pressure. Now go. I'll have omelets ready in ten minutes."

Emma dove past him and into her bedroom, slamming the door behind her before she released the breath she'd been holding. She'd *wanted* him to kiss her. Hell, she'd wanted him to kiss her more than she'd wanted to breathe.

*Get a grip, girl.* The man was only in town for a few

days. Then he'd be gone. And good riddance. Creed Thomas was trouble with a capital *T*.

Straightening her shoulders, she grabbed a bikini, a pair of shorts and T-shirt from her dresser, and hurried into the bathroom across the corridor.

The low rumble of Creed's voice floated down the hallway. The man was singing and talking to Moby. The sound was so natural and warm, it seemed right. And that was *wrong!* Her house had always been one woman and one dog. When she'd been engaged to Randy, they'd spent their evenings at *his* condo, snuggling on *his* couch. Her cottage had been her haven, and he hadn't ever wanted to spend much time there, claiming he wasn't a dog lover.

Part of the problem had been that Moby hadn't liked Randy from the moment they'd met. Every time the man came to pick up Emma, Moby growled and snarled at Randy. Funny how the dog had been a much better judge of character than Emma had been.

Emma ducked into the shower, rinsing off the sweat and shampooing her hair. Granted, she'd be diving in salt water soon, so the shampoo was a waste of effort and soap. But that feminine gene in her couldn't leave her hair sweaty when she would be in the close confines of her kitchen with Creed. No matter how short a time it would be.

As she soaped her skin and water sluiced over her body, the warmth poured over her breasts and down between her legs. She couldn't help but think how naked and wet she was when Creed was just a few steps away. Just the thought made her belly tighten, her thighs quiver, and she moaned out loud.

"Everything okay in there?" Creed's voice called through the door.

The bar of soap squirted from between her hands, hit the wall tiles and bounced off her foot before settling close to the drain. "I'm fine," she said through gritted teeth, her foot throbbing from the soap assault.

"Are you sure?" His voice sounded closer, as if he'd opened the door. "I thought I heard someone moaning."

Her body on fire and her face in flames, Emma pressed the shower curtain to her body and peered around it at Creed.

He stood in the door, a smile teasing the corners of his lips.

"You must have been hearing things. I'm fine." She frowned. "Why are you in my bathroom?"

"I came to tell you the omelets are ready." He winked. "Need any help scrubbing your back?"

Her frown deepened, her body on fire with the possibility of Creed rubbing soap over her back. "I do not."

He sighed. "Doesn't hurt to ask. You're pretty tempting through that practically sheer shower curtain." His smile spread into a grin, and he ducked back through the door as Emma threw her wet washcloth at him.

"I should have let the shark have you," she yelled.

"Now, now, no need getting all upset," he said through the door. "You have a hot body. I call it as I see it."

Emma turned the water to cold and let the spray chill her skin. By the time she stepped out on the bath mat, she was in control and ready to face him. She was a nurse. She'd seen plenty of naked bodies. Having someone see hers shouldn't get her into a flap.

Unless that someone was Creed Thomas, with his smoldering eyes and devilish smile.

She jammed her legs into the bikini bottoms and pulled them up, then she shimmied into her shorts and finished dressing quickly. All the while, she imagined what it would have been like if she'd taken Creed up on his offer to scrub her back.

Sweet Jesus, she was headed down a very slippery path.

When she entered the kitchen, she'd plastered on her best poker face.

The omelet was delicious, and sitting across the table from Creed was a mix of comfortable and nerve-racking. She'd be glad when he left town. Then she could get back to her calm, normal, everyday...boring life.

In the meantime, she only had two days left to find the *Anna Maria*. With Creed occupying too many of her brain cells, she'd almost forgotten her determination to save the Children's Wing Project.

With renewed focus, she gathered her gear and stood on her front porch, staring out over the cape as the sun burned through the clouds. "Ready?"

Creed's gaze was on the large, gleaming white yacht anchored offshore. "I hope so." He turned to her. "You sure you want to dive today? Couldn't you take a day off?"

"No way. I have too much riding on this dive." She frowned. "Why?"

"I don't know. Maybe that shark will be there. It could be really dangerous. I have a bad feeling about it."

"Well, Nervous Nelly, keep that bad feeling to yourself. I've dived with sharks before, and I have too much seafloor to cover to waste time worrying. Are you coming?"

Creed offered to drive them to the marina, but Emma insisted on taking her Jeep, claiming she had errands to run after their dive.

Dave was on the *Reel Dive* sorting tanks and equipment and readying the boat for their dive. "Morning," he said as he latched a tank in place. "Probably only gonna get one dive in this morning."

"Why's that?" Emma asked.

"Looks good right now, but there's a storm brewing off the coast. If it doesn't rain, it'll stir up the waves so much you won't be able to get close to the point later on today."

"Then we'll have to make good use of the time we have." Emma tossed her duffel into the boat and climbed aboard. "At least the fog lifted earlier than predicted."

Creed joined Emma on the deck.

"Same place as yesterday?" Dave asked.

Emma nodded. "Same."

Dave started the engine and revved the throttle in Neutral.

Creed and Emma untied the ropes from the dock, and the *Reel Dive* slipped away from the marina and out into the cape.

While Emma climbed up to the helm to discuss their dive with Dave, Creed pulled a camera with a telephoto lens from his bag and extended it as far as it would go. He adjusted the viewfinder to zoom in on the yacht.

Several men stood on the deck, pointing toward their

dive boat. One lifted a set of binoculars. From the distance, Creed couldn't make out whether or not any of the men was Phillip Macias. He took several photographs. Perhaps the folks back at SOS headquarters could identify the men.

"Thinking of selling insurance to them?" Emma slipped up beside him.

"Never pass up an opportunity to make a buck," he quipped, and stowed the camera in the waterproof compartment of his duffel and set it beneath the bench in the cabin.

Emma followed him inside and set her bag on one of the seats. "We'll be there in ten. We should suit up."

As they pulled on their wet suits, booties and hoods, Creed couldn't help noticing how trim and fit she was. Not a spare ounce of flesh, but curves in all the right places. The bikini suited her body, displaying gently rounded hips and generous, if not overly large, breasts. It was a shame the water in these parts was so cold she had to wear a wet suit to cover all that.

He turned away, jamming his feet into his own wet suit and pulling it up his legs, reminding himself how important it was to maintain body heat to avoid hypothermia. He concentrated on the science of diving, not his dive buddy's beautiful body. Focus kept a SEAL alive.

When he turned back to her, he noted how comfortable Emma was with all the gear that went along with diving. "What made you become a diver?" he asked.

She ran the zipper of her wet suit up from the elastic waistband of her bikini bottom to just below her breasts.

Creed's groin tightened. If anything, the wet suit

only emphasized her curves and made her even more attractive. How did she do that?

"My father got me started when I was fifteen. I loved the weightlessness, seeing the fish and colorful anemones and swimming among the seals. Now, after working at a hospital full of people, noises and smells, I can escape into another world so completely different from the one I live in." Her gaze softened as she looked out across the water. "Down below, all I hear are the soft bubbles and the sound of my own breathing."

Creed understood what she was seeing and hearing in her mind. He felt the same.

Emma turned to him. "When was your first dive?"

"BUD/S."

"Buds?" She tipped her head to the side inquiringly.

"Basic underwater demolition training for SEALs."

"I understand that's pretty difficult."

He shrugged. "Hardest, best thing I've ever done for myself."

"That kind of training makes an impression on a man." She added softly, "I bet it hurt to be kicked out."

The pain in his chest from being kicked off the team had dulled over time, but had never quite gone away. "We're almost there."

Emma's gaze followed him, making him feel like a bug under a magnifying glass. Hell yes, it had hurt to lose the one place on earth he'd felt worth a damn, like he had a purpose in life. SEAL Team 6 had been the only real family he'd ever known. To lose them cut so deeply he'd almost ended it all. Then Royce had come along and given him purpose, a sense of belonging similar to his old team. Worthwhile missions, camaraderie and a new family brought him back from the edge of his own self-destruction.

The boat slowed near the rocky outcropping of the point and came to a halt, bobbing in the swells.

"It's already getting choppy." Dave killed the engine and climbed down the ladder from the helm. "Forget the buoy this round. It'll only slow you down."

Emma nodded and turned her back to Dave as he lifted a tank and harness over her shoulders. She snapped the buckles, settled her mask over her face and grabbed her fins.

Creed slung his harness, tank and all, over his shoulders, slid his mask onto his face and sat to strap on his fins. When he was ready, he stood and waited for Emma to finish.

"I'm moving away from the rocks as soon as you're over the side," Dave said.

"Good." Emma faced Creed. "Ready?"

Creed gave her a thumbs-up.

Holding on to her mask, Emma stepped off the side into the water first.

Creed checked the GPS device on his wrist and turned to Dave. "If another boat comes along with a bunch of badass-looking men, get the hell out of here. There's a gun in my duffel, if you need it, but your best bet would be to leave."

"Whoa, wait a minute." Dave held up his hands. "Should I expect trouble? No one said anything about badasses."

Creed hesitated, not knowing how much to tell him, finally deciding to stick as much to the truth as possible. "I have a feeling the people who shot the man we found yesterday might be back looking for their boat."

Dave scratched his head. "Why? Dead men don't talk or anything."

"I don't know yet. But I aim to explore the yacht wreck and find out."

"I thought we were supposed to steer clear of it until the crime scene investigators had first shot."

"We can't wait. Whoever killed the captain will be back to find whatever he thought was worth killing for."

Emma surfaced. "You coming?" she called out.

"On my way." Creed duckwalked to the edge. "Just remember," he said softly enough that only Dave would hear, "trouble comes, you leave."

"What about you two?"

"We'll manage."

"What about the storm?"

"If we're still out here, wait until the storm's past, morning if necessary. We'll find shelter on one of the rock islands."

Dave stared out over the rocky outcroppings. "Storms make this a really dangerous place. I hope that doesn't happen."

"You and me both." Creed clapped a hand on Dave's shoulder. "Keep your eyes peeled."

Dave gave him a mock salute and Creed stepped off the boat, his hand holding his mask in place. He plunged into the water and came up beside Emma.

Emma's eyes were narrowed behind her mask. "What took you so long?"

Creed grinned. "Cold feet." He stuck his regulator in his mouth, avoiding additional explanations.

"Yeah, Mr. I-learned-to-dive-with-the-SEALs." Emma gave him another look. "Since we're dive buddies for this dive, we stick together. My life depends on you and vice versa. No secrets and no wandering off. Even though you know your way around scuba gear, you don't know these reefs like I do. Stay with me. Got it?"

Creed made no promises. He saluted her, gave Dave a thumbs-up and dove, avoiding Emma's demand by leading the way. The sea surrounded him in a quiet world where all the noise he heard was the sound of his own breathing, the hollow shooshing of each breath he inhaled and the gurgling bubbles of release.

If word got out that the entire west coast was at risk of being blown off the planet, there'd be hell to pay with mass hysteria. If everyone loaded up their vehicles to flee the cities, the traffic jam would be unending and deadly in itself with rising temperatures, fuel shortages and multicar pileups.

The best way to handle it was to stop Phillip before he set the destruction in motion. The people on the yacht had been watching them leave the marina, with more than a passing interest. They had to be part of Phillip's legion of terrorists for hire.

Following his wrist GPS, he made his way back through the forest of boulders and jutting rocks to the sunken yacht, praying that, during this dive, he'd find whatever Phillip was after. Although, given the fact Phillip's thugs hadn't gotten out there this morning first, made him wonder what they were up to. Since he and Emma had found the body and reported the sunken yacht to the local police, it was now a matter of public record that the yacht had been found.

And since they hadn't reported any other find, Phillip might be either biding his time before going out to collect his cargo, or he was counting on Emma and Creed to find it for him and he'd collect it later.

The guy in the car the previous night might only have been there to keep an eye on Emma. And by being there, he'd kept a watch on Creed, as well.

The irony was not lost on Creed as he wove through the rocks.

Emma caught up but stayed a full length behind him.

When the yacht came into view of his headlamp, he paused, checking for intruders, in case they'd missed a dive boat on the surface.

Nothing moved but a school of fish above, their massive numbers creating a shadow over them, changing and undulating as they swam.

Something tugged at his fin.

Creed glanced over his shoulder as Emma swam up beside him. She pointed up and back the way they'd come.

A large white shark slid through the water, keeping pace with them.

They'd have to keep an eye out for the shark as well as Phillip's men.

Creed kicked his fins, making a beeline for the yacht.

Emma quickly followed.

When he didn't swim by, but entered the hatch leading to the cabin level of the three-level yacht, another tug on his fin brought him to a halt.

Emma jabbed her finger away from the boat.

Creed nodded, ignored her and went down into the cabin anyway.

Another tug on his fin would have stopped him, but

he jerked his leg and dislodged Emma's grip, easing into the interior. With no time to appease her, he started his search in the main guest quarters, opening every drawer, cabinet and container. Clothing, newspapers and shoes floated in the water around his head. After searching everywhere, including beneath the mattress, Creed pressed against the wood paneling. Maybe there was a hidden door.

Nothing popped open; no hidden safes or expensive jewelry had been stored in that cabin.

Creed backed out and moved to the next cabin. The woodwork wasn't as fancy, nor was the bed as big as in the main guest cabin. Still, Creed searched the entire room, just as he had the previous quarters. If he repeated the process through all six cabins on the yacht, he'd run out of air before he got to the middle deck and the top deck.

He backed out of the room and bumped into Emma, shining his headlamp into her eyes.

Her frown could not be disguised by the mask clamped to her face. She jerked her thumb over her shoulder, indicating he should get off the yacht immediately.

Creed shook his head and continued upward to the middle deck and entered the lounge, decorated in smooth white leather sectional couches, built in a curve around a low, stationary coffee table. Cabinets lined one wall, and a stereo with an expensive sound system took up another wall. A bank of windows made up a third wall and would have provided a fabulous view of the sea off the back of the ship if it hadn't sunk. Doors leading into the dining area and galley took up the fourth wall.

Without wasting time, he swam to the cabinets and opened one after another. They contained a complete array of wine, beer and hard liquor, and nothing that looked like bomb-making material or anything else that could be used to purchase such devices. What was he missing? Creed needed help if he wanted to complete the search on the current tank of air.

Emma had followed him into the yacht's interior. She turned right and left, her gaze traveling over the lavish decor, then focused on him, crossing her arms over her chest to indicate she wasn't happy with him.

Creed pointed to her, then to the cabinet, then to the air indicator on his regulator.

She shook her head and motioned toward the exit.

A standoff.

Creed completed his search of the cabinets and made a quick perusal of the rest of the room, tapping on wall panels until he reached the door leading to the dining room and galley.

Emma grabbed his arm and pointed at her air gauge.

They were down by seventy percent. Enough air left to swim a little farther in search of her shipwreck and then surface to swap empty tanks for full ones.

He acquiesced and let her lead the way out of the yacht. Creed knew that when they were back on the *Reel Dive,* he'd get an earful from Emma. But begging forgiveness was infinitely easier than getting her buy-in to search a yacht they'd been specifically warned to stay clear of by the local police.

Emma paused at the door leading out of the yacht, looked around, then swam out. Creed followed, searching the underwater landscape for threats, both aquatic and human. So far so good.

Without waiting to see if he'd follow, Emma swam away, heading deeper into the stony stand of rocks jutting up into the air above the ocean's surface.

The deeper they went, the larger the rocks and the darker the shadows, as if the sunshine had been traded for storm clouds.

Emma stopped suddenly. Before Creed could adjust, he swam into her, grabbing her arms to steady them both.

The beam of her headlamp shone on the rocky floor of the ocean where a cylindrical shape jutted out of the rocks, covered in barnacles and rust.

From the silhouette and size, Creed recognized it as the rear end of an ancient cannon.

Emma shot forward, aimed straight for the cannon, her headlamp twisting right and left, scouring the nearby rocks and shadows. When she reached the cannon, she ran her hand across its surface reverently, then looked around, searching for more.

Creed glanced at his air gauge. They had enough to surface safely, but they needed to go, or they'd run out before long. He closed the distance between them and snagged Emma's arm before she could take off again.

Her headlamp caught on a smooth, uniformly curved line like the rib of a giant, reaching out of the rocks. She jerked her arm to free herself of Creed's grip.

He refused to let go, insistent on her surfacing at that moment. They might have to swim a distance to get far enough away from the rocks for Dave to retrieve them.

Creed pointed at the gauge and then to the surface.

Emma glanced back at the rib, obviously torn, wanting to stay and really see what they'd found. Finally, she hit a button on her wrist GPS to mark the spot, then nodded.

They swam back the way they'd come and surfaced to a churning sea.

The *Reel Dive* bobbed crazily a distance away. When Emma blew her whistle, the sound was whipped away by the rising wind.

After Creed and Emma waved for five full minutes, Dave finally saw, jumped to his feet and turned the boat in their direction.

Out of the south, a jet boat burst over the waves, headed straight for the *Reel Dive.*

"That fool's going to hit Dave's boat." She bobbed on the surface, waving at Dave. "Stop!" Her hand clamped onto Creed's arm. "Can't the driver of the jet boat see? Does he even know what he's doing? Sweet Jesus, he's going to hit him!"

Creed feared the driver of the jet boat knew exactly what he was doing by aiming for Dave.

The captain of the *Reel Dive* must have seen the other craft, because he slowed and turned the dive boat hard to port at the last minute before impact. The jet boat glanced off the starboard bow of the *Reel Dive.* The dive boat dipped into the seat and recovered, bouncing on the waves.

"Go, Dave, get out of here!" Creed yelled.

Emma tapped his arm, then grabbed it. "Creed, that boat is coming at us."

He looked in time to see that the jet boat had made a sharp turn and was now headed straight for them. "Dive!"

## Chapter 7

Emma jammed her regulator into her mouth as Creed grabbed her hand and jackknifed, kicking hard to take them down as fast as possible. Flipping her fins, she churned her legs, fighting to get them behind her, before she settled into a tight rhythm that sent her downward, working with Creed, not against him.

The jet boat roared over the top of them, a few feet barely separating them. The backwash from the engines spun Emma around, churning her upward. She lost her grip on Creed's hand and fought the panic threatening to overtake her. Then Creed was there, gripping her hand again.

He struck out, dragging Emma with him, angling down and away, back toward the forest of rocky boulders where the jet boat couldn't follow.

Her pulse pounding in her ears, Emma forced herself to calm. Already low on air, and at the rate she was consuming it, she'd run out too soon. She prayed Dave had gone back to shore and fast. If that other boat had purposely targeted them, it might not stop until it sank the *Reel Dive* and killed the captain and divers.

Emma was in good shape, but she had to work hard not to slow down Creed. The deeper they went into the rocky grove, the more she realized they had to find a safe place to come up and wait out the storm.

Once they were completely surrounded by the rocks and out of range of the jet boat and any rifle its occupants might be carrying, Emma and Creed broke through to open air to get their bearings. Already the swells were rising eight to ten feet, and storm clouds had grown thick and ugly. If they stayed up top for long, they'd be smashed against the rocks.

The wind and waves buffeted them closer and closer to a jagged crag jutting out of the water.

"We can't stay here." Creed held on to her hand, kicking hard to keep them from slamming into the rocks.

"I know a place!" she yelled back.

There was one spot in the forest of boulders where they could come up for air and not be crushed. Emma had been there many times with her father in calmer seas. It wasn't far from where they were. She only hoped they could navigate the opening. It would prove challenging, with the waves creating the amount of churn they were.

Emma motioned for them to dive beneath the frenetic waves. Once below, they sank deep enough to avoid much of the churn. Emma feared if they didn't go directly there, they'd run out of air or daylight before they made it to the pirate's cave hidden among the rocks on the point. It was rumored that pirates hid their treasures in the cave. Emma and her father had been there many times, paddling out in kayaks, never finding anything more than seashells on the sandy floor of the small cave.

She tugged on Creed's arm and brought them to a stop, hovering in the water. Fortunately the cave was one of the points stored on her GPS. She hit the menu button and recalled the cave's location. The screen lit with a contour map of the ocean floor with an *X* in the spot she needed to head toward. As soon as she got her bearings, Emma took off, leading the way.

Within a few hundred feet of the cave's underwater entrance, her air supply registered critically low. In minutes, she'd run out. They had one shot at making it into the cave, when the waves pushed water through the hole and up into the rock's hollowed-out cavity.

This time she grabbed Creed's hand and watched the flow of the water. When it ebbed away from the base of the rocky island, she shot forward, tugging Creed with her. She swam hard, trying to make the entrance before the wave slammed forward. If they got through the entrance, the wave would carry them the rest of the way.

If they didn't breach the opening, the wave would slam them against the rocks.

The flow of the water shifted as they neared a hole large enough to fit a small car through. Emma didn't slow; she kicked harder, the rush of water building behind her.

They cleared the entrance. The wave rushed up behind them, propelling them the rest of the way into the cave and onto a sandy patch of beach.

Emma spit her regulator out of her mouth, her head barely above the water, the drag of the wave's retreat pulling at her legs. "Move!" she yelled, crawling with her elbows, kicking her fins hard against the suction the wave created on its way out of the cave. She was backsliding, losing the battle, being sucked out of the cave they'd barely made it into. She fumbled for her regulator, missed and swallowed a gulp of salty seawater.

Her fingers dug into the sand, but found nothing to hold on to and she was dragged backward, unable to breathe.

A firm hand grabbed her wrist and yanked her out of the water and into strong, capable arms. Creed held on to her as the wave fully retreated. Then he lifted her, scooting backward up the stair steps of slick rocks until he found a point the next wave couldn't reach, and leaned back, breathing hard, his tank braced against the rock behind him.

Emma lay against his chest, the buckles of his buoyancy control device digging into her cheek. But she didn't care. They'd made it.

Laughter bubbled up in her chest and slipped out. In seconds, she was doubled over, laughing so hard it hurt. Soon the laughter turned to tears, and she buried her face in his wet suit.

He removed his mask and hers and set them on the rock above them, the light from their headlamps still shining, casting a soft glow against the damp walls of the cave. "Turn around so I can get that tank off your back."

Emma turned so that Creed could unscrew the clamp holding her regulator to the tank and unclamped the tank from her buoyancy control vest. He pulled the tank free and jammed it into a crevice.

Creed shifted so that his back was to her, and she performed the same task, her hands shaking as they moved over the buckles and knobs. "What the hell just happened?" She pulled his tank out of the harness and handed it to Creed.

"I believe we narrowly escaped being killed."

"I get that part. What I want to know is why?"

Creed didn't answer immediately as he stacked his tank on top of Emma's, then removed his fins and laid them on a ledge over his head.

Free of the heavy, bulky tank, Emma slipped her fins off and handed them to Creed, who stowed them on top of his. She moved as far away from him as she could get without falling off the rock upon which they both were perched. Waves washed up to their feet, reminding her she didn't have far to go to be sucked back through the opening of the cave. "Why are people trying to kill us? We didn't do anything."

"Maybe they think we did."

Emma smacked a palm against his chest. "And maybe you can stop being so damned evasive and give me some straight answers. We almost got killed out there, and who knows how Dave is faring?"

One of the headlamps flickered, the light fading.

"Can we turn these off until we need them?" he asked instead of giving her the answers she demanded.

"Why? So you can hide your face while you lie to me some more?"

He touched a hand to her cheek. "No, so that we can conserve the battery. It's going to be a long day and night."

She hadn't considered the length of their stay in the pirate's cave until that moment. Then the enormity of it hit her. Not only were they trapped, but it would get colder, and all they had to keep them warm were their wet suits and their own body temperatures.

The light flickered again.

"Fine," she grumbled. "Turn it off."

Creed shut off the switch on the winking light.

As he reached for the other one, Emma braced herself for the lack of light.

She wasn't prepared for the complete darkness. Each time she'd come to the cave with her father, they'd brought powerful flashlights and kept them on at all times.

Now, sitting in the dark with hours of the same to come, Emma shivered violently.

"Are you afraid of the dark?" he asked.

"N-no." She hated that her voice shook along with her body.

Big hands reached for her, gripping her arms, dragging her closer.

For half a second, she resisted. "Wh-what are you doing?"

"We need to stay close to conserve body heat."

The nurse in her knew he was right, but the woman was afraid, though not of the dark. She feared what the anonymity of darkness might lead to. Possibly a complete loss of inhibitions. Ultimately, the demise of the wall she'd built around her when Randy left her with the responsibility for the loss of funds for the hospital addition.

She wasn't afraid of the dark, and she wasn't afraid of Creed, so much as her own body's reaction to his nearness in the dark. If she continued to give in to her lusty urges, the overwhelming need to be close to this man, she'd be right back where she was when Randy walked away with all the hospital's money. Only this time it would be different. This time she'd know better. And this time her heart might be more affected.

Emma realized she'd never really been in love, not with Randy. Perhaps she'd been listening too much to her biological clock. While others around her, like Kayla and Gabe, were getting married and having babies, she'd felt life was passing her by. She wanted those things. To be loved, to get married and start a family.

Though her mother had died of cancer when Emma was only twelve, and her father in a car accident a year after she'd graduated with her bachelor of science in nursing, she'd had the best parents and the best childhood. Not all kids had the complete love and support she'd been privileged to have.

With no family left, she'd yearned for that closeness, someone to love. Sure, she had Moby, and he was her four-legged child, but she wanted what her parents had—a home, human children, someone to love and someone to love her in return. She missed being held in strong arms. Having someone else to share her joy and sadness.

Randy had promised all that to get what he'd wanted, and then broke his promises to her and the community she called home, leaving her to pick up the pieces and move on, guilt and all.

Creed had been heading down the same path, lying to her and the police from day one. She'd be damned if she let her lust for the man cloud her vision anymore.

"I'm only staying close to you because you're right, it's going to get cold and we have to share body warmth or die of exposure. But don't think it means anything more than that."

"Fair enough."

She laid her head against his chest, appreciating the solid comfort it brought in the pitch-black of the cave. With the waves crashing relentlessly against the outside and spray reaching up to keep their legs damp and cold, the noise was continuous, almost lulling in its intensity. "Just for the record, I don't trust you," she added, her voice a husky whisper.

"I can live with that, as long as it keeps you alive." He smoothed a hand over her arm, drawing her closer, raising her up so that her feet would remain above the spray of the waves blasting through the cave's entrance.

"You haven't been telling me the truth from the very beginning, have you?"

His hand stopped rubbing her arm, and he didn't answer for so long that Emma thought he wasn't going to. Then he said, "That is correct. I haven't been telling you the truth."

"Since we're stuck in this cave for the night and might not make it out alive, now is the time to bare your soul." She nestled closer. "Start talking, and give it to me straight this time."

His chest rose and fell on a sigh. "Where should I start?"

"Start with who you really are." Her hand rested on his wet suit. "And don't feed me some crap about being an insurance adjuster. I've never met an insurance adjuster who stays in such good shape." She could feel the strength of his muscles, even through the wet suit. Firm, solid. A warrior's physique. "Battle ready."

"You don't think I could be an insurance adjuster?" He chuckled, the sound rumbling against her ear, warming her when she should be shaking with cold. "And I thought I was doing a good job with my cover."

"Aha! I knew it." She lifted her head and stared up at where his face should be, wishing she could read his expressions. When all she could see was black, she lay back against him, her fingers pressing into the insulated wet suit. "Tell me what's going on, and don't leave anything out. I think I've earned the right to know."

Creed laid it all out for her, telling her everything he knew except names of his teammates and boss. Some things were best kept secret to avoid putting the members of his team in any kind of danger, from outright exposure to accidental slippage of information, or in the event someone thought the information was worth torturing for.

When he'd finished his tale with the rumors coming out of Washington, Emma had grown still, barely moving, and he couldn't tell if she was actually breathing.

Several moments of silence passed before she spoke.

"Holy crap." Her head shook back and forth against his chest. "And I was worried about finding the money for the new children's wing. Heck, there might not even be a hospital left if what you say happens. Not that I'm fully convinced I should trust you."

He chuckled. "Jury's still out?"

"Damn right it is. I've been burned before. I won't be burned again by believing everything I hear."

"Hopefully, some of my team will be in Cape Churn

by now, or soon, to corroborate my story. I expect Macias to start pushing for answers. I also suspect he was banking on us finding the cargo today and bringing it up. Thus the attack by jet boat."

"But we didn't."

"And since *we* didn't, he'll be with his men looking for it himself. I imagine he's on a tight timeline with the man he's supposed to be working with to pull off an attack of this magnitude."

"Then he's getting desperate." Emma spoke softly, her breath warming his neck.

Creed's arm tightened around her. "I'm sorry I dragged you into this."

"Who else would you have gotten to help? I'm the best diver in Cape Churn. I know these waters better than anyone."

"I had the GPS tracking device attached to the yacht. I'd have found it."

"You needed a boat, and Dave won't take just anyone out to the point. It's too dangerous to go without a dive partner."

"Then I'm lucky I found you." His arm tightened around her.

Emma stroked his wet suit, the gentle touches stirring a longing inside him he hadn't known was there.

"Where do we go from here?" she asked.

"You're getting out of this. Me and my team will deal with Macias. In fact, is there somewhere you can stay for a while? Away from Cape Churn. They know where you live, and Macias can be a formidable foe. If they think we know what their plans are…" He paused before voicing what had him most concerned.

"He'll whack me?"

Creed burst out laughing. "'Whack me'? Are we in some Hollywood mafia movie?"

"Well? What do you call it, then?"

"He'd murder you." As he said the words, a cold chill raced the length of his spine, a cold so bitter it rivaled the North Pacific waters spitting across their legs.

"I could stay at the bed-and-breakfast," Emma suggested.

"By now, they know I'm supposedly staying there. I wouldn't be surprised if they've been inside to check through my belongings."

"God, I hope they haven't broken into my house and hurt Moby, or let him loose. Once he's loose, he likes to run and he's not always smart enough to come home." Emma pressed closer. "I hope Dave made it back okay."

"Will Moby be all right on his own for a day?"

"If Dave made it back, he'll let the police know what happened. Gabe will stop by my house. He's watched out for Moby when I've gone out of town. And he has a spare key."

"Then there's nothing to worry about. Moby will scare the bad guys away, and Gabe will make sure he's taken care of. All we need to do is concentrate on staying alive until we can get out of here and back to shore."

"It's not that far," she whispered, her voice almost lost against the crashing waves and the wailing of the wind through crevices in the rocks. "Although right now, it feels like we might as well be on the moon."

Creed held her tighter, trying to cocoon her body with his. Before long, she fell asleep, her breathing slowing and growing steady, her body limp against his.

Tired from being awake most of the night, Creed fought sleep for a while, thinking how ironic it was that he'd thought the rental SUV had been uncomfortable. Compared to the hard rocks digging into his back and legs, it was paradise.

He'd known tough times, tougher than this. BUD/S training had been as bad as it gets and he'd survived, earning the distinction of Badass of Hell Week. He'd come out strong, hungry and aching, but he'd never been prouder of his accomplishments.

He didn't doubt he'd come out of this watery coffin of a cave intact. The storm would pass and they would swim out in the morning and find their way to shore. Then he'd get back down to that yacht and rip it apart until he found what Macias was looking for.

On the wave of his last thoughts, sleep overtook him. With Emma cradled in his arms, he slipped into a dream he knew couldn't come true. One in which he and Emma lived in her little seaside house with its white picket fence. Several small children ran through the hallways squealing, chased by a rambunctious Moby, barking as he played with them.

Emma would be coming through the door in her scrubs after a day at the hospital, smiling and holding open her arms for him.

Yeah, it was a dream. Even in his sleep, Creed knew it could never be. He was a secret agent, on the go all the time, fighting to quell one terrorist plot after the other. What woman would want to be a part of that? Only a strong, well-grounded woman who understood what it was like to take pride in hard work and sacrifice and love of country.

Was that woman Emma? The woman he'd known for two days? She'd already proven she could hold up under difficult circumstances.

In his dreams he shut the door to his misgivings and immersed himself in the fantasy, lying naked in Emma's bed with her snuggled close, her silky skin pressed against him. He'd make love to her in the middle of the day with the warm sunlight shining down on her body.

She'd wake up beside him on the days he was home and roll over him to stir him awake in more than one way. Her long, lean body, with curves in all the right places, would fit perfectly with his.

A plume sprayed high, drenching them in cold, salty seawater, jerking Creed out of his dreams. Although much like his fantasy, Emma lay curled against his side, her body completely covered by the thick insulated wet suit. Even if they'd wanted to, the logistics of their perch wouldn't allow them to make love. They'd die of exposure if they removed the wet suits.

Creed took the wave's spray as a slap back to reality. He couldn't have a relationship with Emma, even if he wanted one. There would always be another terrorist and another assignment to save the world.

When he drifted back into a restless sleep, he dreamed of Phillip Macias standing before him, threatening Creed's country and his SOS family if he didn't back off. At first Creed told him to go to hell, that he didn't kowtow to terrorist threats. Then Macias had his thugs drag a woman out of their vehicle and shove her to her knees.

Macias held a gun to the back of her head with one hand, and grabbed a handful of sandy-blond hair and yanked her head back, exposing her face.

Emma.

## Chapter 8

Emma woke off and on all night long, readjusting her body to ease the kinks in her back and legs. Her entire body was cold and damp, her feet the coldest, having been doused most of the night by the plumes of spray erupting from the cave's entrance, but she didn't complain. Creed had to be even more uncomfortable considering he'd allowed her to use him as a pillow.

The pale light of day had found its way up through the cave entrance, turning the sand into glitter at Emma's feet.

"Sleep well?" Creed asked.

"Probably better than you did." She shivered. "I don't think I've ever been this cold for so long, though."

"The only way to warm up is to get moving." He reached for the tanks. "We might have a few minutes of air left on each. Let's get out of this cave and find our way back to the mainland."

"I'm in." Emma helped fit his tank into the straps on the back of his BCD and turned to let him adjust hers. After settling their masks over their faces, strapping their fins on their feet and conducting a quick equipment check, Emma gave Creed a thumbs-up.

Then she eased down the rocky ledge to the sand and water below. The cold seemed to go right through her wet suit to her bones, making her shiver so hard her teeth chattered. She plugged her regulator between them and dove through the cave entrance, following the light to emerge outside in a pale green world.

Still shaking, she hovered, waiting for Creed. When he cleared the cave and swam up beside her, she headed for the surface as she took the final breath of air from her tank.

When she breached the surface, she spit her regulator out, dragged her mask down from her face and sucked in a long, cool breath of fresh air. She darted a look around, praying the bad guys from yesterday hadn't come looking for them today.

Still in the midst of a sea of rocky protrusions, she couldn't see beyond to the bay. She bobbed in the gentle swells, weighing their options.

Creed emerged beside her, slipped his mask off his eyes and removed the regulator from his mouth. "Which way?"

"We can try to swim back to the point, but the swells might make it twice as long a trip than if we get out of this mess and swim back into the open."

"The difference of how much time?"

"Knowing Dave, he'll be back out here looking for us by now. He might even have the coastguard alerted, as well."

"Macias won't attempt a hit if there are too many people around. Let's head for the opening." Creed shifted his snorkel around on his mask and settled the mouthpiece between his teeth. Emma did the same and they swayed back through the rocks, keeping far enough away from them to avoid being smashed up against them. Even in the calmer seas, the swells slapped against the rocks.

Tired, cold and hungry, Emma didn't have the extra strength needed to fight the currents. As they neared the open bay, she slowed, her gaze darting all around, fully expecting a jet boat to come barreling down on top of them.

Instead, she spotted a coastguard schooner at the tip of the point and a smaller fishing boat closer to where they were. The fishing boat wove in and out of the rocks. When it got close enough, Emma could see Dave in the driver's seat. She lifted her whistle from around her neck and blew on it sharply several times.

Already on the lookout, it didn't take long for Dave to spot them and pull up alongside. He killed the engine and ran to the back of the boat, extending the metal ladder into the water. "Am I glad to see you two."

"Not as glad as we are to see you," Emma said, swimming for the ladder.

Creed helped Emma out of her BCD, tank and all, and handed it up to Dave.

Emma ducked her head into the water and slipped her feet out of her fins, tossing them up over the side onto the boat. Then she hauled herself up the ladder, the effort seeming harder than usual. Dave handed her a large beach towel and helped her out of her wet suit while Creed removed his fins and climbed aboard with his tank still on his back.

Once Emma was wrapped in the warm, dry towel, she hunkered down on a seat, as much out of the cool breeze as possible. "Did the jet boat come after you again?" she asked Dave.

"He started to, but I did like Creed said and slammed the throttle forward as hard as I could and got the hell out of there. I was halfway back to the marina before I looked back."

"Creed told you to leave?" Emma glanced at Creed.

The man had shed his BCD and had his wet suit zipped halfway down, exposing his broad, smooth chest.

"We had the shelter of the rocks in case of attack. Dave had nothing."

"You knew it might happen." Emma shook her head. "It would have been nice if you'd told me what to expect sooner. I could have been more prepared."

Dave laid Creed's tank and BCD on the deck and handed him a towel. "How'd you know?"

"I had a hunch." He ran the towel over his head and draped it around his shoulders as he shoved the wet suit down his legs and then sat, unzipped his booties and stepped out of all of it.

Like Emma, his skin was shriveled from being wet for so long. Creed nodded toward the coastguard boat. "Are they looking for us?"

"Yup. I notified the police and the coastguard as soon as I got back to the marina yesterday afternoon. I'm surprised you didn't hear the helicopter fly over. They went up for an hour, but the weather was so bad, they had to call off the search. Then they had some technical malfunction and couldn't get it up this morning, so they sent out a boat."

"Nice to know we were missed." Emma smiled, her lips trembling from cold.

"Oh, and I had Gabe check in on Moby," Dave added.

"Thanks." Emma's heart warmed at Dave's gesture. The people of Cape Churn looked out for each other *and* their dogs. "I'm sure he was glad for the company."

Dave pulled the ladder up in back, stepped over the equipment and settled into the captain's seat. He fiddled with the radio, then notified the coastguard he'd found the two missing persons alive, had them aboard and would take them back to the marina.

Emma huddled low, out of the wind, her teeth chattering. Without the wet suit, the towel did little to keep her warm.

Creed sat on the bench beside her, blocking some of the wind, and pulled her into his arms. She didn't fight it, leaning in to him, his warmth helping to keep her from shaking so hard.

Sal and Olaf Olander, the owners of the marina, hurried across the dock, carrying blankets as Dave guided the boat into its slip.

Emma had never before been so glad to see the marina after a dive trip. Granted, she'd never been on a dive trip that extended overnight in the cold.

Creed climbed up onto the dock and held out his hand to her, pulling her into his arms to steady her.

Sal wrapped a thick wool blanket and her skinny arms around her. "Emma, honey, we're so glad you're okay. You had us worried sick all night long."

Emma smiled at the older couple, whose faces were

lined deeply by wind and age. She was warmed by the sincerity of their worry and the hugs they insisted on giving her at every opportunity. Having spent so much time at the marina, she'd gotten to know the Olanders. They were like the grandparents Emma had never known.

When Sal had been sick with pneumonia, she'd insisted on having Emma as her nurse at Cape Churn Memorial. Whenever Emma got a break, she'd spend it reading *Moby Dick* to the older woman, much to Sal's delight. When she'd checked out of the hospital before the end of the story, Emma had spent her days off parked on a stool in the marina, reading the rest of the book out loud for both Sal and Olie.

Two Cape Churn police cruisers pulled up in the parking lot, lights blazing. Gabe McGregor got out of one and Chief Taggart out of the other, both converging on the dock with the growing crowd around Emma and Creed.

Gabe reached Emma first and wrapped her in a big hug. "Kayla was up all night with Tonya. Neither one could sleep. Kayla was too worried about you. And it's funny how Tonya seems to sense when her mother is upset."

"I'm sorry," Emma said.

"And though Moby was glad for a trip outside, he wouldn't eat his supper without you there."

Tears filled Emma's eyes. "Thanks for checking on him."

"I'm just glad you're okay. Kayla would be lost without you."

"Oh, I doubt that. She has you, Gabe." Emma hugged the big police officer.

Chief Taggart stepped up on the dock. "You might let the two castaways have a little air and maybe a meal. Nora's got the cook on standby at the café. Say the word, and she'll have a feast fit for kings."

"I want a shower and warm clothes first," Emma insisted. "But food would be great immediately following."

Taggart turned to Creed and held out his hand. "Dave tells me you had some trouble out there yesterday."

Creed clasped the chief's hand. "Yes, sir."

"I'd like to hear more about it."

"And you will. As soon as I can get Emma home and find some clean, dry clothes for myself."

"Absolutely." The chief clapped a hand on Creed's back. "Let me give you two a lift to the hospital where they can check you over."

Emma smiled. "Thanks, but I think we're okay."

Gabe chuckled. "Is that your professional nurse's opinion?"

Plastering a serious expression on her face, Emma nodded. "You bet." She ruined it with a grin.

"Then let me give you a lift home," Chief Taggart offered.

"If it's all the same to you, I'd rather take my Jeep," Emma insisted.

"I'll ride with Emma," Creed added.

Emma shot a glance at him. "Don't you want to take your SUV?"

"All I need out of it is my bag." His gaze captured hers, as if telling her he wasn't ready to let her out of his sight.

Emma blinked. Surely she was reading too much

into his look. It had been a long, cold night; she might be just a little delirious. But she didn't care. After what they'd gone through the day before and being holed up in a cave in the dark, she wasn't ready to have him out of her sight, either. Not to mention the matter of the potential terrorist attack. Yeah, she wanted Creed on her side, and close enough to make a difference.

The chief walked Emma and Creed to her Jeep. "Glad you two made it through the night. You had a lot of folks worried."

"We're pretty happy to be back on dry land," Emma admitted.

"Call when you're headed for the café." The chief directed his gaze at Creed. "We have a lot to talk about." The older man walked to his police car and got in, leaving Creed and Emma alone.

Creed's gaze followed the chief. He knew it was time to bring the local authorities into the operation. With a deep sigh, he held out his hand for the key to Emma's Jeep. "Why don't you let me drive?"

"I can drive," she pointed out, but laid the keys in his hand anyway.

"I know, and you're a good driver." He took the keys.

"There's a *but* in there." Emma rolled her eyes, tired but happy to have her feet on the ground and drying. "I feel it coming."

His lips twitching, Creed said, "But you look pretty beat."

"You don't look so hot yourself, and you're running on less sleep than I am." She climbed into the passenger seat and leaned back. "But I'm not complaining too much. It's kinda nice having a chauffeur."

"Do I take that as you beginning to trust me?"

"I wouldn't go that far," she said with her eyes closed.

Tired, her hair hanging in limp strands around her face and shadows beneath her eyes, she was still the most beautiful woman Creed had ever known. With Emma, it wasn't just who she was, but who loved her that made her so appealing. She was surrounded by a town full of people who would miss her if she were gone. That spoke a lot about her character. She was smart, strong and good-hearted, and people loved her for all those qualities.

His pulse quickening, Creed wondered if that was what was happening to him. Was he falling under Emma's spell? Going into their third day together, had he fallen for the hometown girl? Holy hell, perhaps taking her home was a really bad idea. Hadn't he dreamed of her house with its picket fence and him living there as though he actually belonged?

When was the last time he felt as if he really belonged in any one place? Besides on his SEAL team, he'd never found a place he could call home. Growing up, his mother had moved from one house to another, unable to pay rent half the time. He'd roamed the streets rather than stay in the house where no one was ever home.

Emma, on the other hand, had a home, in a community that loved her.

"Where are your parents?" Creed asked.

"My parents?" She cracked one eyelid and peered up at him. "Why do you ask?"

"You've been missing for a day. I'd expect them to be worried."

She closed the eye, her lips turning downward. "They would have worried, but they passed away years ago."

"I'm sorry."

"It's been a while, but I still miss them." Her smile returned. "They gave me the most important gift of all."

"Oh, yeah? What's that?"

"A happy childhood."

Her words hit him square in the gut. A happy childhood was the one thing he'd never had. The very thing he didn't know enough about to give to a child of his own. He was on the road so much, it wouldn't be fair to any woman or child to burden them with coping alone. Emma was loved; she had family in her community. She deserved a man who would be there for her and their children.

"We're here." Creed pulled into her driveway and got out. "I'll see you at the diner in fifteen minutes." He retrieved his bag containing his spare clothing and weapons and started to walk back to the marina and his SUV.

Emma dropped down out of the Jeep, her brow furrowed. "Where are you going?"

"I just remembered something I forgot," he mumbled and continued toward the sidewalk.

Emma hurried after him, the blanket wrapped around her, hindering her steps. "Was it something I said?" She hooked his arm, forcing him to stop. "Tell me."

"Yes. No. Oh, hell." He dropped his bag to the concrete and grabbed her arms. "I'm no good for you. Do you understand?" He shook her slightly, his grip fierce, his teeth grinding together. It took every ounce of will-power not to kiss her.

"And that's an issue because?"

"I'm not staying. As soon as this case is solved, I move on to the next one."

"Did I ask you to stay?"

"No."

Her eyes widened. "But you *want* to stay." She added quietly, "Don't you?"

He squeezed his eyes shut and breathed a ragged breath. "Emma, you have a perfect little life, in a perfect little town. Don't screw it up with a man like me."

"I'm not asking for forever. I was only going to offer you a shower." Tears welled in her eyes. "I've been with you since yesterday morning." She pushed a straggly hair behind her ear. "I guess I wasn't ready to let go." She stared down at his hands on her arms. "You don't have to stay." A tear trailed down her cheek, and she bit her bottom lip. "I'll understand."

When the tear slipped off her chin and landed on his arm, something hard inside him broke, shattering into a million pieces. "Damn it, Emma, this isn't supposed to happen."

She looked up at that moment, her tired eyes awash in unshed tears.

He crushed her lips with his, his arms locking around her like steel bands, holding her as if he would never let her go.

She wrapped her arms around his waist and held on just as hard, lifting up on her toes to deepen the kiss.

Beyond his ability to reason, he cupped the back of her head and eased up, his mouth hovering over hers. "It wasn't supposed to be like this," he repeated.

"How was it supposed to be?" she asked.

He bent to grab his duffel bag, then scooped her up in his arms, blanket and all, and marched back toward the house.

Emma reached down to open the gate to the picket fence.

Once through, Creed kicked the gate shut behind them, without missing a step on his way to the front porch.

Moby barked from the other side of the door, scratching at the wood to get to Emma.

Emma leaned down to unlock the door. "You might want to put me down. Moby will be excited."

Creed reluctantly set her on her feet and pushed the door open.

Moby exploded through the gap and slammed into Emma. She staggered backward, bumping against Creed's chest.

He steadied her with his hands on her hips, counting the moments until Moby settled down and they could continue inside to finish what he'd started on the sidewalk.

With Moby dancing around and lunging against him, the flame of passion simmered, leaving Creed to second-guess his intentions. If there hadn't been barriers between them and the bedroom, he'd have gone straight there and made mad, passionate love to her. Moby's exuberance cooled his heels, reminding him of his duties and responsibilities.

After Moby graced every bush in the yard, he raced back into the house.

Creed held the door for Emma, whose face was flushed, her eyes shining, her mouth swollen from his kiss. He couldn't walk away, but he could give her choices. "Why don't you shower while I feed Moby."

"I know where everything is. I'll take care of Moby while you shower." She headed for the kitchen, leaving Creed standing in the hallway, wishing they could as easily pick up where they'd left off and take it ten steps farther. Ten steps toward her bedroom, getting naked and making love until Moby demanded another trip outside.

With Emma out of sight, Creed should have been able to focus, to get his mind back in the game. He forced himself to enter the bathroom rather than follow her to the kitchen. He closed the door behind him, shed the blanket and his shorts and twisted the handle on the shower until the water sprayed in a warm, steady stream.

He stepped into the tub and closed the curtain, letting the warm water wash away the salt of the ocean. The only bar of soap was the one Emma used, with a fragrant floral scent. Lathering it in his hands, he rubbed it over his body, realizing the mistake as the scent he associated with Emma surrounded him. He braced himself against the shower wall and reached to adjust the water to Cool. Before his hand closed around the handle, the shower curtain whooshed to the side and Emma stepped in behind him, grabbed the bar of soap and collected lather in her hands.

With his back to her, he grit his teeth. "Are you sure this is what you want?"

"Yes." She set the bar of soap in the dish and smoothed her soapy hands over his shoulders, down his back and around to his belly.

Creed groaned. "I'm not staying."

"I know." Her hands slid lower.

His groin tightened, his member jutting out, hard, stiff and ready for when her fingers closed around it.

Every nerve in his body stood up and cheered, sending happy messages to his brain and back to his member, making him even harder.

Her fingers, slick with lather, rode him to the tip and back to the base. She pressed her pelvis against his buttocks, the furry mound of hair brushing against him in a tantalizingly sexy way.

Creed flexed his hips, sliding through her hands, again and again, the tension building to a fevered pitch. When he thought he'd explode, he grabbed her hands and held them still, concentrating on breathing so that he didn't come too soon. Then he turned and switched places with her, letting the water run down over her back and shoulders to drip off her perky breasts.

"You're beautiful," he said. He squirted shampoo into his hands and combed his fingers through her hair, washing and rinsing it until it was squeaky clean.

Emma tipped her head back, letting the water run down over her face and chest. She handed him the bar of soap, and he lathered it in his hands and set it on the dish. With smooth precision and a gentle touch, he ran his hands over her shoulders and down to her breasts, where he pinched the rosy buds into tight little knots. Soap suds bubbled up and slipped down her torso to the thatch of hair at the apex of her thighs.

She shifted her feet apart and guided his hand downward to cup her sex, inviting him in.

His heart thundering against his ribs, Creed forced himself to move slowly, deliberately bringing her with him on the rise to what promised to be an earth-shattering experience.

He slid his fingers between her folds, stroking that nubbin of flesh, that delicate sensory organ packed full of nerve endings.

She arched her back, bracing her hands on his shoulders, her eyes squeezed tightly shut.

When he touched her again, she gasped. "Oh, yeah."

His member pulsed, throbbing, aching to be inside her. But he wanted her there with him, so he pressed a finger into her channel, slick with water and her own juices.

She covered his hand with hers and pressed his finger deeper.

Creed slipped another finger inside her and another until he had three fingers stretching her channel, preparing her for what came next. Then it hit him. "Do you have protection?"

Her eyes blinked open, and she stared at him a moment before she said, "Yes. In the nightstand by my bed."

The water cooling, Creed reached behind her and switched it off, shoved the curtain aside and stepped out onto the bath mat.

"Towels are in the cabinet behind you," she said.

He opened the door and grabbed a fluffy white towel and smoothed it over her body, stopping often to take a tempting nipple between his teeth. She reached around him, snatched another towel and dried him at the same time.

When they were both dry, Creed tossed the towels to the floor, reached down and grabbed her thighs, lifting her and wrapping her legs around his waist. Then he was striding through the bathroom door and into the bedroom across the hallway.

He laid her on the bed, her legs still locked around his waist, and he reached into the drawer beside the bed, fumbling until his fingers curled around a foil packet.

She took it from him and tore it open with her teeth, sliding the condom down over his engorged erection.

When she was done, she lay back against the comforter, her heels digging into his buttocks, urging him to take her.

"Not yet," he said, unlocking her ankles from behind him and dropping to his knees beside the bed. He draped her legs over his shoulders and tongued a path from the inside of her thighs to her center. There, he parted her folds and flicked the flesh, swirling, stroking and sucking on her until her body arched off the bed and stiffened, her fingers digging into the comforter as she cried out.

He strummed her a moment longer, then rose to his feet and entered her wet, slick channel, sliding all the way in.

Her muscles contracted around him, drawing him deeper. She locked her legs around his middle as he pumped in and out of her. With his hands gripping her hips, he settled into a smooth, steady rhythm that built the tension to the edge, and catapulted him into ecstasy.

He held tight, buried deep inside her, his fingers digging into the fleshy part of her buttocks, his manhood throbbing, encased in her warmth. When Creed returned to reality, he slipped free and dropped onto the mattress beside her, his own legs draping over the edge.

"Do we have to go to the café?" Emma yawned and curled into his side.

"I have a feeling that if we don't show up soon, the chief will come looking for us."

"I could sleep for a week." Her hand slipped across his chest, toying with his nipple.

"We need food to keep up our strength."

"I suppose you're right." Emma curled her leg over his thigh, then rose up to straddle his hips, guiding his still-stiff member into her. "But maybe we can wait a little longer."

He didn't know where he found the strength to go again. But with Emma riding him, he revived and ended up flipping her over onto the mattress and driving deep inside her again and again until she clutched his shoulders, her face pinched as her body contracted around him.

When they were completely satiated, Creed carried Emma back to the shower and they rinsed off, touching and feeling every inch of the other's body as they dried off.

Emma dressed in a bright red bikini, slipping a flirty sundress over it that showed off her well-defined calves, while Creed slipped into swim trunks and a T-shirt with a fisherman on the front and the Cape Churn logo across the bottom.

"Are you going to tell the chief what you told me?" she asked.

Creed nodded. "I think it's time."

The smart phone he kept zipped in his duffel buzzed, reminding him that he hadn't checked for messages in a day. While it rang, he dug to find it, locating the device on the fifth ring.

"Thomas here."

"It's Tazer. About time you answered." Nicole Steele, aka Tazer, spoke in a smooth, sexy tone that filled Creed's ear. "I've been trying to reach you since last night."

He chuckled. "My phone was out of reach, and I was out of the coverage area."

"Well, I'm glad you're back. I'm in Seattle with Casanova. The storm delayed us. We should be in Cape Churn in a couple hours. Have you located Macias and his cargo?"

"Negative on both counts."

"Did you think you were on vacation?" Tazer harrumphed. "Guess you can't send a man in to do a woman's job."

"I've been a little distracted." He pressed a kiss to Emma's temple and slid his empty hand around her waist, bringing her close against his side.

"I'd say. Well, we're on our way and, between the three of us, we ought to be able to bring down one badass."

"The badass has minions," Creed informed her.

"That's why we're bringing the big guns. See ya in a few." Tazer clicked off, and Creed pocketed the phone.

"Your team?" Emma asked.

"On their way." With both hands around her back, he leaned down, closing the distance between his lips and hers.

"Good," she whispered against his mouth. "We could use a bit of backup."

"'We'?" Creed frowned down at Emma. "As of now, you're officially off the case."

"Not if you want to get to that yacht before Macias's men do. Is the rest of your team trained in scuba diving?"

Creed thought about it. "I really don't know. But I'll check with the boss."

"In the meantime, your team is on their way and Macias could be out there on that yacht, retrieving his cargo."

Creed didn't like where she was going with this. "I'm not putting you or Dave at risk again."

"You don't have to put Dave and his dive boat at risk." She smiled.

"Damn right I don't. I'll go out on my own."

"You can't go on the surface. They'll try to run you down again. If you want to get to the yacht without being seen, you have to go underwater from the shore."

"It's too far out to go from the marina," he noted.

She touched a finger to his lips. "Remember I told you my father and I used to go out to the cave by kayak?"

He kissed the finger. "Yes."

"There's a road out to the farthest point. It's dirt, but it'll get us there and we can use the DPVs Dave rents out to recreational divers."

"Dave has diver propulsion vehicles?"

"He does. And if we use them from shore, we can avoid detection by the folks on the yacht."

He was already shaking his head. "There you go with that 'we' again."

"We have to get out there before Macias. If we wait for the rest of your team, Macias could retrieve the cargo and disappear."

"First things first. We need to clue in the chief."

"Yeah. Chief Taggart and Gabe."

"Taggart and McGregor. But that's it."

"Deal. Let's get some food in our bellies while we're at it. And we can have Dave prep the DPVs and keep an eye on the yacht while we meet with the chief."

"You're starting to sound like a spy. What kind of nurse did you say you were?"

She grinned. "A damned good one."

"Let's hope folks don't end up needing your services anytime soon. I have a feeling things are going to get a whole lot stickier." He pulled her into his arms and kissed her soundly. "I never should have brought you into this."

"Well, I'm in it now." She tipped her chin upward. "Don't think you can cut me out."

"What about your Spanish galleon treasure hunt?"

"It can wait."

"And the children's addition to the hospital?"

She bit down on her lip. "It'll have to wait, as well. We have a special cargo to locate."

"Why are you so interested?"

"Other than saving millions of people?"

"Yeah."

"He's already tried to kill me once. All that did was piss me off." She grabbed Creed's hand and headed for her Jeep. "We have a terrorist plot to thwart before my vacation is over."

"Some vacation."

Emma snorted. "You're telling me."

# Chapter 9

Emma placed a call to Dave while they were driving to the café. He promised to service the DPVs and meet them at the point in an hour.

As they pulled into the café parking lot, Emma cringed at the number of vehicles parked around the restaurant. It was a normal, busy morning in Cape Churn. Life managed to go on despite the underlying threat of a terrorist attack. What these people didn't know surely wouldn't hurt them, if she had her way.

There were a lot of people crowding the tables and booths. If they wanted a private conversation with the chief, it wouldn't be in the main dining area. They'd have to go to the private dining area in the rear of the building. Fortunately, the private dining section had a good view of the cape.

Emma climbed down from her Jeep and rounded the hood to Creed's side. "Did you bring your binoculars?"

"I did." He reached into his duffel bag and handed her the set.

"In case the chief needs convincing," she explained.

Nora greeted Emma with a hug. "Emma, honey, I'm so glad you're okay. You had us all worried. I barely slept a wink."

"Thank you, Nora. I'm sorry to have kept you up all night." Emma patted the older woman's shoulder. "Where's that husband of yours?"

"I set him and Gabe up in the private dining room. They said they had to discuss business."

"Good."

"What can I get you two? You must be starving."

"You have no idea." Emma's stomach rumbled as she gave Nora her order for two eggs over easy, a side of bacon and wheat toast, hold the butter.

Creed ordered the same and a stack of pancakes. "I could gnaw on a bone, I'm so hungry."

"I can do better than a bone." Nora's chest swelled proudly.

"Nora cooks up a great breakfast, sans the bones." Emma led the way to the private dining room Nora reserved for parties and special occasions.

Chief Taggart and Gabe sat across from each other, plates of half-eaten pancakes soaked in syrup in front of them.

Emma's stomach rumbled louder. "Nothing like a night in the ocean to work up an appetite."

The chief and Gabe rose as she approached. Gabe pulled out a chair beside him. Creed sat across from her, beside the chief.

"Did you order?" Taggart asked.

"We did."

"Good," Taggart said, his jaw set. "Then we can get right down to business."

"Please," Emma concurred. Before they could get started, Nora entered with two mugs and a carafe of steaming coffee. She poured a cup for Emma and Creed and left.

Emma wrapped her fingers around the hot mug, appreciating the warmth after the cold night she'd spent in a cave.

The chief dove in to the discussion. "We found the jet boat that was used in the attack against you two and Dave yesterday."

"You did?" Emma leaned her elbows on the table and sipped the fragrant brew. "Where?"

"On a fairly isolated, rocky beach south of town."

"I don't suppose you found the driver of that boat?" Creed asked.

"No."

Creed's lips thinned. "Were you able to lift prints?"

The chief shook his head. "It was wiped clean. We got nothing but the boat. It's owned by a doctor from Portland. He had it in a slip at the marina. Someone stole it early yesterday morning, before the Olanders opened for business. With over two hundred rented slips to keep track of, they hadn't noticed it missing."

"What we couldn't figure out is why he'd attack," Gabe started.

"When Dave came hauling back into the marina, he radioed ahead and we met him on the dock. The man was shaken and his boat damaged, but it's still usable."

"I'm just glad Dave's all right."

Gabe grinned. "He is, too."

"He also said that you told him to scuttle if anyone

bothered him." The chief turned to Creed. "Seems to me you were expecting trouble."

Creed nodded.

The chief leaned back in his chair. "Care to tell us why?"

Nora entered the back room, bearing two large plates full of steaming food. She set one in front of Emma and the other before Creed. "Anything else?"

"No, thank you." Emma barely waited for Nora to leave before she dug into the eggs. Never had food tasted so very good.

The chief grinned. "Go ahead, eat. We'll talk soon enough."

"No, we don't have much time." Creed gave the chief and Gabe the digest version of what had really brought him to Cape Churn.

"Wish you'd let us in on that little secret from the beginning." Chief Taggart sucked in a deep breath and let it out. "Could have arrested Macias from the get-go."

"It's all rumors and speculation at this point. We have no evidence."

"An attack on Dave's boat and two divers is no longer speculation," Gabe pointed out.

"We couldn't see who was driving the boat from where we were in the water." Creed took a bite, chewed, swallowed and added, "Again, no evidence unless they'd left a trail of fingerprints or were spotted on security camera stealing the boat."

"Would help if we had a photo of this Macias fella," the chief said.

Creed nodded. "I'll get one for you."

Gabe leaned his elbows on the table and interlocked

his fingers. "You say your team is arriving this afternoon?"

"Yes."

"Then we'll have to come up with a good reason to board the yacht out in the cape."

"You might let my team handle that. Macias's men will be fully armed and ready to shoot anyone who threatens them."

"Then they'd have the coastguard and everyone else down on them so fast—"

"Not fast enough. You'd lose men, and they'd get away. He's a master at slipping through the fingers of every agency—foreign or domestic—that has ever attempted to capture him. For all we know, he's not even on that yacht, but calling the shots from here on shore."

"Must have help from someone stateside, then."

"Probably the person he was supposed to meet up with. The one supplying him with the necessary materials to build his bomb, if not the bomb itself."

"It would take a pretty hefty amount of uranium to build a bomb big enough to knock L.A. or Seattle into the ocean."

"It doesn't take much. The amount of highly enriched uranium that supposedly went missing from Iran in 2012 could be used to set off an explosion that could kill a whole lot of people."

"I assume you have a plan," the chief said.

"I'm going back out to the sunken yacht to find whatever it is Macias is after."

"I'm going with him," Emma said.

"Are you sure that's a good idea?" Gabe asked, his gaze on Emma.

"I'm going. I'm the best diver around, and Creed needs help searching that yacht."

"Since he's probably figured out that we didn't find his cargo, he'll be sending his own people down to find the cache of whatever's got him uptight and willing to kill."

"You can't just go boating out there without any backup. They'll know what you're up to and send their thugs out to steal whatever you find, or kill you before you find it. I could get the coastguard to run interference. But I don't know how long it would take for them to show up."

"No, thank you." Creed shook his head. "We're going in with DPVs."

Taggart's eyes narrowed. "From the marina?"

"No," Creed said. "From the point."

"It's pretty rocky there," Gabe pointed out.

"I'm familiar with it, and if we get out there early enough we can avoid afternoon heating and hopefully get there before Macias sends his divers in." Emma pulled out the set of binoculars she'd insisted on bringing in with her. "Check out that yacht. Are they deploying any boats?"

Gabe took the binoculars and strode to the huge picture windows. "I don't see any. That doesn't mean they won't. Heck, they might already be out among the rocks looking for the yacht."

"Then we have to get out there before they find it." Creed took another bite and chewed quickly.

"Let me send one of the police boats with you," Taggart offered.

"No, thank you," Creed said. "It's better if Macias thinks he's scared us off."

"What can we do to help?" the chief asked.

"Keep an eye on the yacht. If they send a boat out to the point, call Game and Fish on them and have them stall their men from diving. Anything to give us time to get in and find what we're looking for."

Emma set her fork aside, her belly full of good food. "It would help if we knew what we're looking for."

"It'll be one of those we'll-know-it-when-we-see-it things." Creed pushed back from the table and stood. "Ready to get started?"

"Ready."

"I'll run interference on your Jeep in case he has someone following you," Gabe said. "Good luck out there."

"Thanks." Emma hugged Gabe. "Kiss the baby for me, will ya."

He grinned. "Kayla would be very disappointed if you didn't do it yourself." His smile faded. "Take care out there."

"I will." She climbed into the driver's seat and waited for Creed to slide in next to her. What had started as a vacation of redemption was turning into something altogether different. Hopefully it would have a happy ending. One in which she and Creed weren't killed and the entire west coast remained where it was.

Creed jumped out of the Jeep as soon as Emma parked beside a truck on the dirt track leading out to what looked like a cliff overlooking the rocky point of Cape Churn.

The truck had faded lettering of Dave's Diving Adventures on the side, but Dave was nowhere to be seen.

"Dave will be waiting below on the beach with everything we'll need."

"There's a beach?" Creed stepped closer to the edge of the cliff before he saw the narrow, steep path winding downward toward a rocky shoreline. He lifted his binoculars and gazed out at the yacht in the bay. Too far away to see the people on board, all he could tell was there wasn't another boat leaving it or floating around the site they'd put in near the rocks.

"So far so good." He grabbed Emma's hand, and they descended the steep path to the pebbled beach below where Dave waited with their wet suits, BCDs, tanks and DPVs. He gave them basic instruction on how to operate the devices and how long the battery would last, and then stood aside as they geared up and slipped into the water.

If possible, the water felt colder than the day before. Probably a residual effect of how little sleep they'd had in the past forty-eight hours. The DPVs had a max speed of a little more than three miles per hour. Fortunately it wasn't far from where they were to the location of the sunken yacht. They'd be there in fifteen minutes or less, depending on current and obstacles. Dave had set them up with twin tanks, extending the amount of bottom time they'd have to find the cargo.

Creed hoped it wouldn't take both tanks full of air to locate what Macias was desperate to find. The longer they were down, the more chance of running into trouble from Macias or the shark they'd seen two days earlier.

Using his GPS dive watch, Creed led the way, keeping an eye out for predators of both ocean and land varieties. Every minute or two, he'd glance back to make certain Emma was close on his fins. As finicky as some DPVs were, he could be way ahead of her before he discovered she wasn't there.

He slowed and let her swim up alongside him. The more time he spent with her, the greater his appreciation for her gumption and commitment to the people of her community. The woman was everything a man could want and more. Nurturing, kind, athletic, fearless and beautiful. How any man could walk away from her was beyond Creed's comprehension.

Emma's ex-fiancé was a fool, choosing money over the love of such a woman. If Creed considered himself a staying kind of guy, he'd have been honored to call Emma his fiancée and worked every day to earn her respect and love.

The fifteen minutes of travel time with nothing but the gentle whir of the DPV's engine and the bubbles expelled from his regulator to distract him gave Creed far too much time to think about Emma. Making love to her had been all he'd expected and more. The woman was beautiful, sexy and passionate. If he had more time in Cape Churn, he'd spend it making love to her. But he was destined to complete this mission and move on. Emma was part of this place and would remain there when he was gone. Why dream of something that would never happen?

They finished the distance side by side, arriving at the yacht together. Creed stopped Emma a few yards short of the boat, hovering near a huge underwater boulder covered in barnacles and colorful sea anemones.

For several long minutes, he watched for movement in and around the yacht. Nothing stirred behind the large glass windows. As he started forward, a dark shadow flitted overhead. Creed shot a glance upward, yanking his dive knife from the scabbard around his ankle, ready to defend himself and Emma from sharks or thugs.

A curious harbor seal dove down to where they were, swimming between the rocks, and then flipped around and circled them. After a few moments, the seal darted away, leaving them alone with the yacht.

When Creed felt certain they were the only human divers in the area, he set his DPV on the far side of the boulder, out of sight of the yacht. Emma set hers beside his. If they needed to make a quick getaway, they'd have them readily available and hidden.

Having searched the cabin level and the middle deck lounge, Creed moved toward the top deck where they'd found the dead captain. The helm was a small room lined with an array of instruments, including GPS, radio and navigational equipment. Behind the observation windows was a wall sectioned off with a number of cabinets. Some were unlocked, others secured with small locks.

Emma started on one end of the cabinets, opening the unlocked doors and peering inside. She, too, had a dive knife she used to pry open the locked doors.

Creed worked from the other end. He found charts, logbooks and a pack of cigarettes, but nothing that looked important enough to kill for. As he moved toward the center and Emma, he jimmied the locked doors with his knife and opened them to find a sextant, a portable GPS device and spare parts for the radio and navigational equipment—backups should technology fail them.

At the center of the wall a small, innocuous drawer was all that remained to be searched. Creed was already thinking of where to look next when Emma popped the lock on it and pulled the drawer open. Inside was dark.

At first it appeared empty. Then Emma dug her knife into the drawer and it snagged on a black velvet bag at the very bottom of the drawer. With limited lighting, they might have missed it.

Emma removed it and turned the bag over, dumping its contents into her palms.

The lights from their headlamps shone down on a pile of brilliantly glittering diamonds. Emma's hand shook and she almost dropped them, her eyes round, shocked.

As many as there were, it had to be a small fortune's worth of the precious stones. A fortune that could purchase enough highly enriched uranium to blow California into the ocean.

Creed helped Emma pour the diamonds back in the velvet pouch and tightened the drawstring, double-knotting it to prevent the diamonds from accidently falling out. He tucked the bag into a Velcro pocket on the side of his BCD and pressed the Velcro in place, locking the stones in.

With Macias's bargaining chips in hand, it was time to get the hell out of the yacht and back to shore before Macias discovered their find.

Anxious to get Emma back to safety, Creed hurried out of the yacht without performing a thorough check of the surrounding seascape.

Out of the corner of his eye, he saw movement. Four divers swam toward them, two carrying spearguns.

Creed snagged Emma's hand and shoved her toward the boulder where they'd hidden the DPVs. If she made it there, she might have a chance to escape. In the meantime, Creed had to divert the divers' attention.

He turned and swam straight toward them, a maneuver he hoped they wouldn't expect. As the two with the spearguns took aim, he ducked behind a boulder and circled around behind them. A spear whooshed by him, barely missing his leg and bouncing off a huge rock.

With his knife ready, he swam up behind the man closest to him and snagged his air hose with the blade, ripping a hole in it. Air bubbled freely, racing to the surface. The man followed the bubbles, opting to breathe rather than fight.

Before the man who'd shot at him with his speargun could reload, Creed swam straight at him, grabbed his hose and would have ripped a hole in it, but the man twisted and dove, taking Creed with him, the other two men racing after them, one of them aiming his speargun.

Creed ripped a hole in the air hose, grabbed the man and twisted around, kicking hard as the man with the speargun let loose a spear.

His spear pierced his own man's leg. Wounded and without air, the man gave up the fight and aimed for the surface, kicking his good leg, the spear firmly lodged in his other leg, blood streaming from the wound in a red cloud, mixing with the seawater.

Which made the odds a little better. Two very angry men against one. Hoping Emma had made it out with her DPV, Creed wove in and out of the rocks, working his way back to the spot he'd left his DPV. As he neared it, one of the men caught up to him and grabbed his fin, yanking him backward.

Creed struggled, let the fin's strap slip off the back of his foot and kicked away from his attacker. No sooner was he free than the other man grabbed his air hose and yanked.

His regulator flew out of his mouth and he struggled to free himself from one man, then suddenly the other had hold of him, too.

Without air, he didn't have long before he lost the fight. He waved his knife, hoping to catch one of the men, but they stayed behind him, holding on to his tanks to keep him from spinning around and sinking his blade into them.

Then, out of the shadows, a flash of bright yellow blew past him—Emma, hanging on to the DPV, sped past his attackers and sliced one air hose. That man let go of Creed and started after Emma, but soon realized he didn't have air and headed to the surface.

With only one man holding him, Creed twisted and turned. A blade flashed in his peripheral vision, and a sharp pain lanced through his arm. Creed fought hard, kicking his single fin to drive himself backward, banging the man against a huge boulder. It didn't faze his attacker, buoyancy making him bounce off the rock. It only distracted him enough to force him to hold on and stop trying to sink his knife into Creed.

His lungs burning for another breath and feeling desperate, Creed reached over his head, grabbed the man's mask and tugged hard.

The man rolled over the top of him and lost his grip on Creed, his mask filling with water, temporarily blinding him.

Emma swung by, grabbed Creed's hand and pulled him out of reach of his attacker, just as the man cleared his mask and was looking around for his victim.

With his free hand, Creed felt over his shoulder for the hose, followed it to the end with the regulator and jammed it between his teeth. He cleared the water and tested the hose's reliability carefully before sucking in a long, much-needed breath. With only a two-yard lead and two people slowing the single DPV, it wouldn't be long before the last attacker caught up with them.

One fin kicking madly, Creed helped propel them forward until Emma slowed enough that he could grab the second DPV from its hiding place behind the boulder. He dragged it along with them and, precious seconds later, had started the engine. He let go of Emma's hand, his own device propelling him. With two DPVs going, they soon left the last attacker in their wake as they sped toward the shore at a whopping three miles per hour.

Creed patted the pocket on his BCD to assure himself that he hadn't lost the booty in the struggle to get away. Now that they had what Macias was after, their lives were in even more danger than before. The suspected terrorist would stop at nothing to reclaim what was his and continue his plan of mass destruction.

# Chapter 10

Emma sat in the shallows, waves splashing up over her, spraying her face and knocking her over several times. Her hands shook so badly it took several attempts before she could release the strap on the back of her fins. She wasn't certain her legs would hold her once she stood. But she had to try. Staying where she was in the water off the point was not an option. They had to get the diamonds back to Cape Churn before they were attacked again.

Creed managed to rise to his feet first, crossing to where she sat. He squatted down and grabbed her fins, looping them over his arm, then took her hand and pulled her to her feet and into his arms, kissing her soundly. When his lips left hers, he whispered, "Thank you."

Leaning against Creed, Emma pressed her face into

the neoprene of his wet suit, letting the past hour's events wash over her. "They almost killed you."

"But they didn't." He hooked his finger beneath her chin and nudged her face upward. "Because of you." He kissed her again.

Emma gripped his arms to steady herself and felt something warm and sticky on her hands. Not the cool wetness of seawater. When she pulled her hand away, it was covered in blood.

Her pulse slamming against her veins, she tried for calm. "Creed, you're bleeding."

"I'm okay."

"No, you're not." She unbuckled his BCD and shoved it over his shoulders.

Creed winced, but let the straps slide down his arm, easing it over the slash in his arm.

Emma took the tanks and BCD and laid them on the rocks, then unzipped Creed's wet suit and tried to push it over his shoulders.

Creed grabbed her wrists and stepped away from her helpful hands. "Emma, we need to get out of here." He turned away and began gathering equipment as though he'd never been injured. Except blood dripped off his fingertips onto the equipment and the ground.

"You might bleed to death before we get up the hill." Emma ran around his side, trying to get a better idea of how deep the cut went and how much blood he was losing. "Stop, damn it!" She stood in front of him and held on to his hurt arm with both hands. "I'm a nurse. Let me help." She parted the cut edges of the wet suit and gazed at the long deep cut and gasped. "Not good, sailor."

"I'll live."

"Emma! Creed!" Dave yelled from the top of the pathway, and waved before hurrying down to help them with the gear. "I was getting worried about you two so I went up top to get a better view." He came to a staggering stop in front of the scuba gear.

"Creed's bleeding." Emma held out her hand. "Give me your T-shirt."

"My T-shirt?" Dave stared at her, his brow furrowed. "But it's my favorite."

"Give it," she demanded.

He jerked the shirt over his head and handed it to her.

Without hesitating, she ran her dive knife through the bottom edge and ripped off a long strip.

Dave gasped. "You tore it!"

"And I'm going to tear it a whole lot more." Emma jerked her head toward Creed. "Help him out of the suit."

Dave tugged the sleeve of the wet suit over the injured arm, while Creed stood resolute, his jaw clenched.

Emma hurriedly tore the shirt into long strips, folded a piece into a thick square and pressed the wad to the open, bleeding wound. "Hold this while I wrap it."

"Did I tell you that I faint like a girl at the sight of blood?" Dave said, his voice teasing but weak.

Emma guided Dave's hand to the spot and pressed down. "Hold it tight. And not all girls faint."

"This one does." Dave held the pad in place, but looked away, his face blanched. "I hate blood."

A tight smile played at the corner of the former SEAL's lips. "It's just a little cut."

"Dave, you pass out on me and I swear to God…" Emma warned, her voice firm, no-nonsense.

"I don't like blood," Dave whined. "Passed out the last time I cut my big toe."

Emma's fingers flew over the wound. "You clean and fillet fish, for heaven's sake."

"That's fish blood, not… Never mind." Dave closed his eyes.

After Emma wrapped a long strip around the thick muscle of Creed's arm, she knotted it snugly over the gash for added pressure. "Okay, Dave, you can open your eyes and remove your fingers from the bandage."

Dave eased his hand from beneath the knot. "Don't make me do that again."

"Trust me," Creed said through gritted teeth. "I'll avoid it the best I can."

"What the hell happened down there?" Dave asked.

Emma eased the straps of her BCD, which still held the two tanks, but didn't remove them. They still had to get Creed and all the equipment up the hill. "We'll tell you all about it, after I take Creed to the hospital."

Creed's tight smile disappeared. "I don't need a hospital. It's just a flesh wound."

Emma shook her head. "Like hell. You need stitches. We're *going* to the hospital."

"Uh, Creed." Dave slung Creed's BCD with the two tanks over his shoulders and gathered the DPVs, one in each hand. "In case you haven't noticed, she has a way of making you do things you always swore you wouldn't." The owner of Dave's Dive Adventures hiked up the path, lugging as much as he could carry.

Creed followed and snagged the fins, draping them over his good arm, muttering, "I'm beginning to learn."

He swayed and steadied himself on the uphill side of the slope.

Emma snorted. "Yeah. Just a flesh wound."

"We don't have time to go to the hospital," Creed argued. "We have to get these diamonds somewhere safe."

"Diamonds?" Dave stopped short.

Creed stumbled into him, and Emma placed a hand in the middle of his back to keep him from tumbling back down the hill. "Delirious, too? *March,* frogman."

"Stubborn woman," he grumbled.

Dave continued up the hill, wheezing by the time he got to the top. "The things I do for women."

Creed made it a little less winded but pale, his lips pressed into a thin line.

While Dave loaded the gear into his truck, Emma shed her BCD and tanks and slid an arm around Creed's waist, letting him lean on her as she guided him to the passenger seat of her Jeep. "Okay, tough guy. Try not to bleed on my upholstery."

"Yes, ma'am." He leaned heavily on her and grinned.

Dave loaded Emma's gear and turned toward them. "You gonna make it all right with him?"

"I'm not that bad," Creed maintained.

Emma nodded. "We'll be fine."

"Then I'll see you at the hospital." Dave climbed into his truck. "I *gotta* hear this story."

"Dave, be careful. Those people who hit your boat were after us. They might make you a target again if they think you're helping."

"Think?" Dave snorted. "I *am* helping you. Dear Lord, does this mean I'll be seeing more blood?"

"Not necessarily." Emma shifted into Drive, her foot on the brake. "Just watch your back."

"Same to ya. Hate to lose Cape Churn's best nurse. In case I have a bleeder like Creed, there." Dave drove ahead of them, bumping along the rutted track until he reached the paved road.

Creed leaned across the seat and hit Emma's horn.

Dave stopped and hopped out, hurrying back to find out what Emma wanted.

"What the hell?" Emma glared at Creed.

"Did you realize Dave just drove away with the diamonds?" Creed unbuckled his seat belt and climbed out.

"Something wrong?" Dave asked.

Creed walked with Dave to the back of his truck. "I need something out of a pocket in my BCD."

"Let me get it." Dave dug around in the pile of equipment and pulled out Creed's BCD.

With his good hand, Creed removed the velvet bag from the Velcro pocket. "Thanks."

"What's in the bag?"

"A whole lot of trouble."

"Those the diamonds?" Dave scratched his beard-stubbled jaw and blew out a stream of air. "I threw diamonds in the back of my pickup?" He shook his head and climbed into the driver's seat. "I *gotta* hear this story."

Creed returned to the Jeep a little steadier on his feet, but Emma wasn't going to let him off the hook easily. He needed stitches and antibiotics to ward off infection. Then they were going to put those diamonds somewhere safe, where terrorists couldn't use them to buy bombs. This whole nightmare would be over, and then maybe the day would turn out as good as it had started.

Her body warmed at the image of Creed lying naked beside her after making love to her. Oh, yeah. The day was going to end better than it started, if she had anything to say about it. She could work around Creed's injury, if he was up to it.

Creed held tight to the bag of diamonds as Emma pulled onto the highway. Dave was already out of sight around a bend in the road.

Now that he had the cargo Macias had been after, he'd revealed only half of the terrorist's story. The other half remained a mystery. Who had Phillip made a deal with? Diamonds for enriched uranium? Obviously someone who didn't plan on sticking around to witness the amount of damage.

Without the diamonds, Phillip wouldn't meet with his contact. Which meant he had to give the diamonds to Phillip, or they'd never discover who had access to the uranium needed to build a bomb powerful enough to put a big hurt on the western coast of the U.S.

When the rest of his team arrived, they'd have to come up with a plan to turn over the diamonds and follow Macias to his rendezvous.

Emma slowed at a stop sign at a junction on the old road and waited for a four-door sedan to pass through the intersection.

The vehicle pulled to the middle of the junction and stopped.

"What are they doing?" Emma grumbled. "I've got a bleeding man in the car. Move!"

Creed's hackles rose as the windows on the sedan

lowered. "Punch it, Emma!" He leaned over, grabbed the steering wheel and jammed his foot on top of hers over the accelerator. The Jeep careened sideways and Creed straightened the wheel, swerving around the sedan as the barrels of two semiautomatic rifles poked out of the windows and the shooters opened fire.

Emma struggled to keep the Jeep from running off the road, while Creed fought to zigzag, refusing to give the shooters a steady target to aim at. "Go! Go! Go!"

He dove for the backseat, reached into the duffel bag he'd brought with him and yanked out his HK40 handgun, wincing as he bumped his wounded arm.

Emma glanced over her shoulder. "Damn it, Creed, you're bleeding again."

"Send me the bill for the upholstery, *if* we live through this."

"Damn the upholstery!" Emma shouted. "What do I do?"

"Drive into town as fast as you can."

A bullet pierced the plastic of the back window on the ragtop Jeep, winged past Creed's ear and shattered the passenger side of the front windshield. If Creed had been in the passenger seat, he well could have taken that bullet in the head. He had to believe it wasn't his day to die. Nor was it Emma's, if he could help it. He pointed the HK40 out the hole in the back and fired on the car speeding to catch up to them. "Faster, Emma," he said, his voice steady and urgent. "They're catching up. Make it to town and they'll have to split off."

"That's three miles!"

"You can do it. You've made a habit of saving my butt. Don't stop now."

"Don't think you're getting out of going to the hospital, just because some jerk is trying to kill us," she cried out, then squealed when another bullet took out the driver's side mirror. "We're not going to make it."

"The hell we aren't." Creed took aim and fired at the driver's window of the other car.

The vehicle swerved and ran halfway into the ditch before it straightened and sped to catch up to them again.

"Do you have the accelerator all the way to the floor?" he called out.

"All the way, frogman. As fast as it'll go."

When they hit a curve in the road, the Jeep tipped up on two wheels, throwing Creed to one side, slamming his wounded arm against the roll bar. He bit down hard on his tongue to keep from yelling. Emma had her hands full, trying to keep from flipping the Jeep while staying ahead of the other car. She didn't need to worry about him.

He pulled himself upright and fired on the car behind them, creating another hole in the windshield but barely slowing the vehicle this time.

"Creed, are you okay?"

He glanced over his shoulder and caught Emma's gaze as she risked looking in the rearview mirror, however brief the moment, before she returned her attention to the road in front of her.

"I'm good," he assured her.

She laughed, the sound bordering on hysteria. "I know you're good, but are you okay?"

"Yes, damn it. Just drive!"

"My dad didn't cover this in driver's ed."

"He'd be proud."

"Damn right, he would." When she took the next curve, Creed braced for it, holding on to the roll bar.

"Town's coming up!" The relief in Emma's voice was palpable.

They weren't home free yet. The long straight stretch into town gave the other car the opportunity to gun it and pull alongside them, their weapons poking out of the open window.

Emma gripped the steering wheel, her knuckles white. Then she jerked it toward the car, slamming into the side of the car before they could fire off a round.

"That's for messing up my Jeep," she yelled and planted her foot on the accelerator, shooting into town at eighty miles an hour.

The trailing car dropped back and did a one-eighty, hurrying off in the opposite direction.

Emma huffed. "Showed them."

Creed grinned. "You sure did."

"Now let's get you to the hospital before you bleed out."

Still traveling a little too fast, Emma blew by the police department and skidded to a stop in front of the emergency entrance to Cape Churn Memorial. Orderlies rushed out to greet them.

"I brought you some business. Knife wound," she said, her voice calm, capable and completely void of any residual effects of the suicidal race into town.

His arm aching, his body bruised and tired, Creed couldn't help but grin. Emma Jenkins had guts and took care of business. His only regret was that Phillip Macias had her in his crosshairs now.

\* \* \*

While the staff on duty in the emergency room prepped Creed's wound and the doctor stitched him up, Emma went back out to her Jeep, stripped out of the wet suit she was still wearing and threw her sundress over her damp bikini. She finger-combed her hair and looked at her face in the rearview mirror. Pale skin, dark circles and lines at the sides of her eyes. What did she expect after being attacked underwater, nearly run off the road and shot at? For a moment, she leaned against the side of the Jeep and allowed herself to inhale several long, calming breaths of fresh sea-salted air.

It did little to settle her shattered nerves, and she couldn't help darting glances in a 360-degree radius of where she stood. Was paranoia a byproduct of being attacked several times in forty-eight hours? How did Creed do this on a regular basis? Having trained and operated as a SEAL, he'd seen combat and been shot at. But *she* hadn't.

*Suck it up, girl. They're just bullets, and none of them hit you.*

A couple more breaths, and she headed back into the hospital and waited outside the room where Creed was being stitched.

"Emma?" Dave joined her in the hallway, his brows drawn together. "I dropped the gear off at the marina and came back to park next to your Jeep. What the heck happened? It's dented, and the windows are shattered."

"Oh, Dave." After hours of holding it together, the wall in Emma crumbled and she leaned into her friend, shaking so violently she couldn't stop.

"Emma?" He patted her back awkwardly. "I'm not good with crying women."

Her laugh ended on a dry sob. "You're not good with blood, you're not good with weepy women...what *are* you good at?"

"I make a mean hush puppy," he offered, holding her against him.

Emma laughed again and forced herself to stand up straight and wipe the tears from her face. Now she could add bloodshot, red-rimmed eyes to the fright she must look like. Not attractive at all to a hot navy SEAL who could have his choice of any woman with only a crook of his finger.

So why did she care? Wasn't she off men? Didn't Randy turn her stomach sour on relationships?

"You gonna tell me what happened?" Dave's hands dropped to his sides, and he rocked back on his worn tennis shoes.

"I'd like to know, as well." Chief Taggart strode down the hall toward Emma and Dave.

Emma glared at the chief. "I thought you were going to distract any divers from going down by the point. What happened to our backup?"

"We would have, but we got a bomb threat here at the hospital. Kinda put the kibosh on our diversion. Once we evacuated all the people and ran a bomb-sniffing dog through, it was too late. Gabe noticed a boat out by the point about the time it was leaving. I was here until fifteen minutes ago, and left for the marina when I got a report over the radio of a speeding Jeep sliding into the parking lot at the hospital. I figured it might be you two."

"Anyone get out to that boat?" Emma asked.

The chief shook his head. "Gabe called out the coastguard, but they were sent out on a rescue mission for a capsized sailboat north of here. So he went out himself, but the boat was gone before he could get there. What happened out there?"

Emma gave the chief and Dave the blow-by-blow account of what happened in the water and then on the way back to town. After describing the sedan, she took a deep breath and looked the chief square in the eyes. "That's it. More fun before noon than I could have banked on."

"What's Agent Thomas gonna do with the diamonds?"

"I suppose he has to give them over to his boss. His team should be here by now."

"Speaking of which." Chief Taggart held up a finger. "Since you and Thomas weren't available, I took a call from a Nicole Steele. She said she was with Thomas. They were waylaid by a traffic accident on the road from Portland. They'll be in later this evening."

Which gave Emma more time alone with Creed. Once his team arrived, he'd be fully occupied with finishing the case. And now that they had the diamonds, he'd have no use for her diving services. She could get back to her original plan to explore the wreck of the *Anna Maria*. After all that had happened over the past three days, she didn't have the heart to go back out and dive. And she doubted Dave would take her. Tomorrow would be soon enough.

The chief scribbled on his notepad, closed it and tucked it into his shirt pocket. "I'll get a BOLO issued on the sedan and its occupants, and I'll see if we can get a warrant to search the yacht in the cape."

"Good."

"If I need you to identify suspects, where can I find you?"

Emma ran her fingers through her hair again. "I'm headed to my house for a shower after I check on Creed."

The chief left, and Dave hung around for a moment longer. "Do you want me to stay?"

Emma shook her head. "No. I'm going to check on Creed and, like I told the chief, head home for a shower and a hot cup of coffee."

"If you need anything…" Dave grinned. "Unless it involves blood—"

"I can count on you." She hugged Dave and he left, his face red. He was a good guy.

Emma straightened her dress, patted her hair back in place and pinched some color into her cheeks before stepping through the door into Creed's room.

He sat on the edge of the exam table, wearing nothing but the swim trunks he'd had on under his wet suit. Thick muscles, tanned skin and washboard abs made him more damn sexy than a man had a right to be. He laughed at something Jenna Watkins, the nurse on duty, said as she wrapped his arm in sterile gauze and tape. His thick black hair gleamed in the overhead lights, and that smile that made her blood sing also took her breath away.

Jenna giggled and a stab of something that felt like jealousy hit Emma in the gut.

The attractive young nurse was fresh out of school, with a sunny smile and rich auburn hair pulled back in a messy bun that made her appear even younger and prettier. She was sweet, funny and gregarious. Everyone on the hospital staff loved her. But at that moment, Emma had a hard time liking her.

Creed had told her from the beginning he wasn't the staying kind of guy. He probably had a girl in every port and didn't like being tied down to one.

Emma had to remind herself she wasn't interested in a relationship. She'd proven she didn't make good choices in men when she'd agreed to marry Randy, who'd used her, stolen hospital money and left town.

What was so different about Creed? He'd used her to get to the diamonds Macias wanted. Now that he had them, he'd be leaving. Only thing he hadn't done was stolen something, unless her heart counted.

Her chest squeezed so hard, she pressed a hand to it and forced a smile. "I guess you're all done here?"

Jenna grinned at Creed. "We wanted to keep him, but he refused our hospitality."

Creed pushed to his feet. "Emma and I have some unfinished business." He gathered the velvet bag from the table beside him and padded across the floor barefooted, looking like a calendar model advertising sex and the sea.

Emma swept her tongue across dry lips.

Creed leaned close and whispered, "You make me crazy when you do that."

He smelled of salt, sun and rubbing alcohol, and he was standing close enough she could have pressed her lips to the smooth, hard curve of his shoulder with very little effort. "Do what?" she asked, her tongue tracing her lips again.

"That." He stared at her mouth. "Can we leave now?" He tossed a glance back at Jenna.

"You're free to go. You'll need to change that bandage at least once every day and keep it clean and free of germs." Jenna handed Emma a roll of tape and a box of gauze. "You might need these."

Emma took the items without looking or arguing that she probably wouldn't be with him to change the bandages.

"I'll have my nurse take care of it," Creed said, his gaze on Emma's mouth.

Emma's cheeks heated, her lips tingled and warmth spread south, low in her belly.

They walked out of the hospital, an inordinate amount of the staff lining the halls to say something to her—mostly females, drooling over the raw masculinity of Creed.

Once they were outside, Emma led the way to where she'd parked her Jeep. "Where to?"

"Since I left my vehicle at your house, I guess we're going there."

"Oh." She climbed behind the wheel and waited as Creed slipped into the passenger seat. After shifting into Drive and pulling out onto the street, she glanced left, right and into the rearview mirror.

"I don't think Macias's mercenaries will try to bother us in the daylight, in the city limits."

"Let's hope not." She drove the short distance to Sand Dollar Lane and pulled into the driveway. "You're welcome to use my shower, rather than going all the way out to the bed-and-breakfast. You're still pale, and I'd hate to think of you passing out at the wheel and driving off a cliff." Emma clamped her lips shut, realizing she was babbling. Her tongue darted out to wet her dry lips.

"See? There you go again, doing that thing that you

know drives me crazy." He leaned across to capture her chin between his fingers.

"What?" She stared at his lips, wishing he'd kiss her.

"This." Creed bent to grant her wish, his tongue sweeping across where hers had been a moment before and darting deeper into her mouth to slide along the length of her tongue.

When he broke the kiss, he rested his forehead against hers. "I really should find out where my team landed."

"Oh, I know." Emma informed him of their delay.

"In that case, I have time to clean up. I should go to the B and B for fresh clothes."

"No need to go all the way out there." Emma cupped his cheek with her hand, calling herself every kind of fool for letting this man into her heart. "I have a washer, dryer and shower."

"Wouldn't be very nice of me to refuse such a generous offer."

"No, it wouldn't." She kissed him, taking the lead this time, her hand circling the back of his neck to draw him closer.

Seconds later they were scrambling for the front door. Moby hit them as soon as it opened.

"If you'll keep an eye on him, I'll drop your clothes into the wash."

"Thanks."

Emma took his duffel bag.

He handed the bag of diamonds to her. "Hold on to these, will ya?"

She took the bag, honored that he trusted her with what could be millions of dollars' worth of precious jewels. No amount of gems compared to the fact he'd decided to stay with her.

She hurriedly laid out a bowl of dog food and fresh water, threw Creed's clothes with some of hers into the wash with detergent and raced into the hallway, looking for Creed.

The sound of the shower sent her pulse into overdrive. She stripped her dress over her head and tossed it to the floor. She pushed through the door into the bathroom at the same time as she flipped the catch on her bikini top.

The outline of Creed's silhouette showed through the near-transparent shower curtain, making Emma's mouth dry. She slid the curtain aside to find Creed facing her, naked and smiling, his member stiff and ready. For her.

Emma closed the shower curtain and joined him in a warm, wet dance that splashed water over the floor of the bathroom.

They made love against the shower wall, on the counter by the sink, and dripped across the floor to her bed and made love again until they were both spent.

As tired as she was, the nurse in Emma wouldn't sleep until she'd replaced the wet bandages with dry ones over his stitches. She switched the load from the washer to the dryer, then returned to the bed and lay against Creed's uninjured arm. Exhausted, she curled up to those thick, hard muscles, the sun shining in through the window, warming her naked body, and relaxed for what felt like the first time in a week.

Life didn't get better than at that moment. She shoved aside thoughts of what came next, basking in Creed's embrace.

If he left, which he would, at least she'd have this memory to keep her warm for a little while. Not that it would be nearly enough, but it was better than nothing.

She draped an arm over his taut abs and slept.

Creed lay with Emma in his arms, wishing he could extend the time like this into forever. The angel lying beside him fit him perfectly. She was smart, athletic, fearless and passionate. Everything a man could want in a woman and more.

He dared to dream of what it would be like to come home to Emma after each mission. She'd be waiting at the top of the steps, a smile on her face. Moby would leap off the porch and race to the gate of that danged white picket fence. And Creed would be happy to see them both. He could picture a miniature version of Emma, a little girl with sandy-blond hair and gray eyes like her mother's.

A muted buzzing sound came from the living room where Creed had left his duffel bag, his smart phone tucked inside. Though he'd rather stay in bed with Emma tucked against his side, he knew he had to answer the call.

Tazer and Casanova were due in soon, and they needed to make a plan. The diamonds would draw Macias back until they were safely stored in a safe-deposit box in a bank vault or given back to Macias for the next phase of the operation. Until then, whoever had the diamonds was in danger of Macias's hit men.

Careful not to wake Emma, Creed slipped out from under her, tucked a sheet over her naked body and left the room, closing the door between them.

The ringing stopped while he was digging for the

phone. He checked the recent calls and noted Tazer's cell number, hit Redial and waited. It didn't even ring on his end.

"We're finally here," Tazer said without preamble.

"Good. Where?"

"At a diner." Tazer's voice faded as if she leaned away from the receiver. "What is this place called?"

"Seaside Café," Casanova's muffled voice came from the background.

"We can meet in fifteen minutes, but not there," Creed said. "It's too public."

"Did you find the cargo?" Tazer asked.

"I did."

"What was it?"

"Diamonds. Lots of diamonds."

"Oooooh. Did you save some for me?"

"Sorry, sweetheart, we have to give them back to Macias."

"So soon?" Tazer's voice pouted over the phone. "Oh, sweetie, don't call me sweetheart, or—"

"You'll have to shoot me." Creed chuckled. He liked that he could kid around with the other members of the SOS team, but when the crap hit the fan, he knew they had his back. "Got it, Nicole. See you in fifteen." He gave them directions to their meeting point, hung up and retrieved slacks and a polo shirt from the dryer, slipping into them before returning to the bedroom where Emma still slept. He gathered the velvet bag of diamonds, feeling the loose stones tumbling within, and stuffed them into his pocket.

Emma barely stirred when he bent to kiss her lips one last time. "I'll be back," he whispered, and kissed her again.

Moby walked with him to the door and whined when Creed told him to stay.

After one last look around, he opened the door, twisted the lock and pulled the door closed behind him, listening for the lock to engage. He couldn't go back in without knocking on the door. It was just as well; he'd been more than tempted to stay and tell his team he'd be off duty until the morning. But what he had in his possession negated that option.

Macias had been willing to kill for the diamonds. He wouldn't stop now, until he got them. He must be on a deadline and desperate. Which could play right into Creed's plan.

If it didn't get him killed first.

## Chapter 11

Creed had given Tazer and Casanova directions to meet him at the point. The fewer people who saw them together, the better his plan would go. And from there, they could keep an eye out for the yacht in the bay as long as the fog didn't roll in.

Tazer met him with a handshake and her cool, blue-eyed stare, wearing a tailored gray pantsuit that could have come straight out of the pages of *Vogue* magazine. She wore her pale blond hair swept up in a neat twist in the back.

*"Hola!"* Casanova hugged Creed tight, with his typical, exuberant backslapping. To Nova, everyone was *familia* on the SOS team—though he toned down his hugs with Tazer to avoid being dropped with a knee to the groin.

As they gathered around the hood of his SUV with a

map of the coastline, they laid out the plan. Royce was
on the satellite phone listening throughout.

Creed had briefed the boss on what had happened
when they found the diamonds and when they'd been
attacked on the road back to town. He finished by ex-
pressing his concerns over deep-sixing the diamonds
and missing the chance to find Macias's contact for
enriched uranium.

"Since they attacked, we can assume they know I
found the diamonds," Creed concluded.

"Which could play in our favor," Royce said.

"Exactly." Creed drummed his fingers against the
hood. "I'm going to play the part of a mercenary op-
portunist looking to make some quick cash. How much
should I ask him for these diamonds? What are they
worth on the black market, Royce?"

"If you're looking for quick cash, you can't go too
high. Hang on, let me get Geek on it." Royce went silent for a couple minutes and came back with, "Ask for
three hundred thousand in twenties. It's not too much
he can't pull it off pretty quickly, but it's not too little
he'd get suspicious."

"Agreed."

Creed would venture out to the yacht in the harbor,
arrange a meeting on land where Tazer and Casanova
would be hiding close by in case the plan went south.
He'd have the diamonds in a safe place until Phillip
produced the cash, at which time he'd make the trade.

"What about the girl?" Royce asked.

Tazer and Casanova both glanced across at Creed,
Tazer voicing what was in their expressions. "Creed's
got a girl? I thought you were the loner of the group."

Creed's lip curled up on one side. "About as much

of a loner as you are, Nicole." As new as his relationship was, he didn't feel like discussing it with anyone else. He wasn't even sure it would go any further than it had, though he found himself wanting it to.

Tazer crossed her arms over her chest, her brows hitching upward. "Since I'm a big-time loner, that means you are, too. So how does the girl fit into this picture?"

"She was with me on the dives," he said, his gaze returning to the map of the coastline. "I wouldn't have found the diamonds without her help."

"You involved a civilian?" Tazer tsked. "That's breaking a few rules, isn't it, Royce?"

"Only when necessary," their boss responded. "However, since she's involved, what are you doing to protect her?"

"Nothing, yet. She lives in town, and it's still daylight. I planned on having her stay at the B and B or with friends until Phillip leaves the area."

"Good. Make sure that happens. She's a loose end Phillip might take advantage of."

"Will do." Creed wasn't sorry he'd have to see Emma again. He did regret the circumstances. If Phillip thought he could manipulate them by threatening Emma, he would.

"Did you get a lead on the license plate of the car that was sitting in front of Emma's place the night before last?"

"I had Geek working on it. It was a rental, but the name listed on it didn't ring any bells."

"Who was it?"

"Randall Wells. He shows up as an executive for an oil company out of Houston, Texas. We're running his driver's license photo through the FBI's facial recognition software to see if he comes up anywhere else. Geek's still working it."

What was an oil exec doing hanging out on Emma's street? Another puzzle Creed couldn't piece together. "Send me a copy of his driver's license photo."

"Will do," Royce acknowledged.

"Anything on the captain of the sunken boat?"

"Our contacts in Russia confirmed his was a boat for hire for anything from tourism to drug running."

"What about the tattoos on his arm and that of the man who washed ashore?" Creed asked.

"Apparently they belonged to the same black-market organization in Russia. It's a pretty nasty crowd Macias is hanging out with."

Creed didn't like that Macias had led the Russian mafia to Cape Churn. "And what have you learned about enriched uranium?"

"We have a contact that confirmed the uranium that went missing from Iran in 2012 is now in the United States. And only recently. It was moved from Russia to the west coast less than a month ago, but we still don't have names."

"You think Macias is moving it?" Tazer asked.

"We think he's in the market to purchase it."

"So we're still operating in the dark." Creed's gut knotted. "And someone's holding on to a stash of uranium sufficient to blow a city-size hole in the landscape." He didn't like it. Too little to go on, and the stakes were so damned high.

"We're working on it on our end," Royce said. "When *we* get a name, *you'll* get that name."

"Got it." Creed folded the map. "I'm tagging the

diamond bag with a GPS tracking device. If Phillip chooses to buy back the diamonds, hopefully he'll arrange to make his other purchase quickly. We can track him to his trade location."

"Good. Keep me informed," Royce said. "If you need more help, get the local police involved. Sean McNeal and I are on our way using the SOS jet. Where should we meet you when we get in?"

"Follow the tracking device in the diamond bag. If we don't have the bag, we're either dead or following it."

Royce laughed without mirth. "I choose to think you'll be following it."

"Thanks." Creed hoped that would be the case. "Glad you're coming. This could be bigger than any of us want it to be. As it is, I involved the local police on a limited basis—the chief and one of his trusted officers."

"Don't let it go any further than necessary. We can't have a local spilling the good news to the press."

"Got it." He figured they'd need all the help they could get if the crap hit the fan. "Should we wait to proceed until you two arrive?"

"No, I have faith you all can handle this. We're just coming in for backup."

The boss rang off, and silence fell over the three.

"Are we all clear on our mission?" Creed glanced across at Tazer and Casanova.

"Sounds like you have it all covered," Nova said. "When do we start?"

"As soon as I can get a ride out to that little boat in the bay." He pointed to the gleaming white luxury yacht anchored in the cape.

"Don't get yourself killed doing it," Tazer said. "I hate the paperwork involved with a dead agent."

"Thanks, Tazer. I feel the love." Creed shook his head, knowing Tazer would be after his killer in a heartbeat. He also knew she'd take a bullet for any one of the team, including Casanova. "Macias won't kill me if he knows I've stashed the diamonds on land."

"Good, because we don't have enough people on the SOS team to handle the caseload as it is," Tazer commented. "We can't afford to lose even one."

"In the meantime—" Creed grinned "—you and Casanova will be the loving tourist couple exploring Cape Churn."

"Not too loving, Nova. Got it?" Tazer elbowed Casanova in the gut.

Casanova bent at the waist, clutching his gut. "Got it."

"How long do we have to be tourists? My feet already hurt in these heels."

Casanova rolled his eyes. "Let's not take too long to find this dude. I don't know how long I'll be able to stand a whiny wife."

"Lose the heels, Tazer," Creed said. "You're in a small vacation town. You can wear flip-flops."

"Thank God." She slipped out of the heels and stood on bare feet in the sandy soil. "Much better."

"Set your watches for 2100. We'll reconvene here and wait for Macias to come sniffing out the bait."

"Do you need backup for the trip out to Phillip's yacht?" Casanova asked. "I could pretend to be a celebrity rapster. Tazer can be my bitch, and we can stop by to check out the yacht's digs."

Tazer pinched her thumb and forefinger together. "You're this close to dead, Nova."

Casanova smiled. "Knew that would piss you off."

Creed shook his head. "No, I've got it covered. I'll report in when I get back to shore."

Tazer frowned. "And if you don't get back to shore?"

"Meet Royce at the airport and turn the diamonds over to him. At least that way Macias won't have them to trade for a bomb."

Casanova saluted. "Got it."

"In the meantime, you're on vacation as a couple. Start acting like it. Roam around town looking for any of Macias's eyes and ears. It would be good to know how many we're up against."

"I might just get to play the rapster after all." Casanova rubbed his hands together.

"Only if you get to be *my* bitch." Tazer climbed into the driver's seat of their rental and plunked a wide-brimmed beach hat on her head. Then, in a really bad Southern accent, she called out, "Come on, Leon, we have some sightseein' to do."

Casanova grimaced. "Really? That's the best you can do? Comin', Eunice!" He hurried to climb into the passenger seat. Before he could buckle his seat belt, Tazer spun out in a one-eighty, kicking up a tail of dust as she headed for pavement.

Creed waited several minutes, giving them time to get way ahead of him, remembering the last time he'd been out on the road and the trouble he'd run into. He drove into town, his guard up, watching the side roads for any sign of the car with the trigger-happy gunmen. Instead of heading for Emma's house, he made use of the remaining daylight to rent a small fishing boat.

Sal and Olie were happy to let him use what amounted to a dinghy. Nothing he considered seaworthy. Thankfully, he was only headed out into the sheltered bay, not the open sea. He bought a fishing hat and a new T-shirt with a picture of a lingcod on the front and Cape Churn written across the bottom. He added fishing poles, a small tackle box and some tackle to go in it.

"You'll need a fishing license, as well," Sal said.

She rang up his purchases and had him fill out a fishing license form. Olie helped him load it all into the fishing boat, along with fresh bait. He showed him how to start the boat, what to do if it didn't crank while out in the water, and handed him a couple oars and a life vest. "Don't stay out past dark. My knee joints are predicting another bout of the Devil's Shroud. You'll want to be on dry land when it hits."

Creed pulled the fishing hat down over his forehead, cranked the dinghy's engine and set sail out into Cape Churn. Clouds had built in the western sky, blocking the majority of the sun's rays. A few shot heavenward, the edges of the clouds tinged a brilliant orange.

As he neared the yacht, he killed the engine, pulled out the fishing pole, set bait on the hook and dropped the line into the water. The little boat drifted toward the yacht while Creed pretended not to notice.

Men with guns stood on the deck, watching as he approached. He counted two positioned on the bow of the boat, one stationed on top in the lookout nest and two more at the stern. All carried what appeared to be AK-47, Soviet-made rifles with thirty-round clips.

One of the men limped to the edge and glared down at him. "Hey!" he yelled.

Creed glanced up at the man who'd probably been the one he'd stabbed in the leg during the underwater fight. Thank goodness, he hadn't recognized him yet. "Hey, who?" He pointed to his chest. "Me?"

"Yeah, you." The man pointed his rifle at him. "Find somewhere else to fish."

"It's a free country. I can fish here if I want," Creed argued. He reeled in his line and cast out again.

The limping man conferred with another sentry. That one left. A few minutes later, a man with dark hair, a dark mustache and goatee leaned over the side of the boat. "Hey, you!"

"Can you keep it down?" Creed called out. "You're scaring the fish away."

"Get away from the boat," Goatee demanded.

About that time, Creed's little dinghy bumped into the yacht. "How about you make me."

Four rifles pointed over the side.

"Not satisfied scaring fish with all your yelling?" Creed didn't break a sweat. "You trying to scare me now?" He stood in the boat and shook his fist. "Let me talk to your boss and tell him how rude you are."

"You can talk to me," Goatee insisted.

"You're just the hired help. Who's in charge?"

"I am." A dark-haired man in a black polo shirt and white slacks stepped up to the side. "What seems to be the problem?"

"You the owner?" Creed continued with his angry fisherman voice.

"I am."

"How do I know? You hiding something behind those sunglasses?"

The man pulled off the glasses.

Based on all the photos Creed had seen of this man, there was no doubt in his mind. This was the one.

"Look, you're irritating my men," he said, waving his sunglasses at the men with the guns. "Why don't you leave and make everyone happy?"

Abandoning his local fisherman role, he stared straight up at the yacht owner. "Because I have a message for Phillip Macias."

The man with the goatee pulled out a pistol and added it to the arsenal, all pointing at Creed.

The man in white slacks stiffened. "And the message is?"

"If you want your cargo, be at the Cape Churn point at eleven-thirty tonight. And it'll cost you three-hundred grand in twenties."

"Why don't I just have my men shoot you now? It will save time later."

"Then you won't have your cargo, and you won't know where it's hidden." Creed held out his hands. "Your choice."

"Tempting." The man's brows drew together, his eyes narrowing. "I'll be there."

"With the money," Creed said.

"With the money," Macias agreed.

"By yourself."

Macias slid his glasses back over his eyes. "Now, what kind of fool would I be to come alone?"

"A smart one."

"I'll be there with my bodyguards."

"I won't, and I'll keep your cargo."

Macias's mouth thinned into a line. "Eleven-thirty. I'll be there."

Creed nodded, sat back in the boat, pulled his hat

down low, started the engine and steered the boat away from the yacht. His back itched. He could feel all five weapons trained on the back of his head, and banked on the fact that they needed those diamonds to make the ultimate deal.

God, he hoped he was right. If he wasn't, he'd need a helluva nurse to patch him up after they used him as target practice.

Emma stretched and yawned, her hand reaching out to find the man in the bed beside her, her grasp coming up empty.

She sat up straight, clutching the sheet to her naked breasts. "Creed?"

No answer.

Moby trotted into the bedroom, his toenails clicking on the wooden floor. He sat beside the bed and whined, his tail swishing like a feather duster across the wood.

One glance at the nightstand gave her the answer she knew was coming. Creed had gone and taken the diamonds with him.

Tossing aside the sheet smelling of their love-making musk, she got up, dressed in shorts and a tank top and hurried through the house. His duffel bag was gone, as well, as were his clothes from the dryer. Her own garments lay neatly stacked on top of the dryer, folded uniformly straight and square.

Emma clutched a T-shirt to her chest and swallowed hard on the sob rising up her throat. Why did she do this to herself? She'd known he wasn't going to stay. Why did she think that after last night the outcome would be different?

She vaguely remembered him waking her to tell

her he was leaving and that he'd be back. How could she believe him when he'd taken everything he owned with him?

The sun had gone below the sea in the distance, a pale glow of pink, fading to dark purple, the only evidence it had been up earlier. Mist rose from the ocean as the cool night air hovered over the sun-soaked warm water. Clouds built in the distance, snuffing out the remaining sunlight with a depressing dark gray.

It fit her mood.

Moby bumped against her leg and whined as if sensing her sadness.

"Wanna go outside?"

His ears perked, and he leaped for the door.

Emma threw on her tennis shoes, snapped the leash on Moby's collar and tucked a key into the hidden pocket of her shorts. "Come on. Maybe I can run him out of my system."

Soon she was out the door and down the street she'd jogged the morning she'd found Creed sleeping in his SUV. The vehicle wasn't there this time, making her heart even heavier. After jogging two miles, Emma realized running Creed out of her system wasn't possible. She'd have to run a very long time, and frankly, she was still tired from her overnight ordeal, the frightening underwater fight and making love with Creed. She'd be better off getting a good night's sleep and use her last day of vacation to explore the *Anna Maria*. Perhaps her luck would change for the better, and she'd find a fortune in Spanish gold to line the coffers of Cape Churn Memorial and get the Children's Wing Project back on track.

And if wishes were horses…she'd probably be cleaning up their crap, too.

The last block before Sand Dollar Lane, Emma dropped into a steady walk, not at all anxious to return home. Without Creed there, it was depressingly empty.

Moby bumped her leg, panting in the darkness. When they rounded the corner, he barked and leaped forward, jerking the leash out of Emma's hand.

"Moby!" Emma ran after him, afraid he'd get out on a busy street and be hit by a passing motorist.

Instead, he flew through the open gate to her little house and ran up on the porch.

"Hey, Moby," said a deep voice, followed by laughter and a stern, "Down, boy."

Her heart pounding against her ribs, Emma entered the yard, hope swelling inside. "You came back."

"I had to."

She frowned up at the shadow of his face, wishing she'd left the light on over the porch so that she could read his expression. "You had to?"

"You need to go stay with someone tonight."

"Why?"

He traced her cheek with his finger. "You're not safe alone."

Emma captured his hand and held it against her face. "I've lived alone for a long time."

"Not with a known terrorist gunning for you." He gripped her arms. "Please. For me. For Moby. Maybe you can stay with your friend Molly at the B and B."

"She doesn't allow dogs, and I can't leave Moby."

"Then what about Gabe's wife? Kayla? Could you stay with her?"

"They live in a small cottage by the lighthouse. They

barely have room for Gabe, Kayla, the baby and Gabe's teenage son."

"You could sleep on their couch. Anyone, anything. Just go stay with someone."

"Can't you stay with me?"

He shook his head. "I wish I could. But I'm working tonight."

Her heart dropped like a wad of lead to the pit of her belly. "Are you going after Phillip Macias?"

Creed stared at her. Without saying a word, she knew the answer. "Why you? If he's a known terrorist, why can't they arrest him and put him in jail?"

"There's not enough evidence to pin him with charges. And he's in league with someone to provide him with enriched uranium. That stuff is hard to come by. We need to catch both men. Phillip to stop his brand of terrorism for hire, and his uranium supplier from supplying extremists with the means necessary to murder millions."

"But why you?" She beat her fists against his chest. "Why do you have to put your life on the line for everyone else?"

He shook his head. "Why are you a nurse? Why do you help people survive horrible accidents, diseases and injuries?" He gripped her wrists in his big, strong hands. "Because it's who we are."

"I don't want you to die," Emma whispered. "I just met you. I want to know you a little longer."

He smiled down at her, his white teeth gleaming in the darkness. "I want to get to know you longer, too. And I don't plan on dying. Not anytime soon." With a sigh, he pulled her into his arms and cradled her gently.

"I came to Cape Churn to find a terrorist. It's my job. I have to do it. I promise, when it's all done, I'll be back."

"Promises, promises." Her voice hitched on a sob. "I'll go stay with Kayla and Gabe, if they'll have me. But if you're not going to stick around, don't bother to come back. You said it yourself. You're not the staying kind of guy. And I'm better off cutting my losses before I get too attached."

She pushed away from him, dug her key from her pocket and opened her front door. Moby raced in, woofed and circled back for Creed.

Emma put out her foot, stopping the dog before he could blow through the door again. "Stay."

"I'll follow you to Kayla's." Creed's voice was stiff, tight.

"I can make it on my own," she said without facing him. "I'm not your responsibility."

As she closed the door, Creed called out, "I'm *following* you to Kayla's."

Emma stuffed toiletries, pajamas and a change of clothes into an oversize tote, grabbed a box of dry dog food and Moby's leash and walked out the front door, down the porch, past Creed to her damaged Jeep. She stowed the tote and folded the front seat down so that Moby could jump into the back. As Emma climbed into the driver's seat, Creed got into his rented SUV and shifted into Drive, waiting for her to pull ahead of him.

For a moment she stared through the cracked windshield. Her heart hurt so badly she wanted to burst into tears. Instead, she pulled up her big girl panties and drove away from her little cottage overlooking the cape. Not a star peppered the sky as the land and sea disappeared, consumed by incoming fog. A portent of things to come?

A shiver raced across Emma's skin. Legend had it that only bad things happened when the Devil's Shroud cloaked the land.

# Chapter 12

"Comm check," Creed said quietly. He stood in the mist on the Cape Churn point, regretting the timing of this assignation and the fog that had crept in like a plague to blanket land and sea.

"Tazer, check."

"Nova, check."

"I can't see a damned thing," Nicole whispered into Creed's earpiece.

"That goes for me, too," Casanova confirmed. "You're gonna be on your own. If something goes down, I'm libel to shoot myself before I find the enemy," he admitted. "This fog is thicker than *mi madre's carne guisada.*"

"Your mamma doesn't cook *carne guisada,* she doesn't have time, working two shifts at the hospital in San Antonio. And it's pea soup. The fog is thicker than pea soup," Tazer said.

"Quiet." Creed cocked his head and pulled the earpiece out of his ear. A soft rumbling sound made the fog seem alive. He set the earpiece firmly back in his ear. "I hear an engine."

"Game on, gang," Tazer whispered. "We've got your back, Creed."

"Wherever it is," Nova added.

A large, dark SUV loomed out of the fog, bright lights bouncing off the low ceiling, blinding Creed. He raised his arm to shade his eyes and waited for Macias to get out.

Four doors opened. *Great.*

"He brought company. Move in." Creed gave the order softly, without moving his lips to form the words. Then he grinned and spread his arms wide, showing the new arrivals he'd come unarmed. "You're late. Have trouble finding the road in the fog?"

"Where are the diamonds?" Goatee Man rounded the front passenger side door, carrying an AR-15 assault rifle, aimed at Creed's chest. The driver and two other men equally armed stepped out of the SUV.

"I might have them here, and I might not." Creed dropped his arms and the smile. "Where's Macias?"

"Couldn't make it. He had another errand to run."

"Sorry, I only deal with the boss man." Creed turned as if to leave.

Goatee Man fired a round that kicked up rocks near Creed's feet.

Touching a finger to his ear, and then speaking loudly so that Goatee Man could hear, Creed said, "Hold your fire, team." Creed glanced back, shaking his head as if at a child needing discipline. "Are all your brains in your beard? If you shoot me, you'll never see those diamonds."

Goatee Man snorted. "You wouldn't have come without them."

"I had a hunch Macias would send his flunkies." Creed crossed his arms. "I bet he didn't even get the cash."

Goatee Man stepped forward, brought his rifle to his shoulder and leaned his cheek on the side, sighting in on Creed. "Hand over the diamonds, or I shoot you now."

"I have a team standing ready to shoot every one of you. Go ahead. Shoot me. And if you make it out of here alive, you'll go without the diamonds and no way to find them."

"You're lying."

"Tazer." Creed spoke softly.

"On it." As quietly as a cat moves in the night, Tazer moved forward, switched on the laser sight of her M4A1 rifle and trained it on the Goatee Man's heart.

Creed almost smiled. Goatee Man didn't know, until the man standing on the other side of the vehicle with his own gun glanced across at him. "Van, your chest."

The man didn't budge. "Shut up."

"Look at your chest, Van," the other man insisted.

Van, or Goatee Man, glanced down. When he saw the red beam on his shirt, he shifted his aim toward the source. The beam blinked off, and nothing could be seen past the reflection of the SUV's headlights against the fog.

"I suggest you go back to your boss and tell him the deal's off if he can't be bothered to show up and make the exchange himself. *Without* his hired monkeys with their toy guns."

Van turned, his aim back on Creed. "I should kill you right now and save us all the trouble. I'll bet those diamonds are around here."

"And if they aren't?" Creed laughed. "I understand Macias doesn't suffer fools. You willing to bank on his mercy?"

Goatee Man's eyes narrowed, his mouth tipping up on one side in a sneer. "Goes both ways, big shot."

Creed bit down on his tongue to keep from asking Van what he meant by that last comment. A bad feeling swarmed over him like a cloud of mosquitoes prickling his skin.

"Load up," Van called out. The other three men, guns and all, climbed into the SUV. Van stood with his rifle to his shoulder, still aiming at Creed. "You'll regret this."

Creed smiled. "I don't so far. I have a bag full of diamonds. I could disappear today and find another buyer if I don't hear from Macias soon."

"Oh, you'll hear from him all right." Van's lips curled in an evil smile. "You'll hear. And I'll lay odds you'll listen."

Van climbed into the SUV, and the vehicle slowly backed down the dirt track until it disappeared except for the glow of the headlight. It, too, faded into the fog, leaving Creed surrounded by a ghostly darkness.

"What do you think he meant by that last comment?" Tazer asked, joining Creed on the track, her rifle pointed at the dirt.

"Yeah." Casanova stepped out of the fog. "What did he mean by 'you'll listen'?"

Creed shook his head, that bad feeling knotting in his gut.

"I don't like it." Tazer set her weapon on Safe, expelled the bullet in the chamber and retrieved it from the ground. "Sounds like he has something on you." She straightened, her head tipping to the side. "Did you get your girl moved to a safe location?"

A rush of adrenaline pushed up into Creed's chest and lodged in his throat. "I did."

"You sure it's safe enough?" Nova asked.

"I thought so, but now..." Creed spun and ran for his vehicle hidden in the brush. For a moment, the fog hampered his attempts to find it. When he practically ran into it, he yelled, "Get in!"

Casanova and Tazer dove into the backseat as Creed slammed his foot down hard on the accelerator, fishtailing out of the bushes onto the dirt track. He fought to control the steering wheel and sped away from the point, praying he wouldn't be too late.

Emma paced the length of the lighthouse cottage, Moby trotting alongside her. Every once in a while Moby stopped and stared at the window. Emma couldn't. If she stayed still, she'd start thinking about Creed, about the diamonds and the men with the scary guns.

"Tonya's fed, changed and ready to sleep through the night. I hope." Kayla, the pretty redheaded artist who'd stolen Gabe McGregor's heart, emerged from the master bedroom at the back of the house, Tonya pressed against her shoulder as she patted her back. The baby burped, bringing a smile to her mother's face. "That's better."

Emma couldn't help but envy the new mother, her own womb aching for a child of her own. She paced faster. You had to have a man in your life to have what Kayla had.

Kayla nestled the little girl in her arms and leaned back against the kitchen bar, overlooking the living room. "You know, pacing won't make the time go faster."

"I know, but I can't sit still." Emma wrung her hands and spun to pace along the big windows that normally looked out over the ocean. Tonight the light from the living room made the windows appear like giant mirrors, reflecting Emma's worried expression as she wore a path across the wooden floors. "I feel like I'm in a mirrored cave or a not-so-fun fun house," she grumbled.

"Gabe and I plan on installing automatic window shades as soon as we can afford to. It is pretty creepy when you can't see out. Especially when those on the outside can see in." Kayla shivered. "I still have nightmares."

"I'm so glad Gabe caught the serial killer before he got to you." Emma smiled across at her friend. "I can't imagine Cape Churn without you and sweet little Tonya."

"We can't imagine living anywhere else but Cape Churn." Kayla tweaked the baby's little chin. The three-month-old grinned up at her, her light fuzz of red hair so much like her mother's it made Emma's chest tighten.

Emma paced to the end of the living room and turned, her heart fluttering when she thought she saw a face in the window. She stopped and stared, but nothing was there except the dense fog. Completing her about-face, she almost ran over Moby as he stood staring at the same spot. Emma bent and ruffled Moby's ears. "Are you seeing ghosts, too?"

"Ghosts?" Kayla asked. "Is the fog getting to you?"

"Yeah. I swear I'm seeing Randy's rat-fink face."

Kayla clutched Tonya to her chest and stared out the window, her eyes narrowed. "Did they ever find his body?"

"No. But they found his car at the bottom of a cliff, almost completely submerged in the surf. The man had to be dead. No one could survive a crash like that."

"And he took the money to his grave. The detectives couldn't trace it through the banks?"

"Sadly, no." Emma made another pass the length of the living room. "I guess the fog's got me seeing ghosts. I'm imagining all the worst things."

"Like?"

"Something bad happening to Creed and his team."

"They're trained professionals. They'll be okay."

"From Creed's description of Phillip Macias, he's a pretty dangerous guy. He'll stop at nothing to get what he wants, and he has no qualms about killing anyone who gets in his way."

"Nice guy."

"Not the kind of man you want to meet in a back alley." Emma clapped a hand over her mouth, remembering too late that Kayla had been attacked in a back alley by a serial killer. "Sorry."

Kayla cradled Tonya with one hand and brushed the base of her throat with the other. "It's okay. I don't think about it much anymore."

"I can't imagine going through what you did and not coming out with some emotional scars."

"It helps to have a loving husband to hold you at night when the bad dreams come." Kayla stared down at her baby. "Tonya and I wouldn't be here if it hadn't been for Gabe. I love him so much."

Emma stopped pacing to stare at the woman and baby, a lump the size of a sweat sock lodged in her throat. An image of Creed formed in her mind—the one of him holding her in his arms as she fell asleep. She'd told him she didn't need him. Didn't want him around when he'd just leave her behind as soon as the job was done. Her problem was that the more she saw of him, the more she wanted to see.

She'd pushed him away to spare her heart, but she feared her heart was already too invested in the man to let go now. Not that it mattered. When they captured Macias and put him away, Creed would move on. He'd said so. He wasn't a staying kind of guy—his words. She'd gone into the relationship knowing that, her mind accepting the temporariness of a fling with Creed. Unfortunately, her heart hadn't listened to that part.

While Emma had been staring at Kayla, seeing Creed, Kayla had crossed the floor and placed a hand on her arm. "Are you okay?"

"I don't know." Emma swallowed hard.

"Is it Creed? Are you worried about him?" Kayla asked.

Emma nodded. "Yes." She was very worried about him. With Macias on the loose and looking for his diamonds, none of his team was safe, especially not Creed. But it was more than that.

"Emma?" Kayla squeezed her arm. "Are you in love with Creed?"

The question caught her off guard. She stepped backward, bumping into the couch. "What did you say?"

"Are you in love with Creed?"

She shook her head, her heart swelling. "How can I be in love with a man I've only known three days?"

Kayla smiled. "I knew the moment I met Gabe. Or at least my heart did. It took a day or two for my head to catch up."

Emma shook her head again. "I can't be in love with him. I know nothing about him, not to mention I'm a terrible judge of character."

"You can't base all your relationships on your experience with Randy. He was a liar, a cheat and a user. Lower than a scum-sucking slug."

"Yeah, and I would have married him."

"But you didn't. Thank God."

"Why is Creed any different? He lies for a living. That's what special agents do. They go in undercover, which is another word for *lie*, get people to trust them, and then pow! He'll be gone, and whoever had the misfortune of falling in love with him will be left alone, empty, pathetic."

"Are you afraid that will be you?" Kayla gave her a sad smile. "You've already fallen for him, and now you're waiting for him to leave."

"He will."

"Maybe not. You're a beautiful woman with a lot to offer a man. Surely he'll see that and come back."

"He told me up front that he wasn't into commitment. Not to get attached. I agreed with him." Emma laughed, her heart empty of any trace of humor. "I agreed with him."

"A man can change his mind. I saw his face when he dropped you off."

"The face of a man glad to get me off his hands?"

Kayla shook her head. "No the face of a man worried about the woman he loves."

"You're seeing things, like I'm seeing ghosts of my dead fiancé."

"Look, you're distraught. Let me get you a cup of hot cocoa. Something to calm you. After you get a good night's sleep, the fog will lift, the sun will shine and everything will be better in the morning."

"You're far too optimistic for me," Emma grumbled.

"Yeah, we've kind of switched roles, haven't we? Being optimistic was your job, but since you're falling down on it, I guess it's my turn." Kayla smiled and offered her Tonya. "Do you mind holding her while I check on Dakota? He's supposed to be staying the night at a friend's house. I want to make sure he got there okay after they went to the movie, what with the fog and him such a new driver."

"Sure." Emma took Tonya into her arms. The tiny baby snuggled against her, yawned and turned her face toward Emma's breast, searching for mother's milk. That single movement tugged so hard at Emma's heart, her eyes misted and she fought to keep from crying. Until now, she hadn't realized just how much she wanted a baby of her own.

Frustrated by the fabric when she was searching for comfort, Tonya stuffed her fist in her little mouth and sucked on the wad of fingers.

Emma swallowed hard on the lump in her throat. "Are you certain she's not still hungry?"

"She nursed for thirty minutes. I'd say she's full or about to go into another growth spurt." Kayla lifted the phone from the receiver. "I'd text Dakota, but I'm not getting any reception on my cell phone. I think the fog plays havoc with the cell towers as well as with road conditions."

"They don't call it the Devil's Shroud for nothing," Emma muttered. "I bet they're going to be busy at the hospital tonight."

"I know. I wish Gabe wasn't working tonight. Things are always weird when the fog rolls in."

Emma tried not to think about how weird. Somewhere out there, Creed and his team had the diamonds Phillip Macias wanted. How far would he go to get them back? He'd already tried to kill them three times.

As much as she loved Kayla and Tonya's company, Emma would rather have been with Creed on a night like this. But she was glad she hadn't stayed at home, alone.

"Hi, this is Kayla McGregor. Dakota was supposed to call me when the boys got back from the movie." Kayla spoke into the phone. "He did get there, didn't he?" She paused to listen, her tense shoulders relaxing. "Oh, good. No. No. I don't want to bother him, I just wanted to know he's safe. The fog's so thick, I worried he'd run off the road. I will. Thank you." Kayla hung up and smiled across at Emma. "He made it okay."

Pushing back her own sadness, Emma forced a smile. "How's life with a baby and a teenager?"

"It's different. Tonya is the best baby…well, besides still getting up in the middle of the night to nurse. And

Dakota is turning out to be quite a gentleman and a very talented young artist."

"With you as a stepmother, how could he go wrong?" Emma glanced around at the easel leaning near the window, searching for anything to keep her mind off the baby, Creed and the fog outside. "Speaking of art, what are you working on now?"

"A portrait I had to put on hold when I went into labor with Tonya. It's for Andrew Stratford." She walked to the window and turned the painting so that the light shone down on it. The painting depicted a small girl with pale blond hair hanging in soft curls down to her waist. She wore a white cotton dress with white eyelet trim. In one hand, she held a doll, while the other rested on a black Labrador retriever almost as big as her. Both appeared so lifelike it took Emma's breath away.

Emma sighed. "It's beautiful."

Kayla's brows wrinkled. "Do you think so?"

"Oh, yes. I do."

"Have you seen Leigha Stratford?"

"Mr. Stratford had me come out to the house once to check her out. She'd fallen and scraped her knee. He didn't want to bring her to the hospital because he was afraid of all the germs." Emma smiled. "She didn't say a word, nor did she shed a single tear as I cleaned the wound and applied antiseptic ointment. You've captured her perfectly."

"I don't know. There's something wrong with her face. It's too…"

"Sad?" Emma finished, her gaze going to the baby in her arms. Tonya had fallen to sleep, a smile curling her tiny lips. So peaceful, content and untouched by the harshness of the world around her. She suspected Leigha had been traumatized sometime in her young life.

"Yeah," Kayla was saying. "I think it bothers me that she looks so sad in the painting."

"But it's her. She had that same expression on her face when I was out there." Emma's heart squeezed for the little girl living a solitary life on her father's big estate. "She needs friends to play with."

"I know." Kayla continued to stare at the painting. "I guess I wish I could paint her happy."

"That would be nice if we could paint our worlds the way we want them."

"Sounds easier than taking it as is."

"In some ways. But then how often do we think we want something, yet it's the opposite thing we really need?" Emma thought she'd wanted to be relationship free. Deep down, she needed the love of another person in her life.

"If I could paint things the way I thought I wanted them, I wouldn't have Gabe in my life. I pushed him away when we first met."

Just like Emma was pushing Creed away.

"You have the magic touch. Look how happy she is." Kayla took the baby from Emma's hands, cradling her in her arms. "She'll sleep most of the night now. I'm going to put her in her bed, and then I'll bring out some blankets and a pillow for you."

"I'm okay, take your time. Moby needs to go outside before I call it a night."

"You might want to keep him on a leash and stay close to the house. You don't want him falling off the cliff because he didn't see it. Or you, too, for that matter."

"I'll hang close," Emma promised. She snapped Moby's leash onto his collar, and he danced all around her as she headed for the door. "You've been a pretty good sport about all this. Let's keep it that way, okay?" Not too excited about stepping off the porch into the fog, Emma leaned back, bracing her legs for when Moby lunged for freedom.

As if he sensed the danger of running off into the fog, Moby stayed close to her heels and walked down the steps with more control than she'd ever seen in him. Though full grown, Moby was a perpetual puppy, even at four years old. Emma wondered when he'd slow down and be less rambunctious, but was glad he still had that youthful exuberance. It kept her on her toes and helped her maintain her own upbeat attitude. Especially when Randy had left her, taking the hospital's money.

Unlike his usual happy-go-lucky self, Moby was stiff tonight and suspicious of the fog.

Emma walked with Moby across the front of the house. When they reached the end, Moby growled, the short hairs on the back of his neck rising. He planted his paws in the damp soil and stood so still he could have been a statue.

"What's wrong, Moby?" Emma's breath caught in her throat, and she strained to listen for any sound of movement. All she heard were the waves splashing against the cliffs far below.

When she tried to take another step, Moby crossed in front of her and stood braced, facing the socked-in, fog-shrouded side of the house, a low growl rumbling in his chest.

Uneasy and a little scared on the wake of talking about serial killers with Kayla, Emma backed up a step, tugging on Moby's leash. "Come on. Let's go back into the house."

Moby didn't budge, refusing to back down from whatever had him concerned.

Emma tugged again, determined to get back inside with the dog.

Moby was having none of it. One moment he was braced for whatever threat he could sense. In the next second, he lunged, yanking the leash right out of Emma's hands.

"Moby!" she called out as the dog disappeared, swallowed by the Devil's Shroud, the only evidence he was even out there the sound of wild barking.

"Moby!" Emma ran around the side of the house, following the barking. It sounded as if it was coming from the back of the house. Every possible scenario flashed through her mind as she ran after Moby. The crashing of waves against the rocky shoreline far below was enough to make her crazy with the fear Moby would run off the edge of the cliff and fall to his death.

"Moby!"

When she reached the back edge of the house, she had to decide whether to follow the dog into the fog and get lost herself or retreat and pray Moby would find his way back without falling over the cliff.

Moby's barking became more frenzied and turned into vicious growling.

"Moby! Come!" she cried out. What had he gotten into? Was there a wild animal out there?

Torn, she balanced on the balls of her feet, her heart booming in her chest. She wished she could see where she was going and what was happening with her dog.

Then Moby yelped, that kind of yelp that meant he'd been hurt. His plaintive whine wrenched Emma's heart, and she ran toward the sound. "Moby?" She couldn't see him, and for a moment thought she might be going the wrong way, when the dog whined again from a few feet ahead.

Emma ran forward, her hands in front of her to keep her from slamming face-first into a tree. She felt as if she was running away from the cliffs, possibly back toward the road, but she couldn't be sure.

The only thing she was certain of was that Moby needed her, and she couldn't stop until she found him. "Moby?" she called out.

The dog whined, his sad cries leading her to him. Afraid she'd step on him, Emma dropped to her hands and knees and felt along the ground. As dark as it was, she might as well close her eyes. No light penetrated the thick fog.

She almost crawled on top of Moby.

The dog lay on his side, whimpering softly as Emma ran her hands over his body. "What's wrong with you, boy? What happened?"

Her hand settled on his ribs and a pool of warm, sticky liquid. The coppery scent of blood filled her senses. "Oh, baby, you're bleeding. What happened?" She wished the animal could talk and tell her. But the important thing was that she'd found him, hopefully in time to help. "We have to get you to a vet. Come on." She rose to her feet, scooped her hands beneath his big hairy body and tried to lift him. He whimpered, his head lolling to the side.

Emma refused to leave her dog out in the fog for whatever animal had attacked him to finish him off. "Come on, Moby, we're getting out of here." She braced her back and lifted with her legs. "What was it you weighed last time we were at the vet? Eighty pounds?" She grunted and straightened, staggering under the weight. "I think you've gained a pound or two."

Moby whined as she jostled his body, walking back the way she'd come. Or at least the way she thought she'd come. "Hang on, Moby. You're going to be okay."

A fuzzy light glowed ahead and Emma aimed for it, praying it was the light from the back porch of the house. As she neared, she realized it was too close to the ground and bobbing. Perhaps it was a flashlight and Kayla had come out to find her.

"Oh, Kayla, you shouldn't have come out. What if you got lost in the fog? No one would be at the house with Tonya."

As she moved closer to the light, it moved away. Emma followed, the light her only beacon in an otherwise foggy black world. "Wait," she called out, barely able to keep up with the heavy load she carried. "Are we headed the right way?"

Why wasn't Kayla answering?

A moment later, she stumbled up a rise and found herself on the blacktop road. "What the hell?" Her Jeep was back at the cottage, and that was a long walk from the road. Her back ached, and Moby wasn't moving anymore. "Hang on, buddy, I'll get you there."

A silhouette stepped through the fog, materializing into a darkly dressed man wearing a black trench coat and black cap on his head, the bill pulled down over his face.

"Put the dog down," said a disembodied voice, one she knew all too well.

## Chapter 13

Creed floored the accelerator, his heart beating so hard he could hear it booming in his ears. He had to get to Emma.

"This is suicide!" Tazer crawled over the console and into the front seat, slamming against the dash as Creed missed a turn, ran into a ditch and powered back up onto the blacktop. "The fog is too bad to be driving this fast. Slow down, Creed."

"I can't," he bit out. "She's in trouble. I can feel it."

"We'll be of no use to her dead," Nova said from the backseat.

"Creed," Tazer said, her voice low, calm, insistent, "we have the diamonds. He probably wants to trade the girl for the diamonds. It's a win-win. We get the girl back safe and sound. He gets the diamonds with the tracking device."

"She's going to be okay," Nova added.

Tazer touched his arm. "We don't even know she's been taken."

Creed pulled his smart phone out of his jacket and tossed it to Tazer. "Dial the number for the McGregors. Hurry."

She activated the phone, and the screen glowed brightly against her pale face. "We aren't getting any reception out here." Tazer continued to stare down at the backlit screen. "There! Two bars." She thumbed through his contact list and pressed the call button. "God, it takes forever to connect."

Creed held his breath, his knuckles white on the steering wheel as he took another corner too fast. With the fog so thick, he hadn't seen it until they were in it, headed for a ditch.

Tazer gripped the handle above the door to keep from slamming into the window, while holding the phone to her ear. "I'm not getting anything."

Creed's foot briefly left the accelerator. "What do you mean you're not getting anything?"

Still holding the phone to her ear, Tazer shook her head. "I mean it's not ringing—nothing."

"Call the chief," Creed urged.

"Looking in your contacts." Tazer scrolled back through his contacts list.

"To hell with the contacts, hit 9-1-1. Hurry!" Creed blew into Cape Churn faster than was prudent in the horrible, foggy conditions. He prayed everyone had stayed home and out of his way, or he'd surely run them over before he even saw them. Nothing was going to slow him down until he got to the lighthouse cottage and Emma.

Tazer hit the three numbers and pressed the call button, set the phone on speaker and waited.

"Cape Churn Emergency Response, what is the nature of your emergency?"

"Get a unit out to the lighthouse cottage ASAP. Emma Jenkins's life is in danger."

"The chief, two units and an ambulance were dispatched to that location five minutes ago," the female dispatcher announced. "Have there been further developments requiring additional emergency support?"

Creed couldn't answer, all his worst fears coming to pass.

"No," Tazer responded for him. "Thank you." She ended the call and sat silent in the seat beside Creed, staring out the window.

Creed's heart slipped to the bottom of his belly. He slammed his palm against the steering wheel. "They got to her."

"We don't know that," Tazer said. "She could be fine. Maybe someone slipped and broke a leg."

He shook his head. "Why else would the chief and all those units be on their way out there?" Once they cleared city limits, his foot hit the accelerator hard. "I should have done more."

"You didn't know," Nova said from the dark backseat.

"I knew what Macias was capable of. I knew he'd had someone watching her house. I should have had a policeman with her at all times. Hell, I should never have involved her. I should know better than anyone not to get civilians involved."

"Shoulda, coulda, woulda. What's done is done. If

she's gone, we go after her." Nova rested a hand on Creed's shoulder. "Tazer and I are in. Right, Taze?"

Tazer slapped her hand on the armrest. "Damn right."

"See?" Nova smiled at Creed in the rearview mirror. "It'll be okay."

"You really have a thing for the girl, don't you?" Tazer asked. "I've never seen you go ape-shit like this over anyone."

"She's saved my life three times in the past three days."

Tazer snorted. "Don't bullshit us. It's more than that. We can tell."

"What does it matter if I have a thing for her? When the mission is over, I'll be out of here. Oregon is on the opposite side of the country from D.C."

"So?" Nova leaned forward, his hand on Creed's shoulder again. "Kat's based out of Alaska, and she has a life outside her job with SOS."

Kat Sikes was on their team and had lived in D.C. until her husband had been blown away on a mission in Africa. She'd returned to her home state of Alaska to recover from her grief, met Sam Russell and decided to base out of Alaska to be closer to him.

"Our missions take us all over the country and the world," Tazer said. "It really doesn't matter if we fly out of D.C. or Cape Churn. We go when and where we're needed."

Kat's case had set the precedent. Since then, basing agents out of opposite sides of the country had proven effective, shortening response times.

"It's not the kind of life for a family left behind." He remembered how devastated Kat had been with the news of her husband's death. As an SOS agent, she'd understood the risks and still had trouble accepting her loss.

"As long as they know what they're getting into, it should be their choice," Tazer said.

"Have you thought about giving Emma that choice?" Nova stared at him in the rearview mirror.

"Like you two are the examples for me to follow? What relationships have you been in that have lasted more than a week?" Neither one said anything. "Exactly. The job keeps us moving. Why are we even discussing this, anyway?" Creed threw his hands in the air, then grabbed the wheel again before they careened off the road and over a guardrail into the ocean. "I've only known her three days."

"Three days is a record for you." Tazer's lips twisted. "The most I've seen you date is a one-night stand. Emma must be special."

"She is." She was smart, caring and sexy as hell. But spouses of agents lived in constant fear of losing their loved one. Creed couldn't put Emma through that. "She deserves better than a washed-up sailor."

"You're not a washed-up anything." Tazer slapped his injured arm.

Creed winced when her fingers touched his stab wound. "Watch it."

"Sorry." Tazer snatched her hand away. "Point is, we're damned lucky to have you as part of the SOS team. If we pull this thing off, you will be saving millions of lives."

"That's a big if," he pointed out.

"Well, we can talk about it, or make it happen."

Nova sat back, his arms crossed over his chest. "I'm for making it happen."

"Me, too. And it starts with getting Emma back and giving Macias his big bad bag of tricks." Tazer leaned back in her seat, arms crossed, as well.

With his team backing him, Creed dared to hope. If Macias had gotten to Emma, they had the bargaining chip to get her back. He prayed she lived long enough for them to make the trade.

He almost missed the turnoff to the lighthouse cottage. If not for the glow penetrating the dense fog from the multitude of vehicles crowding the road into the McGregors' home, he'd have gone right past.

Three police cars, an ambulance and a paramedic fire truck crowded in front of the little cottage.

Creed skidded to a stop, slammed the shift into Park and jumped out, shouting, "Emma!"

Chief Taggart broke away from a group gathered around the front porch. Rescue techs bent over something lying on the wood decking.

His heart leaped into his throat, strangling his vocal cords.

"Creed." Taggart reached out to grab his arm.

Creed shook off his grip and pushed through the crowd, feeling his world crashing in around him. "Emma."

The paramedics knelt around a figure. Creed couldn't see past their uniforms. "Oh, God. Emma."

The paramedics looked up, leaning back, and a gap opened enough for Creed to see what had their attention.

Moby lay on his side, a broad gash along his ribs,

limp, lifeless and still. Creed's heart wrenched, and he dropped to the deck beside the animal.

Emma loved this dog. "Is he alive?" Creed choked out.

"Barely," one of the medics replied. "We have an emergency call out to the local veterinarian. He's going to meet us at his office in town."

Creed ran a hand over the dog's soft, furry head. "Take care of him, will ya?"

"Count on it." The medic nodded. "Emma's our best nurse. We all know how much she cares about Moby."

"Where's Emma?" Creed glanced up into Kayla Mc-Gregor's pale face.

Her eyes were red-rimmed, and she clutched her baby in her arms. "Oh, Creed, I'm so sorry." Her voice hitched on a sob, and she buried her face in the blanket the baby was swaddled in. "She's gone."

Though he knew it before they even drove up to the lighthouse cottage, the world ripped out from under Creed, and his heart fell to rock bottom. "When? What happened?"

Chief Taggart and Gabe McGregor pulled him aside. Tazer and Nova joined them as Gabe told them about Kayla's frantic call and how Emma disappeared with Moby.

They'd gathered as many emergency personnel as they could and spread out around the cottage searching for Emma, even shining lights to the bottom of the cliffs, thinking she might have fallen off in the fog.

When they found Moby by the road and tire tracks in the mud, the chief called off the ground search and alerted other officers in patrol units to be on the lookout for any vehicle passing in or around Cape Churn.

Based on all he knew, he'd come to the same conclusion the SOS team had—Macias had her.

For the length of the story, Creed could barely hold himself together. But by the time Gabe stopped talking, he knew what he had to do. He had to get Emma back. Alive. And he'd do whatever it took to accomplish that mission.

Chief Taggart stared hard at Creed, Tazer and Casanova. "You three are the high-powered operatives. Do you have a plan to get our girl back?"

Creed straightened. "I need to get out to that yacht. Now."

Gabe grinned. "I have Dave on standby. He's at the marina, prepping his dive boat as we speak."

Turning to his team, Creed said, "Let's go."

Gabe stepped forward. "We're going with you."

Creed held up a hand. "I'd rather you stay back in Cape Churn, in case we need a team for hostage negotiations."

Gabe hesitated a moment, then nodded. "Will do. We'll have someone stand by for phone calls."

Creed headed back to his SUV.

Tazer ran to catch up to him. "You know the higher-ups don't negotiate with terrorists."

"They don't have someone they care about whose life is on the line." He stopped long enough to shoot a look back at Tazer. "I do."

The drive back to Cape Churn was no less terrifying. The fog hadn't let up, and it gently choked the landscape. By the time they slid into the marina parking lot, Creed's hands were cramped from gripping the steering wheel so hard he'd probably put dents in it.

Dave met them at the dock. "Creed, I got us all set

up. The Devil's Shroud is giving us hell, but I set the GPS to the middle of the bay where we last saw Macias's yacht. We should be able to get close enough to find it. The good news is that they won't have made it out of the bay in this fog. It's too dangerous."

Creed leaped on board the *Reel Dive*. "Macias isn't known for caution."

Tazer and Casanova untied the ropes and jumped aboard.

As soon as they cleared the marina area with the jetties and anchored sailboats, Dave threw the throttle forward, and the dive boat moved out at a speed of forty knots per hour.

Minutes later, they neared the location Dave thought the yacht would be. He slowed the boat and inched forward. Creed stood at the farthest point forward on the bow, straining his eyes to see through the thick, dark fog.

Minutes passed, and they saw nothing but more fog.

Then Tazer called out and pointed to the starboard. "I see a light!"

Steering for the light and slowly turning as they approached, Dave slid the dive boat alongside the yacht.

"Ahoy!" Creed shouted.

A few moments passed, and no one came to the side.

"Ahoy!" he yelled again.

"Keep your pants on!" A man wearing a robe and a captain's hat appeared at the side, squinting down at Creed. "What's the problem?"

"Let me talk to Macias."

"He's not on board."

"Then let me talk to the one called Van," Creed demanded.

"None of Macias's men are on board. They cleared out today right after you left. Took everything they brought with them."

"Where were they heading?"

"How should I know? They commissioned me to get them here. We're here, and I'm heading back to Russia tomorrow."

"I'm coming aboard." Creed nodded to Dave, who maneuvered the *Reel Dive* toward the rear of the yacht.

"I'll line up the backs of the boats," Dave said from the helm.

Creed waited for Dave to slide the back of their boat up to the back of the yacht, and he waited until they were close together. When the dive boat was close enough, he grabbed the railing on the back of the yacht and climbed onto the deck.

The captain met him, tying the sash around his robe. "I don't know what you think you're going to find. They're gone."

"They kidnapped a woman. If you were involved in any way whatsoever…"

The captain raised his hands. "I had nothing to do with kidnapping. I didn't even know how heavily armed they were until you came by this afternoon and they pulled out their arsenal. You want to look around, go ahead. You're not going to find the woman."

Creed spent the next ten minutes combing over the yacht, startling crew members in their bunks and checking every cabinet, hatch and storage area. By the time he'd completed his inspection, his heart was sick. Not only had Macias gotten away without leaving a trace, he'd taken Emma with him.

With no way to find Macias or contact him, Creed

was at the terrorist's mercy. He'd have to wait until Macias contacted *him*.

He paused before exiting the yacht. "I advise you not to leave tomorrow. The local police will want to talk to you about harboring criminals. Leave, and we'll have the coastguard find you and haul you back in."

Again, the captain raised his hands in surrender. "I'm innocent. I'll cooperate in any way I can."

Creed figured the captain would set sail as soon as the fog lifted, and no one would see him anywhere near Cape Churn ever again. It didn't matter. Emma wasn't here, and he had no way to find her.

Her wrists and ankles bound, duct tape over her mouth, and tossed into the trunk of a car, Emma didn't have any options but to wait until her captor got where he was going and let her out. The black interior of the trunk surrounding her was nothing compared to the darkness of worry in her heart. She'd had to leave Moby on the roadside, probably dying without medical attention. He wouldn't have understood why she'd left him there, abandoning him when he needed her most.

Tears trickled out of the corners of her eyes for the dog she loved as much as a child. He was her only family. The only living creature who'd been there for her when she'd been sad and disappointed. His enthusiasm made her smile and laugh and remember why life was worth living.

An image of Creed filled her thoughts. Moby had liked him instantly, and she considered Moby the best judge of character. He'd hated Randy on sight. Which should have been her first clue.

It hadn't been an animal that attacked Moby. It had

been her former fiancé, apparently risen from the dead.
Or rather, had never died in the first place. He'd run
his vehicle off the cliff at a point where it would crash
into the sea. No one had questioned whether or not he'd
been inside. On a night cloaked in the Devil's Shroud,
he'd planned his fake death to look real.

The ghost she'd seen in the picture window of the
lighthouse cottage had been all too real. Moby had either seen him or sensed his presence, and once he'd
gotten outside, the dog had gone after the menace lurking in the darkness.

Not only had she been stupid to trust Randy with the
hospital's money, she hadn't seen through his smarmy
lies to the real monster lurking inside.

He'd stood there holding a flashlight, shining it in
her face. "Put the dog down."

She'd begged him to let her get help for Moby. "He's
injured. He'll die if I don't get him to a veterinarian."

"Good. Put him down, or I'll stab him again." Randy
jerked the light to the side, revealing the long, wicked
knife in his other hand.

Emma gasped and turned away, knowing Randy
would follow through on that promise, though he'd broken every other promise he'd ever made to her and the
people of Cape Churn. "You're a despicable bastard."

"Maybe so, but I'm going to be a rich, despicable
bastard very soon. Not you, nor that muscle-bound
moron you've been sleeping with is going to stop me."

Before Randy could make good on his threat to stab
Moby, Emma gently laid the wounded animal on the
ground at the shoulder of the road. Hopefully no one
would run him over, and maybe someone would find
him in time to save him. Although, with the fog as

thick as it was, and no one knowing where to look, that possibility seemed unlikely. She patted the dog's head, tears running down her cheeks. "I'm sorry, boy. I love you."

Whining quietly, Moby tried to lift his head and let it fall back to the damp ground.

Randy gripped Emma's arm and jerked her away from the dog.

Moby growled, and lurched to his feet but fell back in the dirt.

"Randy, please. Let me go. Moby needs me."

"Yeah, and I need you more." Before Emma knew what he would do next, Randy slammed the flashlight against her temple.

A shaft of pain ripped through her head, and she fell to the ground, fighting to remain conscious. The fog crept in around her, blocking out all light and sound.

While she'd been out, Randy had zip-tied her wrists and ankles, plastered tape over her mouth and shoved her into the trunk of the car he'd parked on the side of the road.

She had no idea how long she'd been unconscious or where he'd taken her. The scent of tire rubber, oil and gasoline were constant and uninformative.

Emma felt around the interior of the trunk for something to cut the zip ties. Her hands closed around a tire iron, one end rounded for loosening bolts, the other end flat. She worked it around and braced it between her knees where the flat end pointed toward her chin. Her head pounding, she scraped the zip tie binding her wrists over the flat end of the tire iron, the hard plastic digging into her flesh as she pulled it as tight as she could.

The vehicle slowed, bumping over rough ground before coming to a stop. A door opened and slammed shut.

Not enough time. The zip tie still held her wrists. She gripped the tire iron between her hands and half rolled over it, facedown in the trunk.

A key scraped in the lock and the trunk opened, letting in a hazy glow. Probably from Randy's flashlight.

Emma lay still, pretending she was out cold.

When Randy leaned toward the trunk and poked her with the flashlight, she rolled onto her back and swung both arms with all her might, catching the corner of Randy's cheek with the knobby end of the tool and swinging through, knocking the flashlight from his hand.

He grabbed his face, cursing.

The flashlight rolled beneath the car, leaving the trunk in darkness.

Emma shoved her hands out of the opening, leveraged herself with her elbows over the rim and rolled out onto the ground.

Randy reached for her, and she kicked with both feet, landing a good blow in his chest, knocking him backward onto his butt.

With her hands and feet still tied, she tucked her arms close to her chest and rolled as fast and far away as she could, hoping she'd find vegetation to hide in until she could break the zip ties and run.

The more she rolled, the more she realized she was on some kind of weathered asphalt parking lot, complete with cracks and lumps of broken pavement.

Behind her, Randy grunted and cursed, the glow of

the flashlight on the move against the ground, rolling out of the man's reach.

Emma prayed he wouldn't snag the light before she found a place to hide, the asphalt seeming to go on forever. Her arms, legs and face took a beating against the pavement until she finally rolled up against what she thought might be a curb.

Hope flooded her and she inched up the curb, elbows first, then her torso. Before she could swing her hips and legs over, the flashlight caught her in its beam.

Randy laughed. "Go ahead. Roll on over that concrete barrier. I'd like to see you swim without your arms and legs."

Her legs in motion, ready to flip over the curb, Emma looked where the light shone, glistening off water fifteen feet below.

The curb was the edge of a pier. Her legs flailed in the air, teetered toward the ocean and hovered, suspended in time and space for a slow-motion moment.

Not ready to die, she willed her legs back to the parking lot pavement, all hope for escape crushed out of her.

"Thought you might reconsider." Randy stood over her, the flashlight pointing downward, blinding her. Then he reared back and kicked her in the face.

Pain ripped through her cheekbone, and warm sticky liquid dribbled down her chin. Her head spun, and she gave in to the black abyss reaching out to suck her in.

"That was payback." Randy jammed the flashlight on the open wound and leaned close enough she could see his sneering face. "If I didn't need you, I'd shoot you. Hit me again, and I will."

## Chapter 14

By the time they reached shore, Creed's stomach was knotted, and he needed to hit something or someone. No sooner had Dave pulled up to the dock, he was off the boat and running toward his SUV.

Tazer called out behind him. "Don't leave without us, Creed. You hear me?"

They'd have to hurry. He wasn't waiting for anyone.

Nova caught him first. "Where are you going?"

"I don't know. Somewhere, anywhere." Creed climbed into the rental and jammed the key into the ignition. "I can't stand around and do nothing."

"You can't go off half-cocked." Tazer ran around the vehicle and threw herself into the passenger seat. "We don't know where he took her."

Creed shifted into Drive. "I'll kill the bastard."

"Stand in line, buddy. Stand in line." Nova dove into

the backseat and clicked his belt in place, slamming the door shut as Creed spun out of the marina parking lot.

As the vehicle emerged onto the road leading down to the marina, two large, dark SUVs pulled in front of him, blocking his forward movement.

"We've got trouble," Creed said.

"Let's give it back to them." Tazer yanked her HK40 from her shoulder holster and pointed it out the window. "Can you back this thing up?"

Creed whipped the shift into Reverse and hit the gas, slamming into a third vehicle that appeared out of nowhere, trapping them.

He pulled his gun from his shoulder holster, shoved his door wide and dove out, rolling into the tall grasses on the side of road.

Gunfire erupted.

Nova and Tazer knew the drill and had made the same maneuver to escape the trapped vehicle. He prayed they hadn't been hit.

He low-crawled, scooting backward, deeper into the brush until he could determine just how many men Macias had deployed in the three vehicles. Lights glowed from the front two SUVs. Creed counted four men climbing out of each, all carrying AK-47 assault rifles. Eight. Four more men emerged from the rear vehicle. Three carried assault rifles. The fourth was unarmed.

Where were Tazer and Nova? He hadn't heard or seen signs of them since they'd abandoned the SUV. Two men disappeared into the darkness. Four shots were fired, and silence.

Then Nova was dragged into the headlights of the rear vehicle and dropped to the ground in front of Macias. The man pulled a pistol and held it to Nova's head. "Thomas, the diamonds or your friend's life."

Creed touched the bag tucked safely in his pocket. "Where's Emma?"

"The woman?" Macias nodded, and another two men dragged Tazer into view. "She's here. You want them to stay alive, I suggest you hand over the diamonds."

Creed's gut clenched. They didn't know. They hadn't been the ones keeping watch over Emma's house. They didn't know where she was. *Hell. Who had her?*

"Don't do it, CT," Nova said, his voice tight, filled with pain. "Don't give him those diamonds. We can handle this."

"Walk away with the diamonds, and you sentence your friends to death." One of the thugs pointed his AK-47 at Tazer's pretty blond head.

"Get out of here, Creed. Take the diamonds. The lives of too many people, important people, are at stake. Don't worry about us. These guys can't shoot straight anyway." Tazer dropped to her side, rolled backward and kicked the backs of the knees of the man who'd been holding the gun to her head. "Run!"

All Macias's men swarmed in like ants. They grabbed Tazer and Casanova, pushed their faces into the dirt and pressed rifles to the backs of their heads.

"The diamonds, or they die. You have thirty seconds to choose," Macias said.

Creed had no choice. He quietly removed his boot and sock, opened the velvet bag and poured half the diamonds into his empty sock. He slipped his bare foot back into the boot and tucked the diamond-filled sock into his boot, down below his arch. Carefully retying the velvet bag, he called out, "Let them go, and I'll let you have me and the diamonds."

"Not until you show your face *and* the diamonds," Macias said.

Nova pushed up to a kneeling position. "Don't do it, Creed."

"The others need you more." Tazer rose up on her arms.

Nova tipped his head to the side, to avoid the muzzle of the AK-47. "You know once he has the diamonds, he'll kill all of us anyway."

A big, burly thug hit Nova in his side with the butt of his weapon, and he doubled over.

Macias's eyes narrowed. "Your time is running out."

Creed stood. "I only have half of the diamonds on me. The rest are at a safe location. You can have the ones I have on me if you let these two go. I'll take you to the rest."

"No."

"Take it or leave it. You won't get the rest of the diamonds if you don't go for it now. And if you get stubborn, I'll scatter what I have all over." He held the bag of diamonds upside down, the drawstring closure a shake away from releasing a fortune into the rocks and dirt of the seaside landscape. "You have thirty seconds to choose."

Macias's lips pulled back into a menacing snarl. "Shoot him."

"Think about it. If I fall, the bag opens and the diamonds spill. It'll take you too long to find them, plus the other half I have at an undetermined, by you, location. I suspect you need all of the diamonds and less than all of them just won't do. So go ahead, shoot me. You won't get what I have here or what I have hidden."

Macias hesitated a moment longer, then jerked his head. "Tie them to a tree in the brush."

"No." Creed stepped forward. "Let them go free, or the deal is off." Two men stepped between Creed and Macias, AK-47s aimed at Creed's chest.

"And have them circle back and overtake us? I don't think so." Macias crossed his arms. "Show me you're not lying. Show me the diamonds."

Creed turned the bag right side up, untied it and poured diamonds into his palm. "A fortune in diamonds."

"I want the rest."

"And you will get them. When my friends are safe and no longer being threatened.

"I could kill you now, throw your body in the sea and no one would know."

"And *you* wouldn't know where to find the other diamonds." Creed stared hard at the terrorist. "I suspect you need all the jewels, not just half of them."

"Your friends stay here, tied up, or they come with us, tied up. My final offer." The man's eyes narrowed.

"We're going with you," Tazer answered for Creed.

Creed faced Macias, refusing to look at Casanova and Tazer. "Leave them. It's just as well. This is turning out to be another Rain Mountain." Rain Mountain had been an operation he and Tazer had worked together in which they'd run out of all options and had to involve the local authorities to tip the balance of power.

Tazer gave an imperceptible nod.

Unaware of the significance of Rain Mountain, Nova tried one last time. "Don't leave us."

"I never figured you'd turn your back on your friends."
Tazer shook her head, playing the part. "Creed, think about it."

"I have."

Macias jerked his head toward two of his men. "Tie them up, and you two stay and make sure they don't go anywhere. If Mr. Thomas double-crosses us, I'll give you the order to kill them." He nodded to Creed. "I'll take those diamonds now, and you can get in."

Creed handed the bag half-full of diamonds to Macias and started around him for the SUV. If he could get Macias and the rest of his men away from Tazer and Nova, the two guards left behind would prove little challenge to the trained SOS agents.

Macias stepped back. "Check him."

Holding perfectly still, Creed lifted his arms and let the men pat him down, praying they wouldn't find the rest of the diamonds in his sock.

They pounced on the concealed pistol beneath his jacket and the headset plugged in his ear. A cursory pat down of his legs and inside the top of his boots came up empty. They didn't find another weapon, and they didn't find the diamonds that had slid down to his heel. Creed hoped he wouldn't have to run anytime soon. If he had to make a quick escape, he'd find it difficult running with diamonds under his heels.

"Get in." Thug One held open the back door of the SUV.

Creed slid across to the middle. Two of Macias's men climbed in, one on each side of him, each holding a pistol to his head.

"You should be careful where you aim. You don't want those to go off by accident." He glanced at the man in the front passenger seat. "Your boss wouldn't get his pretty jewels."

"They are highly trained at their weapons. If they shoot you, it won't be by accident." Macias spoke without turning around.

The driver got in behind the wheel and pulled out on the road. Another vehicle followed.

Creed glanced back. Their SUV was still parked in the middle of the road, and the two men who'd stayed behind to tie up Tazer and Nova wouldn't know what hit them. Tazer had never met a rope or zip tie she couldn't work her thin wrists out of.

Creed had left the keys of the SUV in the ignition. It wouldn't be long before they took care of Macias's men, met up with the police chief and gathered forces, and then they would follow the GPS tracking device in the diamond bag.

Leaving Tazer and Nova behind didn't bother him. He knew they could take care of themselves. What drove him crazy was not knowing who had kidnapped Emma and why.

They'd traveled in silence for five minutes when Macias's cell phone beeped. He hit the talk button, speaking low and urgently to the person on the other end of the call. "One moment."

Macias turned to face Creed, glaring as he handed the phone across the seat.

Creed frowned. "What is this?"

Phillip Macias held up a pistol, aimed at Creed's face. "Answer it."

A bad feeling rippled across his senses, settling like a bad meal in his gut. "Thomas here."

"Creed?" Emma's voice came over the line.

Creed frowned. "Emma?"

She laughed shakily. "Funny thing happened while I was out walking Moby." Her voice hitched. "I've been kidnapped. It's Randy Walters. My poor excuse for an ex-fiancé come back from the dead. He seems to think I'm some kind of bargaining chip. Ha! The joke's on him."

He could tell by her tone and the false bravado that she was scared, and it made his chest hurt. "I'm coming, Emma."

She went on as if he hadn't said anything. "I told him I meant nothing to you. If he wants to hold me for ransom, he's out of luck. I'm not important to anyone. The laugh's on him."

"It's not up for discussion," Creed insisted.

"I told you, Randy." Her voice faded as the phone was taken away from her. "He doesn't care. Guess you're out of luck."

"Shut up, Emma." A smacking sound echoed through the phone, and Emma grunted.

Randy's voice came over the receiver. "You want to see her alive, get here with Macias and those diamonds, or I'll deliver her to you in pieces."

A stab to the heart couldn't have been more painful. Creed pressed a hand to his chest. "I'll bring the diamonds."

The man's voice came back on the line. "If you don't bring all the diamonds with Macias to our rendezvous location in the next thirty minutes, Emma dies."

"Don't do it, Creed!" Emma shouted in the background. Then she cried out, and there was silence.

"Emma!" Creed yelled.

Macias snatched the phone from his hand. "The

woman back there wasn't Emma." His eyes flashed, his cheeks red. "You lied to me."

"What does it matter? You're getting what you wanted. The diamonds to trade for the uranium."

"Yeah. With the added bonus that you and the girl will die."

Not if Creed could keep that from happening. With part of his backup flying into Portland and then having to drive through the hellish fog, and the other half tied to a tree, being guarded by dangerous men with weapons, Creed's chances of getting Emma out alive looked dismal.

But he refused to give up. As long as he had air to breathe, he had to keep trying. Moby needed Emma. Hell, *he* needed Emma. The damned stubborn, lovable woman had gotten completely under his skin, and he didn't want her to be anywhere else.

He sent a silent prayer to the heavens for guidance, and for time and patience to make the right decisions.

"Where are the rest of the diamonds?" Macias demanded. "Time is running out, along with my sense of humor."

Creed doubted Macias ever had a sense of humor, and he bit down hard on his tongue to keep from saying it out loud. Instead, he said, "They're in a little cottage on Sand Dollar Lane." He had to buy enough time for Tazer and Nova to free themselves and gather the cavalry. Hopefully Royce and Sean were on the ground and headed their way and wouldn't run off the road in this infernal fog spawned by the Devil.

Thirty minutes had to be enough time to stall the big showdown and for his troops to gather. With Macias's army of mercenaries and whatever Randy had waiting with him and Emma, Creed would need all the help he could get to extract Emma alive.

At Emma's house with Macias and two of his armed guards, Creed broke the back window on the kitchen door and unlocked it, stepping over the broken glass. He walked through the house, picturing every kiss he and Emma had shared.

Bringing Macias and his men in her inner sanctum felt like a violation of her space, and he regretted it. But if he could somehow distract Macias and his men long enough for him to pull the diamonds out of his boot, and maybe retrieve Emma's gun from her night-stand, he'd have a party favor to take to the big event.

The men waited just inside the bedroom door. Creed paused beside Emma's bed and opened the drawer he'd seen her pull lace underwear and a foil-packed con-dom from. While he rifled through, pulling out silky, lacy, skimpy underwear one by one, he slipped his other hand beneath her pillow, his body blocking his hand and arm. He purposely dropped bright, red lace panties on the floor. When the men's gazes followed the underwear, Creed grabbed the HK380 Emma kept hidden beneath and tucked it into the back of his jeans.

Macias and his men watched the lacy underwear, completely unaware of Creed's other find.

Once he had the gun hidden beneath his shirt, he squatted lower. "I know it's in here." He pulled out another pair of panties, lifted the sock out of his boot, palmed it and shoved his hand deep into the remaining lingerie. "Ah, there it is." He withdrew his hand and dangled the sock in front of Phillip. "Just like I said."

Macias snatched for the sock. "Give them to me."

Creed jerked it out of his reach. "The man wanted

*me* to deliver the diamonds, and you were to come with me. I suggest we go along with his wishes. You'll get what you came for, and I'll get Emma."

Macias's lip curled back. "I should have killed you."

"Yeah, well, now you can't without jeopardizing your trade, can you?" Creed straightened, aware of the hard metal digging into his back. His shirt and the leather jacket he wore covered it, but all it would take was for one of Macias's men to bump into him, and he'd be caught. He glanced at his watch. "We have exactly twenty minutes to get to the rendezvous point. I hope you know where it is. I get the feeling Walters doesn't like it when people are late."

Creed left through the door they'd used to enter and hurried to take his seat in the back of the SUV. He'd stalled all he could and hoped it was enough. One HK380 wasn't nearly enough firepower to take out an army of terrorists.

Emma blinked her eyes open to a splitting headache and one eye swelling enough to impair her vision. Her wrists were still zip-tied, but Randy had cut the ties binding her legs so that she could walk inside the empty fish processing plant. A single battery-powered lantern, sitting on what appeared to be a metal case perched on top of a large crate, cast a soft yellow glow in a wide circle in the middle of the room. The place still smelled of fish, though it appeared to have been closed for years, with lacy spider webs filling every corner and a layer of dust covering the horizontal surfaces.

Movement at the door drew her attention. A man turned toward the light. He carried an assault rifle and extra thirty-round magazines tucked into a utility belt around his waist.

Randy stood at a grimy window, staring out.

Emma forced words out of her dry throat and cracked lips. "He's not coming."

"Shut up." Randy remained with his back to her.

"He doesn't care about me like that. He wouldn't risk his life to save mine."

"The man shacked up with you. He'll be here."

"Just because a man slept with me doesn't mean he loves me. Look at you." She pushed to her feet, working the zip tie she'd damaged while still confined to the trunk of his car. It had to have been compromised. If she wiggled it enough, surely it would break. With only two men in the warehouse, she could figure a way out of this nightmare.

Randy glanced over his shoulder, a sneer lifting his lip on one side. "I only slept with you to get the money I needed."

"The money you needed to buy the uranium?" Emma nodded toward the metal case. "Is that it? Is that the uranium you're willing to sell to a terrorist?"

"What do you know? You're just a dumb nurse from a small town. You were nothing but a means to an end."

"Maybe so. But I learned from the best liar there was not to trust people." She nodded toward the window. "I learned what it felt like to be in over my head. And let me tell you. You're in way over your head with Phillip Macias. He's an extremist with an army of fanatics at his disposal."

"Shut up." Randy turned toward her, pointing a forty-five caliber pistol at her. "I know what I'm doing. Just shut the hell up, or I'll gag you." He glanced back out the window, keeping his gun pointed in her general direction.

"Did you use the hospital's money to buy the uranium?"

"It's none of your business."

"It was my business when my former fiancé, whom I'd recommended to the board, stole the money. The least you can do is tell me what you did with it."

"Yes! I bought the uranium. Are you happy? Now shut up."

"You realize they're going to use the uranium to make dirty bombs and blow up Los Angeles and Seattle?"

"I'm not stupid." He snorted. "I plan to be on the other side of the ocean when they attack."

"And all the people they kill, the men, women and small children…don't you feel the least bit sorry for them?"

"There are too many people in this world as it is. As a graduate of the foster care system, I know firsthand. People throw their kids away. They're better off dead."

"You were one of them. Do you think you would have been better off dead?"

"Hell, yes! Then I wouldn't have been beaten by my own mother, farmed out to abusive foster parents, bullied by other kids in the so-called system and forced to run away when I was fourteen to escape it. Fourteen, on my own, on the street. Who cared about me? No one. Not a single damn soul. Why should I care about anyone else but me? They're better off dead."

Emma's heart went out to the kid no one wanted, but she couldn't discard the ones who still had a chance at a future. "I'm sorry you had a tough childhood, Randy. But taking it out on others won't make it better."

"I don't care what happens to the others. I'm taking my diamonds, and I'm going to sell them a little at a time and live on an island paradise where I can do anything I want, have anything I want by just snapping my fingers." He snapped his fingers as if to prove his point.

"Those diamonds won't buy happiness, Randy. It's not too late to stop this."

"Emma, you talk too much. Shut up!" He pointed the pistol at her feet and fired, kicking up a puff of dust.

Emma flinched but didn't back off. "You're not as hard-hearted as you let on."

"I killed your dog, and you can say that?" He laughed. "You loved that dog more than you ever loved me."

Emma swallowed the lump in her throat, forcing back the image of Moby lying on the side of the road, hurt, lost and looking to her to make things right. She wanted to bring harm to Randy for what he'd done to Moby, but so many people's lives were on the line. She couldn't think only of herself and Moby.

"You don't have to do this. There's still time to turn yourself in. Cut a deal with the feds to hand over Macias. You'll be a hero."

"Bullshit. I'd go straight to jail, I would not pass go, I would not collect two hundred dollars. I've been there. I won't go back. Ever."

"Randy, it's not too late—"

"Enough! It *is* too late, anyway. They're here." He crossed to the suitcase, moved the lantern to the floor beside it, opened it and clicked a few buttons, the electronic beeping the only noise Emma could hear in the room.

"What are you doing?" she asked, a bad feeling filling her gut.

Randy grinned. "Protecting myself and my investment."

# Chapter 15

When Philip Macias's two SUVs pulled into what appeared to be a deserted warehouse on a remote road south of Cape Churn, Creed stiffened, a hundred scenarios roiling through his head. At least he still had Emma's pistol. Macias's bodyguards hadn't frisked him or knocked it loose from where it was snugly tucked into the back of his jeans.

As far as he knew, he was alone in this event. Until his backup arrived, he had to stall any shootings and stay alive long enough to get Emma out in one piece. The only way his team would find them was tracking the bag of diamonds with the GPS device sewn into it. It had to be enough.

Creed suspected, between Walters and Macias, they planned on killing the witnesses. That would be Emma and himself. They'd be considered loose ends. And

Macias would give the kill order for Tazer and Nova as soon as the trade took place.

He wouldn't put it past Macias to kill Walters, as well.

Phillip climbed down from the SUV, pulled a pistol from beneath his jacket and waited for the driver to round the side of the SUV and provide cover for him before he moved forward. The two men in the backseat with Creed got out, one of them jerking Creed with him.

"I'm getting out. I don't need help doing it," he muttered, praying the gun wouldn't dislodge and fall on the ground at his feet. He scooted across the backseat, climbed out as quickly as he could and performed a quick scan of the surrounding area.

Armed guards stood at each corner of the building, semiautomatic weapons aimed at Phillip and his nine men. There had to be more. Walters had gone to a lot of trouble to make this trade; he had to know Phillip Macias would come with enough firepower to insure he got what he came for and possibly leave no witnesses, as was his usual way of doing business.

"Walters!" Phillip called out. "I have your diamonds."

The door to the warehouse opened and another armed man stepped out, followed by a man Creed recognized from the picture he'd seen hanging on Emma's refrigerator of her and Walters with the bright red $X$ drawn through Walter's image.

"Where is Emma?" Creed demanded.

"Ah, you must be the man who'd shacked up with her to get to the diamonds. You're not much different from me." He reached inside the door and yanked

Emma out to stand in front of him, pointing a nine-millimeter pistol at her temple.

Her wrists were bound in front of her, and her right eye was swollen almost shut. "You shouldn't have come," she said through split lips.

Anger boiled up inside Creed, and he fought not to charge across the cracked pavement of the parking lot and choke the man with his bare hands.

Phillip strode forward, his bodyguards moving with him. "I came here to make a deal, not argue over women. Where is it?"

"Show me the diamonds," Walters said. "And I'll show you the uranium."

Phillip handed the velvet bag over to one of his men who walked it across to where Walters stood. His guard stepped in front of him, his weapon pointed at Macias's man. Macias's man held out the bag, and Walters's man took it.

"Open it." Randy trained his pistol on Phillip.

The man slung his gun over his shoulder and emptied the bag into his palm.

Randy stared at the diamonds, his eyes widening, then narrowing. "That's only about half of them. Where are the rest?"

Phillip nodded toward Creed. "The girl's boyfriend has them."

"I want all the diamonds, or you don't get the uranium."

Creed fished the sock full of diamonds from his pocket and held them up. "Let the girl go, and I'll give you the diamonds."

Randy laughed. "You must think you have leverage in this situation."

Creed grabbed the sock from the other end. "Let her go, or I scatter the diamonds everywhere."

"Oh, don't be so melodramatic." Walters glanced at his watch, then turned to Macias. "You have exactly five minutes to give me all my diamonds, or the deal's off."

Phillip's eyes narrowed. "What's to stop me from shooting you and your men and taking the diamonds and the uranium?"

Walters shook his head. "I wouldn't do that if I were you." He glanced at his watch again. "Four minutes, thirty seconds."

"Or what?"

"I helped you out a bit by assembling the dirty bomb for you, complete with a timer set to go off in—" he looked at his watch "—four minutes."

Phillip gasped "Are you insane?"

Walters shrugged. "How else was I going to get out of this alive? Your reputation precedes you, and I wasn't going to be the next moron to fall to your ruthless negotiation methods. All you have to do is give me the diamonds." He looked from Phillip to Creed. "All of them. I'll leave and, when I'm well out of range of your bullets, I'll text the code you can use to stop the timer."

"How do we know you're not lying?" Creed asked, his gut churning at how this mission could potentially end.

"I saw him set the timer," Emma said, her tone flat, the rest of her face pale beneath the dark purple shiner.

"Three minutes, thirty," Randy said. "It takes time to get out of the parking lot and to text back. I suggest you make a decision now."

Phillip pointed his pistol at Creed. "Give him the damn diamonds."

Creed saw no other option. If the bomb went off, they'd all be dead, and probably all of the people in Cape Churn, too. "Let Emma go."

"You don't have the choice. Give me the diamonds," Randy said.

"Give him the diamonds!" Phillip fired a shot at Creed's feet.

Creed had stalled all he could. His team wouldn't make it there in time to save them. If he didn't give the diamonds over and let Walters go, it wouldn't matter anyway.

"Okay, take them." Creed slung the sock full of diamonds in the air like a slow-pitch softball, aiming for the guard beside Walters.

As the guard reached for the diamonds, shots were fired from the darkness of the fog. The guard reaching for the diamonds jerked backward, slamming into the wall of the warehouse. The sock full of diamonds plopped against the concrete, unclaimed.

Four of the men who'd come with Phillip collapsed where they stood, two lying still, unmoving, one clutching his chest, moaning, the other trying to lift a shattered right arm and failing to raise his gun to fire back. The two men beside Phillip jerked backward, hit the SUV and slid to the ground.

Creed dropped to the ground, low-crawled to the front of one of the SUVs, yanked the gun from the back of his jeans, aimed the HK380 at the shins of two of Phillip's men and fired twice, hitting both men. They went down, screaming and clutching their legs. Not knowing how many rounds he had left, he rolled over and pointed his weapon at Randy Walters.

The man wasn't there, and neither was Emma. The door to the warehouse slammed shut with the two of them inside with an unexploded bomb.

"Cover me!" Creed yelled to his team, scrambled to his feet and ran for the door.

A bullet winged past his head as he reached for the knob, turned it and threw himself inside, tumbling to the side and rolling up onto his feet behind a stack of pallets.

A shot rang out, hitting the concrete bricks over Creed's head, spitting concrete down over his head.

"Two minutes until the bomb goes off. Are you willing to sacrifice thousands of lives?"

Creed's eyes adjusted to the limited lighting provided by a single lantern in the middle of the room. It sat beside a silver metal suitcase he assumed contained the bomb.

Movement on the other side of the lantern alerted him to Walter's whereabouts.

"Give it up, Walters. You won't get out alive," Creed warned.

"If that's the case, we all die." The man laughed. "And you won't need Emma."

"Let her go, disable the bomb, and I promise I'll get you out of here alive."

"I want my diamonds," Walters insisted.

"Fine. I'll get you out of here *with* the diamonds," Creed said.

"How can I trust you?" Walters asked.

"You have the word of a navy SEAL."

The man snorted. "And that's supposed to reassure me?"

"Let Emma go and take me as your hostage. I'll help you get out." Creed held up his hand with the gun. "I'll throw down my weapon as soon as you let her go."

Walters had Emma firmly in front of him, her body blocking any good shot Creed could take. "Throw it down first, and I'll let her go."

"Don't do it, Creed, he's going to shoot you," Emma cried out.

"I told you to shut up!" Walters hit Emma across the temple with the butt of his gun. Emma collapsed against him, her head lolling to the side, giving Creed a clean shot at Walters.

Creed aimed the little HK380. The pistol didn't have enough power to slam the man backward. His hand steady, Creed prayed he wouldn't hit Emma, and he squeezed the trigger.

Walters screamed, dropped his hold on Emma and fell to the ground.

Creed scrambled across the floor toward Emma. She lay on the fringe of the lantern's glow, her body still, her eyes closed. He felt for a pulse, found it and breathed a short-lived sigh of relief.

"Creed! Look out for Macias!" A voice shouted from outside.

Someone dove through the door and rolled to his feet into the shadows.

Creed figured they didn't have much time left before the bomb exploded. Even if they got out of the building and drove away as fast as they could, the bomb would blow them all away and everyone in Cape Churn with them.

Creed grabbed the nine-millimeter pistol Walters had dropped, left Emma lying on the floor, figuring she was better off low to the ground, and moved back into the shadows. Using every ounce of stealth training he'd learned during his stint as a navy SEAL, he stepped carefully, laying his feet down so quietly, he could only hear his heart thumping inside his chest.

A scuffling sound came from his right. He turned, aimed his weapon at the sound and waited for a silhouette to materialize.

Like an apparition disengaging from one shadow to move and blend into another, Macias slipped sideways. Creed squeezed the trigger. The weapon kicked harder than the HK380, but Creed's hand held steady.

A grunt was followed swiftly by a thump, and all was still and silent but for the sporadic gunfire outside the building.

Creed edged back to the lantern, grabbed it and lifted it high. Phillip Macias lay against the floor, a hole in his chest, where bright red blood stained the front of his shirt. He lay still, his eyes open, vacant.

Behind him, Emma groaned and pushed to a sitting position. "Creed. We have to stop the bomb."

"We don't know the code."

"He didn't use one to open the case." She crawled across the floor to the metal suitcase and flipped it open. "Oh, dear God, we only have twenty seconds left."

Creed raced across the room, raised the lantern and dropped down beside her, holding it high enough to see what they were doing.

"What do I do?" she asked.

"It's wired to the timer." Creed stared down at what

appeared to be a case within the case and an electronic timer.

"Nine, eight, seven." Emma spoke the numbers as they changed on the clock. Then she grabbed Creed's face and pulled it down to hers. "In case we don't make it, I just wanted you to know, I think I love you."

With one second left on the clock, Creed reached in, twisted his fingers around the wires leading out of the timer and yanked as hard as he could. The clock ticked over to zeros.

Creed held Emma's gaze. His breath caught and held in his throat.

The clock buzzed like an alarm waking the late sleeper.

Emma jumped, but nothing happened.

Creed pulled her up and into his arms, hugging her close, his hands skimming over her body. He wanted to memorize the feel of her in his arms. "When you disappeared, I thought I'd never see you again."

"You found me and saved me." She cupped his face and brushed his bottom lip with her thumb.

"No, you saved us all." He bent to kiss her, pressing gently.

She winced. "Ouch."

"What did that bastard do to you?"

"Just a few bruises. I'll live." Her eyes rounded. "Moby."

"Is being cared for now. The entire fire department was looking out for him."

She leaned her good cheek against his chest. "Does this mean your mission's over and you're going back to wherever it is you came from?"

He brushed the hair away from her forehead, careful not to touch her bruises. "I guess that depends."

"On?" Her fingers slipped across his shirt.

"Our first real date."

"Are you asking me out?"

"Sounds like it."

"Will it involve diving?"

"No."

"Ducking bullets?"

"No bullets."

"Smuggling diamonds?"

He chuckled. "No."

"How will you possibly keep me entertained?" She grinned up at him.

"High maintenance, aren't you?"

"I have my standards." She slipped her hand beneath his shirt, her cool fingers feeling great against his heated skin. Even with her eyes swollen and her lips split, she was the bravest, most beautiful woman Creed had ever seen.

"Umm." He skimmed a hand down her back to cup her bottom. "I'll come up with something to occupy you."

"Creed, Emma?" Tazer called through the door. "I'm coming in." The muzzle of an assault rifle preceded Tazer as she edged around the door and into the shadows.

"Walters is on your left. Check for a pulse, will ya?" Creed said. "My hands are full."

Tazer dropped down beside Walters. "Ha. Got a pulse, a weak one. But we might be able to salvage something to interrogate."

Casanova stepped through the doorway. "Royce will be glad to hear that."

Another man entered behind Casanova. "I'd be glad to hear what?"

"That our uranium dealer might live to spill." Creed held Emma close to him. "You clean up outside?"

"We got thirteen. Nine dead, four wounded." Sean McNeal entered behind Royce.

"Glad to see the cavalry arrived," Creed commented.

"Chief Taggart has ambulances on the way."

Royce glanced around. "What happened with Macias?"

"He's over there." Creed turned toward the body on the floor in the shadows.

At the exact moment he realized Macias wasn't where he'd left him, a shot rang out.

Emma jerked, her fingers curling into his skin. "Damn. I was looking forward to our date." Her eyes rolled to the back of her head, and she slid down his side.

Four bullets hit Macias at once, while Creed gathered Emma against him and lifted her. "Emma." She didn't respond. "Where's the ambulance? Where's the damned ambulance?"

Creed hurried toward the warehouse door, Emma lying limp in his arms, his heart crashing down around his knees. "Emma, hold on, girl. You're not getting out of this date that easily. And Moby's counting on you for treats and walks. He'll be on his feet and looking for you. Damn it, Emma, wake up."

Before he knew it, he was outside, surrounded by police, SOS agents and paramedics.

"Creed, let the paramedics help her." Royce touched his shoulder. "She'll be okay."

"She has to be."

The emergency personnel dragged a gurney out of the back of an ambulance.

Creed laid Emma onto it and stepped back while the techs applied pressure to the wound in her gut and hooked up an IV.

Another EMT ran a handheld radiation detection device over her and then moved on to Creed. When he was satisfied they were within acceptable levels, he gave a thumbs-up.

Helpless to do anything, Creed stood by, afraid to breathe, afraid to watch but more afraid to look away.

"Blood pressure's dropping," one medic said.

"We're losing her," the other said.

"Not tonight," the man working over her growled, his jaw set, his hands moving over her. "The Devil's Shroud isn't getting Nurse Jenkins. Not only would every doctor and nurse at Cape Churn Memorial hate me, my wife would divorce me."

"Then let's make sure that doesn't happen." They bent to the task of saving Emma.

"Must be some internal injuries. We have to get her to the hospital." They raised the gurney and ran it toward the back of the ambulance, sliding it in, then jumping in with her.

Creed followed. "I'm going with her."

The ambulance driver grabbed his arm to keep him from getting into the ambulance. "Sorry, they've got their work cut out for them and need room to do their jobs." He closed the door behind them.

The EMTs went back to work forcing air into

Emma's lungs while the driver secured the door and ran for the cab, calling over his shoulder, "We're taking her to Cape Churn Memorial. You can follow us." The ambulance pulled out of the parking lot and up onto the highway.

Creed glanced right and left. He'd come with Phillip and his thugs. One of their vehicles stood with the doors wide-open, bullet holes in the sides. He ran for it, jumped into the driver's seat and reached for the key in the ignition.

"Creed, let one of us drive." Tazer stepped up on the running board and laid a hand on his shoulder. "You're upset and in no condition to drive."

"Get down." He shifted into Reverse and backed up with Tazer still hanging on to the door.

"Damn, Creed, you trying to kill me?" She held on tight. "If you're not going to let me drive, at least stop long enough for me to get in."

"Me, too." Casanova jumped through the open passenger seat door. Tazer dropped down off the running board and spun around the back door and hopped in, pulling it closed as Creed spun out of the parking lot.

"She's gonna be okay, buddy," Nova said. "You saw those medics. They love her almost as much as you do."

Creed's chest felt as though it was caught in a vise grip and someone was tightening the screws. Phillip was supposed to have been dead. Emma was supposed to be okay. How could he be so careless?

"You can't blame yourself," Tazer said from the backseat. "You couldn't know he'd shoot her."

"I should have checked on him as soon as we secured the bomb."

"You thought he was dead."

"But he wasn't, damn it!"

"He's dead now," Nova said. "One less terrorist in the world. Millions can sleep easier, knowing they have a better chance of waking up in the morning."

"All because of Emma," Creed said softly.

"How so?"

"She found the diamonds. And she saved my life three times. And I couldn't save her once."

"You saved her from a ticking time bomb and Randy Walters. He would have killed her."

Creed didn't listen—he couldn't, not when it took all his concentration not to run off the road. He stayed back far enough from the ambulance and set his pace slower, not wanting to risk running into the back of the vehicle and injuring Emma more or the people working to keep her alive.

By the time he reached the outskirts of Cape Churn, his hands and arms were cramped and his head and chest ached with all the thoughts swirling around inside. Was Emma okay?

Creed pulled up behind the ambulance in the emergency entrance, jumped out and followed as they wheeled Emma into the hospital. Her face was pale beneath the oxygen mask, and she was breathing through a tube.

They rolled her into the hospital.

"Sounds like she has a collapsed lung, and no telling what other internal injuries," the lead EMT said.

A man in a white coat ran alongside the gurney. "We'll need to get her prepped for surgery." They wheeled her past the examination rooms and straight into the elevator. With so many attending, Creed couldn't fit with her. As the elevator doors slid closed,

Creed watched Emma's face, praying it wouldn't be the last time he saw her.

"Sir, you can wait in the surgery waiting room, if you'd like." The pretty nurse Jenna touched his arm. "I'd be happy to show you where."

"Creed." Tazer ran toward him. "We parked the vehicle out of the way. What's happening with the girl?"

"Emma." He ran a hand through his hair, standing it on end. "They took her straight to surgery."

"That bad?" Nova asked. "Poor kid."

"Emma's a fighter. I've never known a nicer, more compassionate nurse, or a stronger woman," Jenna said with a soft smile. "She'll be okay."

Creed wanted to believe Jenna. The alternative wasn't thinkable. The few days he'd spent with Emma had been crazy, hectic, dangerous and more wonderful than any other time in his life. He wanted to dive with her again. To explore new places and to experience life with her by his side, pointing out how he could make a difference.

Emma made him feel useful, loved and like he had a real purpose in life. Having just found her—no, having *finally* found her—he didn't want to lose another day with her.

Jenna led the way to the waiting room on the second floor, fixed a fresh batch of coffee in the coffeemaker and left him in the company of Tazer and Casanova.

With nothing but time and worry on his hands, Creed called the police dispatcher and asked if she knew the status of Emma Jenkins's dog.

"Moby? Since I've had more calls about Emma and Moby than anything else tonight, I got hold of the vet who reports that Moby is going to be fine. He's all stitched up, has been given antibiotics and a sedative and should sleep through the night. By morning, the vet expects he'll be yowling for Emma."

Creed thanked the dispatcher, amazed at how this small town looked out for everyone else *and* their dog.

Royce and Sean McNeal entered the waiting room an hour later.

"We left the police to clean up the mess of Macias's and Walters's hired guns."

"What I want to know is how Walters got enriched uranium?"

Royce grinned. "Once he knew he wasn't getting away with anything, Walters was ready to squeal like a stuck pig. From what we'd learned through our background check and what he told us, Randall Walters worked for an oil company out of Saudi up until a year ago when he quit his job. But not until after he'd made a few contacts and discovered, among Iranian dissidents, the source of the stolen enriched uranium. He came back to America to find a quiet location along the coast to bring in the uranium and lucked into the job at the hospital, where he got the funding for his little project.

"He made the plans and had the cargo shipped to the States in the crate you saw in that warehouse. We have the biohazard team working on moving the uranium to a safe location."

Creed glanced up when the nurse passed in the hallway outside the waiting room, his mind on Emma, not uranium.

"So what happens now?"

"The uranium will be disposed of, and Walters will go to jail."

"Good." Creed ran a hand through his hair. "What's taking them so damned long?"

Tazer laid a hand on his arm. "Emma's tough. She's going to pull through just fine."

Another hour passed, and still no word on Emma.

Creed paced, Tazer and Nova stopped trying to re-assure him and Royce took a seat—all his teammates were there for him, no matter the outcome.

Sweat beaded on his upper lip the more he paced and the longer it took for the doctor to complete his work and deliver his prognosis for Emma's recovery. Night crept into morning. The fog lifted enough that they could almost see the cape and the flotilla of sailboats anchored near the marina. The sun had broken through the low-lying clouds and started on its upward climb into the sky by the time the doctor stepped through the doors into the waiting room.

"Ms. Jenkins has stabilized. We patched what we could find that was torn or broken when the bullet went through her. She'll be out of it, probably until tomorrow morning, in a drug-induced sleep. You might as well go home."

"I'm staying," Creed said.

"We're moving her to ICU for the night, but we expect she'll be ready to move into a regular room by tomorrow morning. She's lucky the bullet went all the way through and didn't hit any vital organs." The doctor gave them a tired smile. "We're just glad she made it. Nurse Jenkins is special."

And how Creed knew it. "Can I stay with her in ICU?"

The doctor frowned. "ICU visiting rules are five minutes at a time, and relatives only."

His hopes crushed, Creed scrambled for some reason, excuse or argument that would satisfy the hospital rules. He had to see her. Had to know she was going to be okay throughout the night.

"She doesn't have any relatives," Jenna said.

Tazer stepped up beside Creed. "Does a fiancé count?" She elbowed Creed in the midsection.

"Why, yes, it does." The doctor grinned. "This is news to me. Why didn't she tell us? Who's the lucky guy?"

"Me." His heart beating faster, Creed dared to hope he could get away with this ruse. "It's all so recent."

"I bet she didn't tell anyone because she's probably still embarrassed after her former fiancé ran off with the hospital money." The doctor shook his head. "We told her it wasn't her fault. But she took it so personally. She's been donating most of her paycheck to the children's wing fund to repay the money lost."

The doctor clapped his hands together and stared at Creed. "So you're her fiancé." The doctor stuck out his hand. "She's a great girl. Any man would be lucky to have her. And I'm glad to see she's chosen someone who really cares about her."

Creed felt like a fraud. They weren't engaged, and he had no right to be in her room. He opened his mouth to tell the truth, but he couldn't. And what was the truth, anyway?

He wanted to be with Emma for more than just her stay in the hospital. He wanted to be by her side for the long haul. When had he come to that conclusion? And did it matter? The important thing was to get Emma well and back on her feet so that he could take her out on that honest-to-goodness date he'd promised. Then he'd work on making their engagement the real deal.

The doctor clapped a hand on his back. "I think we can arrange for her fiancé to stay with her, if you don't mind sitting up in a chair all night."

"Not at all."

"I'll see to it." The doctor left the waiting room.

"Where's Emma?" Dave Logsdon entered the waiting room, his eyes wild. "Oh, please tell me I'm not too late."

"Another one of Emma's fan club?" Royce smiled.

Creed met Dave at the door. "She came through surgery just fine."

Dave's shoulders slumped. "Oh, thank goodness. All I heard was she'd been shot."

"Now that you all know Emma's going to be okay," Jenna said, "you can go home and get some rest." She herded them out of the waiting room. "Emma's not going to wake until morning. Sitting around the waiting room won't make her wake sooner." As the others headed for the elevator, she snagged Creed's arm. "You can come with me."

She led him down the hall, passing ICU rooms, opened one and held it for him. "They just settled her in."

Amidst wires and monitors, Emma lay with a breathing tube in her nose, her eyes closed, the bruises on her cheek and eye the darkest spots on her face.

Jenna pointed toward the chair. "Have a seat. I'll get you a blanket. It gets cold in here at night."

"I don't need one. But Emma might."

"I have one warming for her. I'll be right back." Jenna smiled and left the room.

Creed stood beside the bed, staring down at Emma. He'd been with SEAL teammates caught in the line of enemy fire and had them die in his arms. That helpless feeling of not being able to do anything made his knees weak and his heart ache.

He lifted her hand and threaded her fingers through his. She had long, supple fingers that nurtured the sick, swam in the ocean and cared for those she loved. The woman was amazing, and he'd be lucky to have her in his life. If she'd have him.

After an hour hovering over her bedside, the steady beat of the heart monitor calmed Creed enough to pull a chair up beside her bed and lean his head against her hand. After all that had happened and being awake for two whole days, exhaustion tugged at him. He fought it, wracking his brain for what he could do to convince Emma to give him a chance to win her heart. When the idea came to him, he let go of consciousness and slept, knowing he had a tough task ahead of him and he needed to be rested to accomplish it.

# Chapter 16

When Emma woke, her chest hurt, her tongue was dry and she was hungry.

Kayla McGregor sat beside her. "About time you woke up. We thought you were going to sleep through the rest of your twenties."

"What happened?"

Kayla's brows wrinkled. "What do you remember?"

"Creed shot Randy, and then he kissed me. It's all a blur after that."

"Must have been a heck of a kiss." Kayla counted off on her fingers. "Let's see. That Macias guy shot you last night. You almost died. The doctor patched you up, and you're going to be fine." Kayla took Emma's hand and pressed it to her cheek, blinking back tears. "And promise me you won't scare me like that ever again."

"I promise." Emma squeezed Kayla's hand and asked, "How's Moby?"

"The vet kept him overnight. He's probably driving the vet techs at the clinic nuts by now."

A heavy weight lifted from Emma's heart. Moby would be okay. "How long have I been out?"

"It's almost seven o'clock now. That's p.m., for those of us who slept for almost two days. And they are more than ready to move you to a room of your own and out of ICU. I had to twist a lot of arms to get in to see you here, and there are a lot of others who want their turn."

"You shouldn't have come. But I'm glad you did." Emma's eyes widened. "Who's watching the baby?"

"Gabe's at home with her while I'm visiting."

"He can change a diaper?"

"He's actually pretty good at it." Kayla squeezed her hand. "Anything I can get you?"

"Water and breakfast."

Kayla smiled. "You're hungry. I take that as a good sign. You had me worried for a while there. Thought I almost lost Tonya's godmother."

"No way. I plan on sticking around for her wedding." Emma stared around the room, disappointment bringing ready tears to her eyes. She'd been out of it for two entire days. With Randy dead and the plot to destroy the west coast foiled, had Creed moved on? Without saying goodbye?

"If you're looking for Creed, he had to leave around noon yesterday to, as he put it, take care of business."

"Oh. He was here?"

"All night long for the past two nights. He had the nurses in ICU checking on your every blip."

Warmth stole over her, filling her with hope. "Did he say whether or not he'd be back?"

"No, but the rest of his crew cleared out of town today."

"Oh." Which meant if he hadn't gone with them, he'd be following soon enough.

"I'll get that water and see if I can get them to scrounge up some food for you."

"Thanks, Kayla. You're a good friend." Emma's eyelids drifted closed, the sedatives dragging her back to sleep. The next time she woke, Kayla had gone and Jenna was there with another nurse to help her onto a gurney. "We're moving you to a room of your own, out of ICU. Dr. Matthews said you're doing better than expected. He thinks you should be released soon."

Emma made the move, checking the hallway as they went for any sign of Creed. Nothing. Jenna administered more pain meds before Emma could protest, and she was out again, her sleep filled with dreams of Creed there beside her, holding her hand and kissing her lips. She wanted to wake up to look into his eyes and tell him she was falling in love with him, but her eyelids were too heavy. She contented herself with holding his hand in her dreams, wishing she could do a whole lot more.

When she woke the next morning, she was alone in the room. Kayla wasn't there to cheer her up, Jenna had gone off duty and the day shift was probably busy distributing morning meds and helping other patients. Emma had grown up in Cape Churn and had always felt a sense of family there, even after her parents had died. Maybe it was a side effect of the pain meds, but despite this being her home, she'd never felt as lonely or depressed as she did at that moment.

What did she have? A house, a dog, a good job and

great friends. A lot more than many people. But she didn't have what she wanted most. What Kayla had. Someone to love, to come home to and build a family with. All the years that she'd told herself she was fine and happy with the way things were, she'd been lying to herself. She wanted what her parents had. Love.

Right then she'd have been happy to have that date Creed had promised her. One lousy date. But she hadn't seen him since the abandoned fish warehouse. He might be regretting that promise.

The day dragged on, filled with visitors, everyone including Gabe, Sal and Olie, the chief of police and his wife, all congratulating her on helping stop a terrorist plot. After they all left, Emma was allowed a shower, where it was all she could do to wash her hair. She was tired, ready to be home and ready to have Moby by her side. She took one look at her black-and-blue face, and she could see why any man would run away.

Emma returned to her hospital bed, having brushed her hair, leaving it to dry around her shoulders. The sun was setting, melting into the ocean like molten fire. Her week of vacation had turned out a lot different from what she'd planned, and she'd never gotten back to the wreck of the *Anna Maria* to search for Spanish gold to give to the hospital expansion fund. So basically, she was back to square one, and she'd used up her vacation. She sighed.

"Great view, huh?" came a voice from behind her.

Her heart bumped hard in her chest, and she turned slowly to find Creed standing in the doorway.

Emma raised a hand to her face, wanting to cover the ugly bruises. "I thought you'd be gone by now."

Creed crossed to where she stood and gripped her

wrist, pulling her hand away from her face. "I couldn't leave yet. I'd made plans."

His warm hand around her wrist spread electric jolts all through her body. "Plans?" she whispered.

"We have a date."

She dipped her chin. "I can't go out on a date looking like this."

"Well, you'll have to get well enough to leave the hospital gown behind so that you don't offend the prudes. Other than that—" he tipped her face up "—you're the most beautiful woman in this hospital."

"With a swollen eye, cut cheek and a scar across my chest."

He gathered her into his arms, treating her as if she was delicate china to be handled with care.

Her heart filled and spilled over, pushing tears from her eyes. "Don't be so nice to me."

"Why?"

She wanted to say, *Because it'll hurt too much when you leave*. Instead she said, "Just because."

He pressed his lips to her forehead. "I have another surprise for you."

"Surprise?" She shook her head. "I don't like surprises."

He grinned. "You're gonna like this one." Creed turned toward the door. "Bring him in."

Moby jerked Gabe through the door and bounded toward the bed where Emma lay.

"Oh, baby." Emma leaned over the side, ignoring the pain as she stretched the stitches over her incision. She draped her hand over the side of the bed and petted Moby's head with the tips of her fingers.

Apparently it wasn't enough for the golden retriever.

He jumped up, planted his front paws on the side of the bed and woofed.

Emma laughed, her chest hurting, but loving every minute of seeing her dog, with the big white swath of bandages wrapped around his middle. "He's okay?" she asked.

"The vet fixed him right up, and he's staying with me and Kayla until you can come home."

"Thank you."

Gabe faced Creed. "Did you tell her?"

Creed shook his head. "Not yet."

Tired, but too delighted to see Gabe and Creed to send them away, Emma asked, "Tell me what?"

Creed turned to her. "I haven't been here during the day because I've been out exploring the shipwreck we'd found before."

Emma leaned forward, her pulse speeding. "And?"

"I'm sad to report that we didn't find a coffer of Spanish gold or anything else of value."

"Oh." Emma laid back against the pillows, her eyes closing to the disappointment. The children's wing project might never be completed. Maybe when she was up and running again, she'd think of something.

"That was the bad news," Creed continued. "The good news is that since you found the diamonds on board the *Pelageya,* you get to keep them."

"What?" Emma's eyes opened wide, her mouth falling open, her pulse slamming against her veins. "The diamonds? I get to keep them?"

"Well, after the government takes their share." Creed held up the velvet bag they'd rescued from the yacht. "They are all yours to do whatever you want with."

"But half of them should go to you. You were there, too."

"Then I will donate my half to Cape Churn Memorial Hospital."

Emma felt as if her face would split, she was grinning so broadly. "They'll get that children's unit. Oh, Creed. That is good news."

Gabe cleared his throat. "I'd better take Moby back to the house before he wears out his welcome."

"Thanks for bringing him by, Gabe. Give Kayla a hug for me."

"We want to see you up and moving soon. Kayla misses your coffees at the marina."

"I'll be back soon." Emma scratched Moby's ears and watched as Gabe led the dog out the door, making her more determined to get out of bed and back to life.

She took a deep breath and asked the question that had been eating at her since she woke. "Now that your case is solved, when are you leaving?"

Creed took her hand in his. "I haven't decided. I kind of like it here at Cape Churn. The people are friendly, the cape is beautiful when it's not fogged in, and I haven't had my date with the best nurse in town."

Emma's cheeks burned. "We're still on?"

He carried her hand to his lips and kissed her fingertips. "As soon as you're up to it."

"Umm," she moaned, her insides heating all the way to her core. "I'm feeling better already."

He gathered her into his arms and held her gently. "Good, because I can't hardly wait for that date and many more to come. Ms. Emma Jenkins, you've helped me to discover something about myself."

She could barely think when he was so close, his lips brushing across her eyelids. "Oh, yeah? What's that?"

"I didn't think I was, but now I know—I'm a staying kind of guy, and I have a thing for white picket fences and a woman who loves scuba diving and dogs."

"Good thing." Her heart soaring, Emma placed her hands on either side of his face and stared into Creed's eyes. "Now kiss me like you mean it, frogman."

\* \* \* \* \*

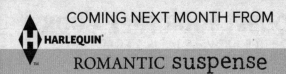

COMING NEXT MONTH FROM

**H HARLEQUIN®**

# ROMANTIC suspense

## Available February 4, 2014

### #1787 RISK TAKER
*Shadow Warriors* • by Lindsay McKenna
Black Hawk pilot Sarah Benson is known for her risky flights to save lives and SEAL Ethan Quinn is just one more mission. But when she needs rescuing, it's Ethan who infiltrates enemy territory, and her heart.

### #1788 CAVANAUGH HERO
*Cavanaugh Justice* • by Marie Ferrarella
When a serial killer targets his own, it becomes personal for Detective Declan Cavanaugh. But as the investigation ramps up, so does the attraction between Declan and his partner, Charlotte—can they survive the heat?

### #1789 ARMED AND FAMOUS
*Ivy Avengers* • by Jennifer Morey
Bounty hunter Lincoln Ivy steers clear of the redheaded spitfire next door, who looks like trouble. But when an arms dealer tries to kill her, he intervenes, only to learn she's not the woman he thinks she is.

### #1790 MOVING TARGET
by Kimberly Van Meter
In the wrong hands, Dr. Kat Odgers's miracle drug is a weapon—and the wrong hands are after Kat. Agent Jake Isaacs will do anything to keep her safe, even deny his dangerous attraction to her.

---

**YOU CAN FIND MORE INFORMATION ON UPCOMING HARLEQUIN® TITLES, FREE EXCERPTS AND MORE AT WWW.HARLEQUIN.COM.**

HRSCNM0114

# REQUEST YOUR FREE BOOKS!

## 2 FREE NOVELS PLUS 2 FREE GIFTS!

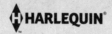

## ROMANTIC suspense

*Sparked by danger, fueled by passion*

**YES!** Please send me 2 FREE Harlequin® Romantic Suspense novels and my 2 FREE gifts (gifts are worth about $10). After receiving them, if I don't wish to receive any more books, I can return the shipping statement marked "cancel." If I don't cancel, I will receive 4 brand-new novels every month and be billed just $4.74 per book in the U.S. or $5.24 per book in Canada. That's a savings of at least 14% off the cover price! It's quite a bargain! Shipping and handling is just 50¢ per book in the U.S. and 75¢ per book in Canada.* I understand that accepting the 2 free books and gifts places me under no obligation to buy anything. I can always return a shipment and cancel at any time. Even if I never buy another book, the two free books and gifts are mine to keep forever.

240/340 HDN F45N

| | | |
|---|---|---|
| Name | (PLEASE PRINT) | |
| Address | | Apt. # |
| City | State/Prov. | Zip/Postal Code |

Signature (if under 18, a parent or guardian must sign)

### Mail to the **Harlequin®** Reader Service:

**IN U.S.A.:** P.O. Box 1867, Buffalo, NY 14240-1867
**IN CANADA:** P.O. Box 609, Fort Erie, Ontario L2A 5X3

**Want to try two free books from another line?**
Call 1-800-873-8635 or visit www.ReaderService.com.

\* Terms and prices subject to change without notice. Prices do not include applicable taxes. Sales tax applicable in N.Y. Canadian residents will be charged applicable taxes. Offer not valid in Quebec. This offer is limited to one order per household. Not valid for current subscribers to Harlequin Romantic Suspense books. All orders subject to credit approval. Credit or debit balances in a customer's account(s) may be offset by any other outstanding balance owed by or to the customer. Please allow 4 to 6 weeks for delivery. Offer available while quantities last.

**Your Privacy**—The Harlequin® Reader Service is committed to protecting your privacy. Our Privacy Policy is available online at www.ReaderService.com or upon request from the Harlequin Reader Service.

We make a portion of our mailing list available to reputable third parties that offer products we believe may interest you. If you prefer that we not exchange your name with third parties, or if you wish to clarify or modify your communication preferences, please visit us at www.ReaderService.com/consumerschoice or write to us at Harlequin Reader Service Preference Service, P.O. Box 9062, Buffalo, NY 14269. Include your complete name and address.

HRS13R

# ARMED AND FAMOUS

Maddie barked and moved closer to Remy, protecting her.
Remy stepped outside and the dog did, too. Remy was tempted
to run.

Wade, appearing at the open door, aiming his gun, stopped
her. Maybe Maddie would go next door, or her barking would
alert Lincoln.

She reentered the house and closed the door before Maddie
could follow. Her heart wrenched with the sound of frantic
barking.

"In the living room," Wade ordered her.

Maddie's barking stopped. She was running next door.

"You've been sneaking around again," Wade said, stepping
close to her with dangerous eyes. "What were you doing at my
store three days ago?"

"What are you talking about?" She played ignorant, the
same as she'd done the last time he'd come accusing her of
spying on him and his friends. That time she'd followed him
when he'd met some men she hadn't recognized. Nothing had

been exchanged, but she suspected he'd gone to discuss one of his illegal gun deals, deals that he expected her to execute for him.

He leaned close, the gun at his side as though he didn't think he needed it to keep her under control. "You know damn well what I'm talking about. You're supposed to be working with me, not against me."

"If working with you means breaking the law, I'll pass."

With a smirk, Wade straightened. "You've already done that. And if you don't start doing what I tell you, the cops are going to find out."

Because he'd tell them. Soon, he wouldn't be able to threaten her like this. Soon, she'd be able to call the cops herself and have *him* arrested. But for now she had to be patient.

Remy spotted Lincoln at the back door. She'd left it unlocked for him, hoping he'd retrace Maddie's path. Sure enough, he had. Wade's back was to him. Careful not to shift her eyes, she used her peripheral vision to watch Lincoln enter.

"I'm only going to ask you once more," Wade said.

Before he could repeat the question, Lincoln put the barrel of his pistol against the back of Wade's neck. "Put the gun down."

**Don't miss**
**ARMED AND FAMOUS**
**by Jennifer Morey,**
**available February 2014 from**
**Harlequin® Romantic Suspense**

HRSEXPO114

# HARLEQUIN®

*A Romance* FOR EVERY MOOD™

**Stay up-to-date on all your
romance-reading news with the
*Harlequin Shopping Guide*,
featuring bestselling authors, exciting new
miniseries, books to watch and more!**

The newest issue will be delivered right to you
with our compliments! There are 4 each year.

Signing up is easy.

## EMAIL

ShoppingGuide@Harlequin.ca

## WRITE TO US

HARLEQUIN BOOKS
Attention: Customer Service Department
P.O. Box 9057, Buffalo, NY 14269-9057

## OR PHONE

1-800-873-8635 in the United States
1-888-343-9777 in Canada

Please allow 4-6 weeks for delivery of the first issue by mail.